Possessed By the Leonid King

Felix Orbus Galaxy
Book One

S.C. PRINCIPALE

D1528004

Copyright Information

Editing: Evil Commas Editing at Evilcommas@gmail.com

For questions or further information please contact: scprincipaleauthor@gmail.com

Table of Contents

Dedications and Acknowledgements

To the people who encourage me to write weird romances with monsters, shifters, vamps, and now...science fiction with hot, cat-man aliens. I blame you and I thank you. I'm looking at you, people from Monster Brides Monster Fans and MDK. I love my job.

Thank you to Judy, Rachelle, Sofia, LoLo, Terry, Judy I., Grace, Mikayla, Michelle, Dawn, Ingrid, Amy, and my massive long list of writing support sisters.

To my own King. You've possessed my heart, right from the start.

Introduction

L ayla and Rupex should never have crossed paths.

But now that they have—they could be each other's salvation.

Rupex is the King of a decimated pride and the captain of the *Comet Stalker*, a starcraft traveling through the Felix Orbus Galaxy on a quest to avoid more loss and heartache. After Queen Fever killed almost all the pride females of cub-bearing age, the Leonids are facing a population crisis. Rupex needs to start living again after losing the women in his life. Could a human surrogate carry his child and reawaken his interest in life?

Layla is a scrappy survivor from Sapien-Three, a ravaged planet where most humans sell themselves to the highest bidders in hopes of staying alive. When an unexpected encounter with a towering, savage-looking lion-man shows her a better way, she jumps at the opportunity. Layla knows that being his surrogate could set her up for a comfortable life where she'll never struggle again. She just has to get the proud, stubborn King to see her as an equal and accept her proposal!

"Surrogacy is not an option. Surrogacy is medical, clinical, and the father of the child has a purely professional relationship with the mother."

"If you pay me, that makes it professional." Layla gave him her best, brightest smile.

The elevator car shook with the force of his sudden enraged roar. "This isn't a joke, human!"

"I wasn't laughing, Leonid!" I wasn't laughing at all. I might have peed a little...

"My medical officer has been researching a way to make human eggs compatible with Leonid sperm. It can be done. What cannot *be done is artificial insemination. Our systems are compatible but different. I would have to breed you. Do you know what it is like to be bred by a Leonid?*

2

It's not a single occurrence. I would have to possess you, over and over, day after day," he panted, towering over her, his glowering eyes inches from her own.

Layla shook her head, jaw popping open as his massive frame covered hers. She was able to see ridge after ridge of muscle through the snug material of his uniform coat, and the muscles of his thighs stood out like ropes.

And there was something sizable between them, something proportionate to the head-sized paws pressing into the steel walls on either side of her face.

No, I can't imagine what it would be like to be possessed by the Leonid. But I want to find out...

Chapter One

"Felids shouldn't have been using them for food. They have far more value."

Rupex turned to face Marcus, a scrawny specimen of a Leonid with a scraggly, graying mane and slender paws more accustomed to manipulating data than the firing mechanisms on starcrafts or assault weapons.

"Only the poorest prides on the extreme outer rims eat humans. That's primitive nonsense. Probably just rumors." Rupex paced with a sickened sneer, his long tawny tail tapping on the floor of his craft as it swished between his black boots. Humans. Too stupid to negotiate with their betters properly. Selling themselves into contracts that spoke of "whatever service deemed necessary." Ha. Some Felids deemed a meal a necessary service of their employees.

"I've heard plenty of prides on the outer fringes do it. But if my data is correct—and it usually is—human females can be far more beneficial to our species as mates rather than meals." Marcus hurried forward, personal computing device outstretched. "Look. One minor chromosome booster delivered in the female's heat cycle makes human eggs compatible with Leonid sperm."

Rupex paused in his pacing. A ripple of disgust ran down his spine, forcing his thick yellow-brown fur to a constricted stand under his protective black suit. "What... what *sickness* made you consider such an experiment?" Rupex demanded, his voice slick and threatening, a snarl in every word.

Marcus met his eyes over thick spectacles perched on his graying muzzle. "You know very well what sickness, Ru."

Rupex took a step back, eyes wide.

No one liked to talk about the Queen Fever.

SIX YEARS AGO...

Marcus spoke to Rupex and the rest of the crew, ten Queens and three Knights. Ru, as commander of the ship, was considered the King of the pride, at least until they docked and disbanded.

"I do not recommend we resupply at Tigerite-Three, sir. There are rumors of a contagious infection that doesn't respond to any treatment."

"This Queen flu? Males are immune, is that correct?"

"No, sir, it isn't that males are immune." Marcus' voice was suddenly thin and tight. "It's that males don't die. They get the fever, but it seems to pass harmlessly within a few days."

"Then why would it impact a female differently?" Silvia demanded, striding forward, her black uniform highlighting the magenta waves of fur that trailed down her neck. "That makes no sense."

"It could have something to do with the females' heat cycles. Males don't have them. When a female is in her heat—"

"Enough of the school cub lectures, Marcus!" Rupex quickly shut his medical officer down. "We need supplies. Only males will go on-world and get what we need. We'll be in and out of port in a day. Queens, males will quarantine on A-Deck. You will assign yourselves to rooms on B-Deck. There will be no fraternizing for the entire heat cycle, just to be on the safe side."

PRESENT

Rupex sat in his captain's chair and looked out at the sprinkled black and purple vista ahead of him.

Marcus had been right. Queen Fever did have something to do with heat cycles. And it was incredibly contagious. They'd soon realized there was only one option to prevent death once a Queen caught it—an immediate removal of her reproductive organs to stop the heat cycle that seemed to turn the fever into a lethal illness. Sometimes it was already too late. If her hormone levels had started to build, nothing could be done. Even injections of male hormones and prophylactic pills didn't fool the virus.

Within six years, most females of cub-bearing age had been sterilized. The only female Leonids who would be able to bear children were still children themselves. Girls who hadn't entered their first heat were safe.

"Now we have a vaccine, sir. But in the meantime..."

Ru nodded. People on certain planets complained about the population. They begged couples to cease reproducing with incentives and contraceptives. Ru had a special bitterness for those worlds. They had no idea what they were really asking for.

Imagine having no new births for six straight years aside from a rare litter here and there. And imagine most of the females of your kind disappearing within a few months of the disease breaking out. They'd only thought of surgery after the first few waves had swept through the Felix Orbus Galaxy.

The situation was desperate indeed.

"It would only be a temporary measure. I thought you ought to know. If we could test it here, I'd report my findings. It could be a stop-gap solution, just until the younger generation of females matures."

"Hm," Ru answered with a single grunt, raking his paws through his dark, honey-colored mane. It wasn't that Leonid hybrids didn't exist. The Leonids were old-fashioned about their pride structures, but within the pride, interspecies couples were common. There were mostly Felix-Leonid couples, but in a few cases, the pairings were more unusual. Why, his own sister had raised eyebrows when she married a Canid from the Sirius Federation.

But that was for love.

And it was never with a human. Sapien planets (all measly three of them) still had the unevolved mammalian, avian, reptilian, and aquatic species. Human interactions with those species seemed to be permanently ingrained within most of them. They were unaccepting of different social structures. The ones he had met years ago still seemed to consider Leonids and Canids dumb animals they needed to condescend to, even while taking their money for trade and contracts.

There was the whole human "structure" to consider, too.

"Humans are so...furless. And weak. They're barely sentient. No Leonid in his right mind would want to mate with one."

"The chromosome modification would allow the Leonid genes to be dominant. Yes, the child would have some human characteristics, but they could be bred out in a few generations."

"No."

"A lighter coating of fur. No tail perhaps. Poor night vision. You know our evolutionary matrix crossed with a sapien at some point or else—"

"I said *no*, Marcus."

Marcus sighed. "Sir, I didn't want to bring this up, but this bulletin arrived from the Department of Health's senior officer at Serval-Five."

Ru snatched the screen Marcus was holding out.

"'Possible Queen Fever mutation linked to deaths aboard a Sirius Federation pleasure ship.' Bastet's whiskers!" Ru pushed the device back into Marcus' paws. "It's jumping species?"

Marcus made a mewing noise in his throat. "It could be. They'll know soon. They'll know how to treat it, too."

"But how could this happen now? It's been six... Oh." Rupex didn't finish his sentence. When Queen Fever first struck in the Felix Orbus Galaxy, interplanetary and intergalactic trade and travel had been halted in nearly all cases. It had opened up slowly this past year, now that the fever was almost eradicated and vaccinations were widespread.

The Serval planets were closest to the Sirius Federation.

He could add two and two together to create a very grim picture.

Marcus injected a note of hope. "Our vaccine will probably work on most mammalian peoples." He waited for a moment, a hesitant smile coming over his face. "And because of the structure of Queen Fever, it's not compatible with humans. Humans will be immune."

Ru groaned. He didn't like when Marcus was smug, but he might have earned the right this time.

Chapter Two

Layla paced. Boredom had finally latched onto her after ten days aboard the craft. At least she *hoped* it had only been ten days. Time seemed slippery in isolation. She was the only human on board, and she wasn't a passenger. She was *cargo*. She'd been sold by her no-good-not-even-boyfriend. A one-night stand gone horribly wrong on Sapien-Three, and now she was being sold as permanent help—or worse—to someone in the Felix Orbus Galaxy.

She'd heard rumors that the Leonids ate humans like humans ate the unevolved cows and pigs. She also heard that Leonids were a proud race who despised humans. They didn't want them around, so maybe they'd be just as happy to let her work off a passage back to Sapien-Three, where she would track down Paul Bermauger and ship *him* to the other end of the solar system.

"Miss Human?"

Miss Human. At least her captor was polite. And to give him credit, it wasn't his fault that she was cargo. You could buy hired help legally anywhere in the galaxy, although the beings being bought were supposed to do the negotiating and bartering themselves, like a modern form of indentured servitude.

"Yes, Mr. Lion?"

"Mr. Leonid, please. Miss Human, you are being taken to a human clearinghouse on Lynx-Nineteen. Was that your intention?"

"No. I was hoping for something on Sapien-Three." She was hoping for anything, anywhere, honestly. A human without an elevated degree or a family had pretty crummy prospects. "Actually, I was hoping not to be on this ship at all, at least not in the cargo bay!"

The old lion-dude crept forward. She could see him now. She usually only heard his voice on the intercom making sure the service droids had delivered adequate food and water. Her "cell" was the size of four bunks pressed together and twice as wide. It had a bed and a minuscule shower/waste removal unit, a sink, and a media viewer. Of course, all the shows were from the Felix Orbus Production company, but still... She was getting into shows like *Pride to Pride* and *Cubs Say the Strangest Things*.

She'd seen pictures of Leonids back on Sapien-Three, her home planet. They were huge, usually about seven-feet tall with lashing tails and manes the size of a walk-in closet. This guy reminded her of her hopeless fourth-grade math teacher, who had finally given up on teaching and let them play games on their comms all year. He had the same air of wizened exhaustion to him, even if he did tower over her through the partition.

"Could you clarify, Miss Human?"

"Layla. Miss Layla, Mr. Leonid. I said I'm not supposed to be in your cargo bay."

"Why not? That is the usual way humans travel aboard off-world ships on long journeys when they haven't paid a passenger fare. If you only pay cargo rates, this is what you get. You have adequate space to sleep and eat."

"Yeah, but I'm not supposed to be cargo! I wasn't even planning to go off-world!"

The shaggy gray brows shot up and got lost in wispy gray fur. "You didn't negotiate your own contract?"

"No. I'm trafficked. I told you that."

"You did not! You most *certainly* did not! Leonids do not hold with slavers. What your owners do with you once you're paid... that's their business. But a subject must negotiate their own purchase. Sweet Bastet." He flapped one paw to his cheek and knocked his own glasses off.

Layla tried to remember the first few days on board the ship. She had been drugged out of her mind and sleeping a lot. That wasn't their fault, that was Paul-the-Wonder-Slug's fault. *Maybe I dreamed I had a conversation. Or maybe I did have it, but I slurred so badly that I made no sense.*

"Miss Human, our craft is not going to Sapien-Three, or even out of the Felix Orbus Galaxy. I can arrange for someone to refund your purchase price to Lynx-Nineteen."

"Good luck."

"Yes, well... That's only one small problem. Here is another. You *are* cargo on our vessel. You are listed on our manifest. Your passage was paid as part of the contract price. With the contract refunded, you owe us passage fees."

"Good luck getting that, too. I'm broke. I would negotiate a contract with your captain if he needs someone to cook or clean. I'm good at those things." Layla leaned against the glass partition between her accommodations and the rest of the ship, hoping Leonids couldn't smell liars. She could clean just fine. Cooking was a work in progress, but you had to have food and a heat source at the same time to practice.

"I have another proposition for you. It's much easier work. All you have to do is hold still."

RU SAT IN HIS QUARTERS. As captain and owner of the ship, his quarters were the biggest and best—but they weren't much in the way of luxury. Once, he would have gone in for all that finery, but new jade carvings or silk sleep hangings didn't mean much anymore. One concession to luxury was the bejeweled frame that held Silvia's picture. It mocked him as he looked at it from his empty bed, and he put it hastily away. He didn't like to look at those laughing eyes, didn't want to imagine her bold voice or her flirtatious purr.

He'd missed his shot there. A captain wasn't supposed to fraternize with his requisitions officer, even if he was King of the pride. He'd planned to ask her about a courtship once her year aboard was officially up for renegotiation.

Well... speaking of shots to take... he could use a shot of Leonid homebrew right now. Or even one of those weak little human cocktails.

Marcus was going to ask the only remaining human in the hold, a female, if she'd like to transfer her contract to the crew of the *Comet Stalker*.

The crew was currently Marcus and himself. Marcus had already made it clear that he would be having no part in this experiment. He was much older, and he assumed his sperm viability wasn't the best. That meant this insemination business was up to him.

"But I'm not ready to be a father!"

That wasn't exactly true. With cubs being in short supply and almost every planet seeming like a motherless wasteland and Queens being all graying or young kits...the idea of family danced through Ru's dreams on a regular basis.

It's just like paying for a surrogate, Ru tried to reassure himself. Some wealthy Leonids had done that, paying for a female who would enter her first heat in a few years, booking her womb for a litter in the future.

Gods, what desperate times.

Marcus knocked on the sliding hatch to his room, then entered the access code without waiting for a reply.

"I told the girl she would perform a personal service for you. I didn't specify what. I figured you'd prefer to tailor your explanation to your tastes. By the look on her face, I think she suspects it's at least a bit sexual in nature." Marcus gave Ru a guilty nudge.

"But it isn't. This is medical. Why didn't you tell her the precise nature of your 'experiment'? You'll be the one who collects my *contribution*—well, not personally," Ru preferred not to use the anatomical terms at the moment considering his shock, "and sees that it manages to find its way into the correct receptacle. Right?"

"Inject? Oh, goodness. No. You see, humans don't give off visible signs of heat. Their body temperatures may not even elevate! It happens once a month, in a two-day window, but it can come early or late. Many things can influence it, too. Diet, stress, exercise, weight—"

"Marcus, spare me the lecture. What are you saying?"

"I'm not a doctor of reproductive science. I'm a medical officer with a new hobby, thanks to this terrible disease we've lived through. I'll do my part and research the most expedient method of conception between a human female and a Leonid male. That's how I can help. If *you* want to help the Leonid population, you're going to have to do this the old-fashioned way. Mate the girl every day for a month, or thereabouts."

"We'll be docking in two weeks! We're picking up a new crew at Leonid-One!"

"It's a simple enough matter to get word to the crew you've hired that they'll still be paid and they'll have two weeks initial leave. I can assign them tasks. We have an entire bay that's unfilled. Set them to acquiring cargo. Besides... if the outbreak aboard that Sirius vessel *is* a mutation of Queen Fever, all ports except designated survival ports will be closed for a month or two."

Ru hung his head in frustration, a growling groan echoing in the large, domed captain's quarters. "That a Leonid should lower himself..."

"Maybe humans aren't the intellectual planetoids you think they are. I spoke to the cargo today and found her competent."

"The *cargo*. The fact that they ship themselves as cargo and not passengers—"

"Because they're poor, Rupex. Their planets are longer established and more decimated by war and want, yet most stubbornly refuse to even leave Sapien-One, the original Earth." Marcus' nose twitched, and his tail did a nervous pit-pat on his ankle.

Marcus had been with Rupex for the last seven years. The grizzled old lion had been the only one to stay with him through the Grounding when all starcraft were only allowed to dock on their original home worlds or their designated survival ports. This wasn't necessarily by choice—medical officers were in critically short supply and every ship was now required by law to have one or have their ship's registry rejected. Ru didn't always enjoy Marcus' company, and the ship was large enough to allow them to avoid one another on most occasions. Still, Ru knew him well enough to recognize the signs of impending bad news.

"What is it?"

"What's what?" Marcus avoided his eyes.

"Your tail is *fluttering*. Don't tell me. The mutation has been confirmed to be Queen Fever?"

"Oh. No. I haven't heard one way or the other. It'll probably be a day before they send a new bulletin. No, it's about the cargo. The girl."

"Girl? A cub!"

"No, no. A woman. A young lady named Layla. She wasn't intending to go to Lynx-Nineteen."

"I hope not. They'd eat her. That's an almost entirely primal backwater."

"She was sold. As in, someone sold her. She didn't negotiate her contract."

Ru's mane bristled out and his claws unsheathed in rage. "What? *What*!?"

"Calm down."

"I will not! You volunteered to take over the cargo assignments while I was down with the post-vaccination reaction! I leave you in charge for two days and you take on a trafficked human? Manes and tails, Marcus! We're going to be permanently grounded for this!"

"I picked the cargo up from a vessel that wasn't going to the outer reaches of the Felix Orbus. I didn't know she wasn't moving of her own volition, Rupex. She was asleep, which is standard for most humans on a galaxy jump. Nothing twigged my suspicions, and I hope you won't pretend she would have aroused yours, either. You've been on autopilot since—"

"Quiet. That's an order."

Silence filled the deck. They both knew what Marcus would have said. Rupex had been on autopilot, functioning automatically since he lost his sisters and the Queens of the *Comet Stalker*. He took on skeleton crews and long-haul freights that would keep him on his ship for as long as possible. Planets within the Felix Orbus Galaxy seemed permanently touched by death and sadness, with a dearth of cubs and Queens, and many citizens (especially on the smaller and more distant planets) were claiming they should either remain in isolation or revert to feral states to cope with the new reality.

"The stars feel familiar." Rupex double-checked the navigation settings and the alerts before stalking away.

"Ru... We're not going to rebuild without change. Do you want to stay stuck in the past, where we were helpless? Or do something to fix it?"

Rupex had to get away from Marcus before he clawed him. He could feel the dagger-like tips of his claws passing through the soft sheath of his paws. There was no fixing this.

But maybe the older Leonid has a point.

Somehow, someway, he would have to move forward. The *Comet Stalker* could jump galaxies, but it couldn't travel back in time.

Chapter Three

Layla felt smug. And worried. And irritated. Whatever that emotional blend was, she wanted to patent it and sell it.

Instead, she was going to sell herself to some alien cat-man.

The idea of selling her services, whether it was having sex or cleaning a bunker didn't bother Layla. Growing up poor on Sapien-Three meant that you were always looking for any way to make cash. That was one reason she hadn't struggled too hard when she woke up in the hold of some strange vessel. Part of her had been relieved when she realized the accommodations were clean and the food was good and plentiful. Another part of her, while still worried, had been curious about what kind of contract she'd been sold into. A contract meant money, or at least food and shelter.

She hadn't known until she'd explored the media viewer and the limited number of books that she was on a Felix Orbus craft. Most people from the Sapien planets preferred to stick close to their three human-friendly rocks. Those who did leave didn't usually go to the Felix Orbus planets. Layla wasn't sure why. But in the last handful of years, ever since she'd been forced to start looking out for herself, she hadn't met anyone who'd been to that galaxy. The smug feeling was the most comfortable, so Layla tried to hold onto it while she paced in her little room.

Ha. Leonids, Servalis, Lynxians, and Tigerites were so aloof. So stand-offish. They wouldn't dream of coming to the Sapien planets. They weren't at any of the Galactic Games that she could remember.

But here I am, taking up space, and we're weeks away from wherever we're supposed to land, and what does the big horny lion-man want to do?

She didn't know.

Curiosity came back. *Maybe he just wants a good belly rub?*

It wasn't that interspecies dating wasn't a thing—it just wasn't *her* thing. On Sapien-Three, interspecies couples were rare and were usually just there for refueling. She could count on one hand the number of interspecies couples she'd met personally.

He doesn't want to be a couple. He's probably bored and doesn't have a sex droid. The first one pays for my passage and the rest he can pay for with cold, hard credits.

How much should she charge?

Her friends who traded in carnal pleasures usually asked for a thousand credits or more per exchange, but they were *good* at it. They were professional seductresses with skills and moves.

Layla didn't even have a dress. She had the black blouse and faded jeans she'd been wearing on her date and a simple white robe that came with the clean linens the service droids brought every day.

They're clean. Everyone says cats are clean. It'll probably be basic in-and-out stuff.

I wonder if they have fur on their—

"May I enter?"

Layla jumped off her bed so fast that she stumbled and smacked into the glass partition. That wasn't the little old lion-man. This was a different voice, deeper and...wider somehow. It was almost like a different frequency, radiating in her ears and sliding down to rest in her middle.

"Yes. C-come in." She tried to lean seductively against the edge of the bed, praying he hadn't been watching her on some corridor camera to witness her spectacular burst of clumsiness a moment ago.

The being who stepped up in front of the glass partition was easily seven feet tall. He wore a black suit that looked like it might be a cross between silk and leather, which Layla recognized as Thermagyle, a polyblend of fabrics recommended for extended time in space because of how it adapted to temperature changes and gravitational force fluctuations. Above the suit, which seemed to consist of a tight, chest-hugging shirt and fitted trousers, was a massive head.

A massive head with dark golden eyes spanning a wide feline nose, rounded ears perched above hard brows, and a tawny, brownish-yellow mane that flowed past his shoulders.

Thoughts spilled into her brain.

Tall.

That head! It's huge.

I wish I had hair like that. I wonder what conditioner he uses?

"Miss Layla?" The voice that rumbled out was businesslike and disdainful.

Layla nodded, her entire perspective changing. *Nope. This is not a sex call. This is a "Will you kindly attend to returning my communications and hanging up my suits?" deal.*

"I am Rupex, King of this pride, captain of the *Comet Stalker*. Welcome aboard as a passenger." He pressed one paw to a panel on the side of her chamber.

The glass vanished with a whooshing shift, sliding up into the ceiling. Layla was staring at his paw. It was the size of her head, thick and furry with light brown pads. She wondered if Leonids still had claws, and when did they use them if they weren't typically on display?

"I am Layla Threewood. Domestic and retail worker. Personal services provided based on a contract-by-contract basis." Layla hoped she sounded professional and polished, keeping her eyes locked on the Leonid's face. She refused to look away, even though she was growing twitchier inside with every passing second. Leonids were supposed to be as intelligent as humans, maybe even more so... but when she looked at those golden eyes with oval pupils, she felt like she was looking at something incredibly foreign and wild, something lost and intimidating.

Rupex nodded. "Would you like to move your quarters to A-Deck? It's usually for crew, but we are currently en route to pick up our new crew."

That would explain why she hadn't seen other people milling about or heard other noises and voices on the ship.

"Sure. Thank you. Better than being considered 'cargo.'" She knew her tone had dipped into the "sassy" category by the way Rupex's eyes glinted and his massive muzzle, which was somehow flatter and more human than what she remembered from the pictures of lions she'd seen in old books about earth animals, scrunched up to reveal long white canines.

"You humans are the ones who book yourselves off-world and sell yourselves to the highest bidders, making yourselves 'cargo.'"

"I didn't. And do you know how weak Sapien credits are when compared to most other galaxies? Sometimes it's the only way we can afford to get off-world and travel to a place where we can get a job. Cargo or starvation. Hmmm." Layla held up both hands and pretended to weigh the options. "I know you Leonids wouldn't understand that. You stay in your own galaxy and keep with your own kind, right?"

Yes, she was being a brat, but his tone had touched a nerve—and so had the mention of her poverty. Sapien-Three had once been the jewel of the solar system. No more.

"Keep to our own kind? Stay in our galaxy? Wh-what *ignorant* rock have you been hiding under for the last decade, human?" Rupex spat the words like a vile curse.

"Excuse me? Ignorant? Ha! They were right about Leonids. You're all proud—jerks." Layla substituted the word quickly for the less offensive option. Those teeth were big, and that mouth... He could probably bite her arm off in one nip.

Rupex curled his fists. She could see the tips of claws now, dark, sharp, and short. "Queen Fever, fool. Heard of it?" Rage was practically sweating out of him. His fur bristled, and his whole form seemed to swell.

There was a line here. And I crossed it.

"Nn-no?"

"Wait? No?" The anger didn't dissipate, but it was suddenly coupled with confusion. "Are you joking?"

"No! We don't even have queens on Sapien planets. We're all democracies. Or worse."

"A Queen. A female Leonid or Felid of cub-bearing years. Queen Fever raged for over two years, killing almost every female from fourteen to fifty."

Layla could tell when she blushed. She could also tell when all the blood vanished from her face. "Oh my God. Like the Maximus Virus in 2800?"

"Yes, except that ours was deadly only to Queens. Something to do with their hormone levels." The Leonid looked away. "Millions died. Millions more sacrificed their ability to have cubs to stave off the disease. Some wealthy families in the Felix Orbus Galaxy actually went so far as to 'reserve' the reproductive services of young female cubs who wouldn't mature for years in advance, hoping to have offspring of their own later."

Layla felt a drizzle of warmth for the big beast who was now pacing in a perfect line, turning in sharp right angles at the end of the walkway in front of her former quarters. "I'm so sorry. I honestly didn't know. I didn't get to sit down and hear about the intergalactic news and affairs growing up. I was in survival mode, just like your people were. The reasons were different, but the struggle was real."

The hulking figure in black paused in front of her long enough to nod and then paced away again. "Poverty is a greater problem on Sapien-Three because humans are reluctant to innovate and trade with other mammalian species."

"And we have a shitty environment, corruption, war, and disease. But sure, blame the stubborn jackoffs who won't buy cheap groceries from the interspecies couple down the street."

A growl that rippled the air around her made Layla bite her tongue. *They could eat you, you know. Or just kill you. Starve you in that little glass cell. They could do all of that, and no one would ever know.*

No one would ever care.

"Reasons aside, Leonid credits exchange at eighteen to one with Sapien credits."

Layla blinked. "That much? Damn. Never mind. Take me to the kitty planets."

Rupex slammed a paw to his forehead and squeezed his eyes shut. "Kitty planets? No. No, this is pointless. Worthless. Insane. Goodbye, Miss Layla. I will prepare quarters for you and hope your stay is comfortable. We will find a ship to take you to a planet where you can negotiate a contract for your services."

"But I thought the little old lion-man said *you* wanted my services!" Layla protested, the sound of credits inflating her pitiful account drowning out the irritation and woe in his voice.

"That was before I talked to you!" Rupex pushed a button on the wall and it lit up, showing a warm green light under the pads pressing it down. The silvery panel of the wall slid up, and he was gone.

Chapter Four

Marcus was a cruel, sadistic bastard to toy with his hopes like this. Even if the girl herself had spirit.

Even if she was suitably curvaceous and pretty (for a human) and would not damn his offspring with undue ugliness, scrawniness, or temerity.

Rupex stalked back to his quarters, a growl clawing at his chest, longing to break loose like a feral hunter of old.

We don't do that. We would scare the humans and timid species if we did that. We can't alienate anyone else or we'll die out.

"Rupex! Captain! Wait!"

Curse his canines. She had followed him.

"Go, Miss Layla. Marcus will escort you to a guest chamber when it is prepared. *Later.*"

"Look, I'm sorry I offended you. I didn't mean anything by it! I just said kitty planets. If someone called Sapien-Three a human burrow, I wouldn't get huffy."

He smirked. "Wouldn't you?" Somehow he doubted that.

"Maybe a little. Depending on who it was coming from. I know it wouldn't make sense to a King, but I'm from a mean cesspit of a city where you get a thick skin and a big mouth. I'm sorry. Should I bow?"

Rupex shook his head in wonder. How were humans so... different? "A King is the term for the male leader of a pride. It is not a term that requires scraping and bowing. It means loyalty from my pride and denotes that my responsibility is to them above myself, at all times. Queen Fever proved that in many cases King is an empty title. I could not save the females in my pride. None."

To his surprise, the little human who barely came a foot above his waist reached out and tried to pat his arm. She drew her hand back at the last second, but the gesture was... thoughtful. And her wide eyes with their odd blue color and their perfectly round black pupils were wet and woeful looking. "That's horrible. I know it's not the same, but I kind of get it. I couldn't save my 'pride' either. There were four of us assigned to the same shelter in the Sapien-Three Public Childcare System. I was the oldest and I couldn't prevent the other three—um—cubs, I guess you'd call them—from being taken from me."

She looked so pained—and it had been so long since he had anyone but Marcus to speak to about anything other than freight rates and schedules—that Rupex let his curiosity get the better of him. "What happened to them?"

"They weren't chosen for adoption by the time they were fourteen, so they had two choices—get out of the system and find work and shelter, or hand their working papers over to the Sapien-Three Public Contract Auction. All three were bought by the labs."

"The labs? Laboratories?"

"Right. Labs are always looking for test subjects to try new medicines, regeneration techniques, and other things. Selling your contract to the labs should be safe. It is supposed to be regulated and safe. Maybe it is." Layla shrugged. "I tell myself it is," she whispered, arms sliding around herself and pushing in like she was holding herself together by the sheer pressure of those thin little limbs.

Rupex studied her. He hadn't often had the opportunity to observe humans at close range. How could the middle of her have such generous dips and curves and her arms and legs be so *twiggy*? Humans. A puzzle, indeed.

"They didn't die, your friends?"

"No. I don't think so. I don't know. I tried to tell them they could live with me, that we'd make enough money to stay together, but they didn't believe me. Looks like they were right." She gave him a sudden, bitter smile. "So, here's the deal, King Rupex—"

"Captain or Rupex is fine." He didn't feel like a King anymore, and this woman would never be part of his pride. That was a grim reminder that this was wrong. No one but a Queen should bear his cubs.

Yet, he was still considering it.

"Rupex, the older Leonid said you needed a human for a contracted job. What kind of job? I know I'm a smartass, but I'm also a survivor and a hard worker. I'm smart, too. I can figure things out on a ship, even though I haven't been to school. Well, not a *lot* of school. Seriously, if you show me just once or twice, I can do most of the basic tasks."

Rupex slowly started walking, hoping if he kept moving, he could avoid the words that were pushing past his fangs, tickling the inside of his muzzle.

Layla followed. Her voice was soft when she spoke, so soft that only someone with excellent predatory hearing could have caught her words. "You don't have to tell me. I can figure it out. Your civilization lost its women. I'm a woman. You need me for something only a woman can do." Her tiny feet caught up to his massive ones which arched in their thick black boots. She wore the simple white stretchy slippers that the ship provided. They expanded or shrank to cover the feet of most beings. The tiny white ovals looked so strange next to his polished black boots that flared out to follow the shape of his long, arched feet with wide pads designed for digging in and springing off after prey.

"I do not need you." Rupex shook his head and considered the matter closed.

The human was persistent. "Well, maybe your species needs me, huh? Is that the job you were going to offer me? A surrogate?"

LAYLA WASN'T READY to be a mother. She had proven that she couldn't keep kids safe. Her little pseudo-family hadn't trusted her to keep them alive and together. They'd let themselves be sold to the labs, herded into long white transports with dark glass windows rather than risk squatting in the abandoned basement apartment she'd found for them.

Why hadn't she gone with them? At sixteen, she could have offered her contract to the labs. They were always willing to pay, especially for young, healthy adults. They were the hardest to come by because they could still get other types of work.

Had she been too afraid of dying? Too untrusting of the labs?

Whatever. She'd become harder, faster, and stronger alone.

And more prone to stupidity and numbing herself with alcohol as long as the guy paid—hence her one-way ticket from Paul.

Her blurted words were purely financial. The Leonid wanted her to carry his cubs. Fine. She could carry them if interspecies couples were anything to go by. She just couldn't *raise* those cubs, and with surrogacy, she wouldn't have to. That would be ideal. She could have the credits—top prices, too, bolstered by the Leonid-Sapien exchange rate. The kids—cubs—would be cherished, adored as new life in a galaxy that had vacancies to fill. She wouldn't have to watch them suffer on Sapien-Three. If she worded it right, maybe she could even go home and buy a place to live and then work on buying the contracts of Dax, Wendy, and Elio. Maybe...

The big Leonid hadn't replied to her in words. After a few tense huffs of air, his panting breaths so heavy that she felt their warm wetness on her cheek, Rupex had slammed his paw down beside the double steel doors of an elevator. The doors slid apart.

"A-Deck!" he growled, stepping inside.

She was too quick for him. "Are my quarters this way?" Layla asked.

What am I doing? Why am I pushing this?

Why did I just get in a little metal box with a giant grumpy alien-lion who looks like he would like to bite my head off?

"Surrogacy is not an option. Surrogacy is medical, clinical, and the father of the child has a purely professional relationship with the mother."

"If you pay me, that makes it professional." Layla gave him her best, brightest smile.

The car shook with the force of his sudden enraged roar. "This isn't a joke, human!"

"I wasn't laughing, Leonid!" *I wasn't laughing at all. I might have peed a little...*

"My medical officer has been researching a way to make human eggs compatible with Leonid sperm. It can be done. What cannot be done is artificial insemination. Our systems are compatible but different. I would have to breed you. Do you know what it is like to be bred by a Leonid? It's not a single occurrence. I would have to possess you, over and over, day after day," he panted, towering over her, his glowering eyes inches from her own.

Layla shook her head, jaw popping open as his massive frame covered hers. She was able to see ridge after ridge of muscle through the snug material of his uniform coat, and the muscles of his thighs stood out like ropes.

And there was something sizable between them, something proportionate to the head-sized paws pressing into the steel walls on either side of her face.

No, I can't imagine what it would be like to be possessed by a Leonid. But I might want to find out...

Chapter Five

He was ashamed. He had acted like a King of old, a selfish King with many Queens to satisfy, hot-tempered and short, thinking only of himself.

Leonids had evolved from that. They were monogamous. They were not feral.

But there was still a month-long heat cycle multiple times a year. For each cycle, a Queen was in need of satisfaction three or four times a day until her hormones settled or conception occurred.

That was the King's job—providing satisfaction and progeny.

Rupex contented himself that his body was confused and acting on long-unused muscle memory. One particular muscle was giving him insistent reminders. All male Leonids had penile spines. These short, soft, flexible spines were designed to swell and embed into the soft, spongy paradise of a Queen's walls like they were starcrafts docking, locking them together for long moments where waves of pleasure coated them and endless jets of cum filled her. The fullness of the torrents of sperm put pressure on the already tender, aroused flesh inside a Queen's tight sheath, causing her to orgasm over and over as she milked her lover dry.

Only after completion would the spines shrink and release.

Rupex wondered how much tighter, how infinitely tighter this human's sheath would be around him, how full of his seed she would be, how helpless she would be, pinned down by his paws and held captive by his spines...

He had the unmistakable urge to rut.

A sweet, salty smell tickled his nose as the elevator juddered to a halt and opened behind him.

"I-if that's what your people do to impregnate Queens, who am I to judge? Most human men don't last five minutes. Daily 'possessing' could be a perk."

Rupex wondered if his eyes would drop to the floor. "Have you no shame?" he asked, practically falling from the elevator in his haste to leave Layla behind.

In answer, Layla looked pointedly down at his crotch.

Betrayer. Rupex was glad that his golden fur hid his blush.

"No more shame than your body." Layla scoffed as her eyes took their time to travel back to his face. "Look, I'm not a whore. If I were, I'd be living more comfortably—well, probably. But surrogacy is noble. I don't care how it goes. Plus, you can pay me a surcharge per 'coupling.'"

"No. Per day." Wait, why was he thinking of this? He hoped the sweet, tempting smell that was familiar yet foreign would vanish and release his fevered imagination.

"No deal."

"The cost per day would be prohibitive! You know nothing about Leonid lovemaking."

"This isn't lovemaking. It's biology." Layla argued, crossing her arms under her bust.

It was a small bust, but he suddenly wondered how they would feel. Humans were so soft and so much less muscular.

Is she that soft all over?

"It's madness." Rupex stormed off.

His little sweet-smelling shadow followed, tempting him to think lewd thoughts—and to consider her proposal.

How had this happened? They were supposed to be discussing *his* proposal, a purely business endeavor. Now she had him wondering if it would be possible for them to start tonight if they could agree to terms.

Her voice echoed in the empty tunnel-like corridor of A-Deck, surrounding him, teasing his mind with her words like she teased his nose with her scent. "This is a mad galaxy. Look, daily surcharges and a monthly womb-rental fee. Plus a bonus for additional cubs. Leonids have litters, right?"

"You are a—a cunning female!" Rupex stopped halfway down the corridor to insult her.

Layla shrugged. "I want a better life. This could be my big payout, and it helps you, too. Win-win."

That shut his mouth. Money was plentiful. He had no one to buy trinkets for. Salaries and overhead for the *Comet Stalker* had been far below his intake. Credits had flowed freely into his paws as crafts began to fly again, but he had maintained a skeleton crew and taken the long-distance, high-pay jobs few wanted. While many preferred to be "safe," he preferred to be off-world, and he didn't care if he flew with few in his pride. The smaller the pride, the better. He'd rather have double the work than risk losing so many.

"What would you charge?" Rupex finally asked.

"How many months would this take?"

He had to think for a minute. It had been so long since he had celebrated the arrival of cubs. "Five months is a typical gestation period for Leonid Queens."

"It's nine months for humans. Split the difference and figure on seven?"

Seven months of her company? He might go mad.

But at the end of that time... he would have cubs. Maybe daughters. The next generation of Queens. Names for them popped into his head.

Silvia.

Alana, after his late sister.

Maybe he'd get lucky and have three.

And these daughters would live. If he had to take them out of the Felix Orbus Galaxy, he would.

Or maybe they would inherit their human mother's immunity.

By Bastet! What if he could give his daughters a fighting chance simply by choosing a human and mixing in a little science?

Years of feeling helpless and lonely seemed to vanish in a rosy (if tarnished) dream. He could do something for his people. He could do something for this human.

They would have to write up a contract. They would have to write up several. What if he and the human weren't even compatible? What if Marcus' booster didn't work?

Layla's voice was low and without her brashness of a moment ago. "So? What do you think? Want to try it? I can negotiate on the price. That cub bonus thing might have been pushing it on —"

Rupex stuck out a paw and seized her hand. He completely wrapped around her hand and wrist with plenty of room to spare. Dainty little thing. Not something one would say about a Leonid Queen, that was certain. "We will write up terms to our mutual satisfaction."

She smiled at him, breathing out a shaky little sigh. "To our mutual satisfaction."

WHILE LAYLA SETTLED into the rooms down the corridor from his, Rupex went on a research binge. He looked at the costs of properties on Sapien-Three. For the cost of a shack on Leonid-One, he could have a modest estate on Sapien-Three. He had his eye on one, a white house on a lake, well-gated and a reasonable distance from other dwellings. For some reason, Rupex liked the look of it and wanted to imagine Layla there, safe and protected, away from men who would harm her and sell her, away from these "labs" that sounded like something out of old horror tales, rounding up children to experiment on!

But it would be her money. She could do as she liked with it.

Rupex tapped the com screen and punched in Marcus' code. "Marcus?"

The grizzled face appeared. "Captain?"

Oh no. Formal titles. Marcus was upset. "What is it?"

"You first."

"How can you be sure the chromosome booster will work with Layla—our current human guest?"

"Whose blood do you think I was using for my initial research? I took a pint while she was sleeping. Standard protocol when taking cargo transfers from off-world. Well... a sample. A pint wasn't regulation size, I admit."

Rupex groaned. He was a bit of a rule-breaker himself, but Marcus seemed to have reached the "Fuck it all" stage of his career. "Marcus, you're going to get us banned by the trading unions!"

"Knock a hundred credits off her passage. Say I bought it. Then it's legal." The Leonid in the white lab coat shrugged.

"Saying that the booster works—"

"It will."

"That helps her get pregnant. What will help her stay pregnant?"

"Routine injections of the booster. Here, look at what the simulator has generated."

Rupex watched the screen shift from Marcus' face to his own, then Layla's, and then both side by side with scrolling letters and numbers dancing across them as the simulator took over.

Rupex gasped and almost dropped his comm when the formulas stopped buzzing across the screen and revealed a final product.

"She's... she's beautiful. Could that be—would that be what a daughter of ours would look like?" Rupe asked, his voice faint with awe.

The image on his screen showed a young Queen with fine fur that was pale and silvery, a cross between his golden fur and Layla's peachy-white skin, he supposed. Her muzzle was small and had a faint uptilt like a human nose, and her eyes were blue, not amber or yellow. Unlike Leonid Queens, she had long hair on the top of her head as well as down the back of the neck, a white-blonde swirl that covered one of her small, oval ears.

He was in love.

That is my daughter.

That is my daughter, all grown up.

"Show me her as a cub," he demanded.

"I can't do that. I only had adult images of you and the human to work from. I'll run some more simulations later and see what I can work up. But you approve?"

"Yes." One word contained a world of meanings. *Yes, we can do this. Yes, I'm going to be a father, I'm going to protect my cub, I'm going to have a cub!*

"Want to see what a boy would look like?" Marcus asked and didn't wait for an answer.

Rupex let out a startled purr as the screen changed.

My son.

The male Leonid-human hybrid on the screen had that same thin, whitish fur and a riotously full tawny mane, a narrower muzzle than normal, and wide blue eyes.

"He's a handsome specimen. Humans have been known to comfortably gestate three at once, with some assistance at delivery and careful monitoring. Leonid litters of three are the norm, so I expect you'll have at least two. Still, some singletons occur. Weren't you and your sister both a litter of one?"

"We were."

"Rupex, you are monosyllabic, even for you. Cold paws?"

"No. No, I'm preparing the contractual end of the matter, now that the science is in our favor."

"Plenty of things could go wrong, but I'll give it a solid 80% success rate," Marcus said cheerfully. His face reappeared on the screen and Rupex could see that the Leonid's expression didn't match his tone. "Another bulletin from Serval-Five. They're locking down all ports and denying entry to any ships carrying non-Servali citizens. Sound familiar?"

"I'll be up to the cockpit in five minutes."

The last time ports closed... they hadn't reopened for months, in some cases years. It wouldn't be so bad this time. Right? The vaccines worked against mutations. Right?

Last time he hadn't had a human onboard, either.

In the cockpit, Rupex changed course slightly.

The automated voice of the *Comet Stalker*'s navigation system spoke in its friendly artificial tones. "You've changed course by 38 points. Former destination: Leonid-One, Bastet Bay Space Port. New destination: Leo Falls Island, port unspecified. Is this correct?"

"Correct."

"Warning. There is no official docking procedure established and no flight command to report to on Leo Falls Island. Do you wish to proceed?"

"Proceed."

"Course changed."

Rupex sank back and watched the black, starry space shift slightly as the *Comet Stalker* altered its course.

He wasn't going to risk having Layla and his chance for a family taken by the Fever or the quarantines that came with it. If the ports closed... this time he'd rather be at home. Well, the one place in the galaxy besides the *Comet Stalker* that still felt like home.

Chapter Six

Layla was pacing in front of his quarters when he returned from the cockpit. Her pale face lit up when she saw him, relief in her eyes. But then the relief was overtaken by worry. "Hey. The voice in the walls was talking to me."

"The what?"

"The automated lady who speaks from the walls?"

Rupex squinted. "Have you *never* been on a starcraft before?"

"Yes!" Layla said defensively. Then she blushed, shrugging. "No. Not exactly. I've been on little in-planet transports and atmosphere planes, but never a real starcraft."

"You're hearing the ship's communication system. That's all. What alarmed you?"

"It said we were changing course. Why? What's going on?"

Rupex wondered if the worry in her eyes was because she feared him or feared the end of their deal. He had always believed humans were rather timid, defenseless creatures who lacked natural courage and ingenuity. "Queen Fever has mutated and caused deaths aboard a Sirius Federation ship."

"Sirius. Those are the puppy planets, right?"

"First kitty planets, now puppy planets. At least you are consistent in your disrespect. Yes, the Sirius Federation is closest to the Serval planets within the Felix Orbus Galaxy. We believed the Queen Fever virus was localized to Felid species. Planets were locked down and people didn't travel in and out to non-Felix planets. Vaccines and countermeasures were developed. It now looks like we were wrong in believing the virus to be species limited, so other planets will need to co-opt our vaccine technology. It shouldn't take them long to test and create, now that we've laid the groundwork." Rupex nodded, muttering to himself as he opened his quarters. "It makes sense. Canids from the Sirius Federation have similar heat cycles, I believe." Although if his sister's overheard gossip was to be believed, the Canids lacked penile spines and resorted to something called "knotting."

"And humans?"

"Don't. You are immune. You are not a recent mammalian evolution. You are at the peak of natural adaptations for your species, at least if the last 10,000 years are any indicator. Any changes in humans these days are a matter of circuitry or science."

Layla followed him into his room and stood awkwardly by the door. When it shut thirty seconds after it sensed no further activity at the threshold, she jumped, knocked into the little red table where he drank his solitary morning cup of protein and caffeine, and caught it just before it hit the floor.

So much for Leonid grace. Even those bumblefooted Lynxians were more agile than she was.

"What does it mean for us? Now? Are we unable to dock? Do we have supplies to survive for a few weeks?" Layla rubbed her side from where it had knocked into the table. Seeing her in his quarters made Rupex realize just how small she was next to a Leonid. The table his knees fit under comfortably came to her bust. His bed was luxuriously large, allowing him to sprawl out like a seastar if he wished. She would probably fit on a single pillow if she curled up on her side, knees to her chest, as he had seen in pictures.

"Hello? Rupex?"

Her voice interrupted his thoughts. "We are closer to Leonid-One at this point. That's my home planet and where the *Comet Stalker's* registry is held. We can go to Leonid-One... but I'm not sure what will happen to a non-Leonid, non-Felix Orbus citizen. Would you be quarantined? I do not know. Hopefully, they would allow us to remain on the ship. We have enough supplies to last twenty-four cycles."

"Cycles?" Layla's brows knitted together. "Oh. Like lunar cycles. So I'm not in any danger of being on the menu?"

"I would not eat a human. It's uncivilized."

But suddenly he could imagine tasting her. Licking her where that sticky, tangy scent was coming from, making his whiskers twitch. And while he would not eat her, the way she moved sometimes, like now, fast and nervous, made his predatory urges come out. He wanted to chase her. Catch her. Wrap his paws around her and pin her down, and then sink into her to the hilt, stretching her sheath open and embedding in her, forcing her to take load after load of his hot cum.

"Sorry, Mr. King and Captain. I'm a scruffy little commoner." Layla tried to laugh.

He tried to smile. He couldn't. His body was reacting so strangely around her. It was almost as if—

"Layla. Did Marcus, the 'old-lion dude' give you anything when he spoke to you earlier today?"

"No." She shook her head. "Should he have? Oh God! Am I going to have to take a vaccine in order for us to dock? What if it gives me fur? No offense, fur looks awesome on you, but it wouldn't on me."

Those little fluttery movements again, hand to her cheek, hand to her hair, smoothing it back behind her ear, and those white slippers on her feet reminded him of something small making tracks in the snow.

It brought out his natural dominance, but that shouldn't make him think of rutting her. Even the thought of coupling should have been clinical. Procedural.

"We're not docking on Leonid-One. There are a bunch of small uncharted planetoids in the liquid belts around Leonid-One."

"Liquid belts with planetoids? Like... oceans and islands?"

"Exactly." He gave her a pleased look. "They used to be smugglers' outposts, but now they're mainly used for pleasure excursions. Ru's Rest is one of the smaller planets on the outer rim. We're going there."

"Ru's Rest? As in Rupex? You own an *island*? Are you rich?"

"By no means. I don't own the whole island, just a little beach shack on it—but I'm the only one who has a house on it, last I checked."

"So technically, it's *like* you own a whole island?" Layla pressed, arching one eyebrow.

"Sure, in the same way a human might own a rusty old rowboat and call it an ocean liner."

"You sure know a lot about humans."

"No, I know that humans aren't so different from the other mammalian species." Rupex gave her a half-grin.

It was nice to have someone to smile with again.

"I was thinking about the contract and what it entails." Rupex hastily crossed back to his desk and flicked his paws across the keys. The screen on the wall flickered to life with the image of the gated property on Sapien-Three. "Would you accept the purchase of a dwelling place as compensation in exchange for your services as a surrogate? It is on Sapien-Three and seems to be well protected. If this particular property has been purchased by the time you return to the planet, I would secure another similar property for you. If my calculations are correct, this is a fair value and comparable to what you would earn in credits. Of course, if you'd rather have the credits, we could do that."

Layla came over and stood beside him, a hand to her mouth and her eyes wide. "This place?" Her voice was awed. "I could never live in a house like that. That's a house for rich people."

Rupex spread his paws. "Well, if you would accommodate me as your partner in reproduction for a few months, this would be yours, wealthy or not."

Layla hesitated. Rupex could see her eyes moving hungrily over the screen and he felt like a successful hunter who realizes he's just discovered the right sort of bait.

"That's a database computer, isn't it?" Layla asked after a long moment of waiting silence.

Rupex nodded. "It is, and a reasonably good one."

"Could you see how much it takes to buy out someone's laboratory contract?" She moved closer to him, hands pressing together at her waist. "Because I need a place to live, and that's a *really gorgeous* place to live, but if I had a smaller place and some credits left over, I could rescue my— I mean, I could get my friends' contracts back from the labs. They might not want to leave." Layla gave a jerk of her shoulders and her hands fell limply to her sides. It was not a defeatist gesture, more like one of relinquishment. This woman had long ago accepted there were some things she couldn't have, even if she wanted them.

He could relate.

"But even if they don't want to leave, I'd like to have enough credits to offer them a way out if they'd like the option."

Leonids admired loyalty more than beauty or even intelligence. Rupex felt his attraction to the human growing. She would have made a good Queen in that respect. "How many friends are you intending to 'set free'?" he asked, his paws curving into quote marks in the air.

"Three," Layla murmured. "If all three are still alive. At least I can try."

At least we can try. By Bastet, if that hadn't become the unofficial motto of every survival-hungry family in the Felix Orbus Galaxy these past six years...

"Humans typically produce one offspring at a time, but Leonid births are typically two to four with three being the most common size. Single births do happen. I was a singleton."

"Me, too." Layla interrupted him, her hesitant smile growing, stretching to fill her petite face.

"Hrm. Well, Marcus, the medical officer, thinks three cubs may be possible in our situation. Would a contractual addendum of credits per cub—past the agreed upon price of a Sapien-Three dwelling—be acceptable?"

"What if it was only one child? I mean, cub? I still need credits to get the lab contracts."

Rupex licked his lips and took a perverse pleasure that was totally foreign to him in watching her shiver. "I'm sure we can arrange something. Maybe some other services can be performed once conception is achieved?"

Layla nodded so quickly that her hair shook loose from the long tail at the back of her head.

He liked her hair like that, free and flowing, a mottled blonde and brown. It reminded him of a Leonid mane in its coloring, but it looked much finer and softer. He wondered just how soft other parts of her were, and why that made his mouth water.

She was watching him. She was staring at him as he looked at her like a starving beast, nose twitching, whiskers vibrating, and paws flexing on the edge of his chair. Humans and Leonids may be equals in civilized behavior, Rupex thought ruefully as his tongue flicked out and caught the sweet-salty notes drifting through the air.

I need to stop. I need to remain in control. The contract isn't signed. Or even written! She has to be in heat—or whatever passes for human heat. She has to have injections, and probably read some basic literature about the breeding process.

Calm, Ru. Be calm.

How was he supposed to be calm when she left his side, but didn't leave the room? How was he supposed to write a contract when Layla went and sat on the edge of his bed, a silky, soft white island in a sea of dark, lonely sheets?

"It takes around twenty-four hours to have a contract registered once the written and signed document is submitted." Rupex's tail tapped the ground impatiently, his body urging him to action while his mind told him to wait.

"I know. But uh... well. I'm twenty-two. This probably won't shock you, considering that Leonids were isolated from our galaxy for my entire adult life, but I don't know anything about how humans and Leonids—" she looked up at him, eyes boring into him as time seemed to slow down, *"fit together.* Should we have a good faith 'interaction' to make sure this works?"

His mind, usually agile, seemed to topple and flail to a halt.

Wait. Mate her just to see if it works? I suppose that's practical.

Layla scooted back on the bed and tucked her knees up under her, a position that sang of vulnerability and seduction at the same time.

How does she do that?

Why do I like it?

This is not how a Leonid female behaves...

"If you don't want to, that's okay." Layla's head dipped and jerked back up suddenly, her eyes wide in alarm. "Oh my God. Is this gross to you? Is this like... *taboo* for Leonids?" She put her hand up to her mouth, pale skin bright pink.

"Yes," he rumbled.

She scrambled off the bed and his predator instincts launched.

With a single spring, he was out of his chair and against her, pushing her to the wall of his quarters as she gasped. "I'm sorry. No, it is not repulsive. Yes, it is taboo. But you were right earlier when you said my body had no shame."

Pressed close to her, he could inhale Layla's scent in great waves, and the smell that he now knew was arousal washed over him and made him lust-drunk. "It's been a long time."

"I guess so."

He was still pressing into her, feeling the difference in their sizes. She was a third of his width and maybe two-thirds his height. A perfect, pretty little morsel with a fierce mouth and the will to survive.

That thought troubled him, even through the haze of lust and the tempting squirms she gave against him. She was not struggling to get free, as that would have caused his immediate retreat. No, Layla was inching around to face him instead of having her small curvy rear backed into the base of cock. His body was reacting like a juvenile before his first rut as she shifted and shimmied, finally looking up at him.

So different. But quite lovely.

"You must answer a question honestly," he said, voice low and grave, supple spine bending so his muzzle was just above her head.

"I'm clean. They got a blood sample, right?"

"Not that. Is this purely a financial exchange? If you have to *force* yourself to do this, I would rather not continue."

She sprang up on her toes and kissed the flat of his nose, startling him. It was only with an effort that he stopped himself from swatting her with his paw. "To get pregnant? Yeah, that's for the money. I'm not ready to raise kids." Her hand slid over to where his paw was suspended in mid-air and traced the thick fur on the back, then slid to the rougher pads on the front. Her touch was light and tentative, her eyes working from his paw to his face and back. "But forcing myself to try this? No. Not even a little."

He had to swallow the rush of wetness in his mouth. Her fingers went down into the crevices of his paw, exploring him so innocently. In return, Rupex imagined doing the same to her, his tongue between her legs and down her back, nuzzling her naked body as she sprawled open for him on his bed. "Do all humans choose partners so quickly?"

The smile on her lips turned sad. "No. Just the unlucky ones like me. We don't get to do long-term plans."

With a low purr that surprised him, he cupped her face with his free paw. "Well, now you can."

Chapter Seven

Layla found herself airborne and then cradled against Rupex's chest. He held her easily in one arm and carried her as if she was a satchel, light and inconsequential. It was a pleasant but strange feeling. Layla was used to being strong and having no one to care for her. Being carried, even for a second, made her heart clench.

And the thing nudging her rear made her thighs clench. Was there Leonid porn floating around out there on the intergalactic media collective? She should have watched some so she knew what to expect. Then again, why would she have bothered? Never in a million years would she have expected this!

Did Leonids kiss? Rupex seemed surprised but happy about her little peck on the muzzle. As she sank into the criminally wide bed, she reached for him again, her breath catching as he came to rest beside her.

Her hands stroked up his cheeks and over the rounded ears nestled in his luxurious dark honey-colored mane. Was he furry all over?

"You are a most curious human." Rupex sighed as she massaged his head with one hand and worked her way down his chest with the other.

"Very curious. How does this thing even open?" Her hand roved over his skintight black suit feeling for buttons or catches and finding none.

"Up at the collar and down it goes. It's all one piece. Easier when you have a tail."

As if wishing to highlight the said appendage, Layla felt a smart swat on her bare calf. The feathery tip of his tail was tapping along her leg now, brushing so gently that it tickled. "That's nice," she closed her eyes and allowed herself simply to feel, taking a break from her usual hyperaware stance of loner and survivor.

I'll be okay. He won't hurt me on purpose. If he did, he'd be the one paying for it. No surrogate, no cubs.

She felt safe. Potentially, she could feel safe for seven months or more—the first vacation she'd had in...ever.

A rush of affection for the big Leonid beside her made her wrap her arms around his neck and tug open the black collar. "Let's get you out of these," Layla giggled.

"Only if you'll do the same." His laugh was deep and rippling, making her skin tingle. Her nipples hardened as his paws bumped over her body, untucking her shirt as she tugged and stretched his clinging suit from him.

Her eyes opened and remained that way, wide and hungry.

Wow.

Leonids were nothing but fur and muscle. Forget about six-pack abs, this guy was sporting a dozen. Each edge and ripple was covered in soft, thick fur that she wanted to rub all over her bare skin, allowing herself a private, forbidden luxury.

And speaking of forbidden...

It should be illegal to own anything that large. Layla's eyes locked onto the erection between Rupex's thighs. A heavy, dangling sack with two beautifully defined balls was the base of his cock. The fur on his shaft was light and cream-colored, and several slick pink inches protruded above it. With a grunt, he reached down and pumped the shaft once, pushing out another solid six inches of pulsating bright pink flesh—and this second cylinder was completely wrapped in spiky protrusions.

"They're not sharp if that's what you were wondering," Rupex groaned, his fist still pumping.

"I wasn't wondering that," Layla replied truthfully. *I was wondering if that's completely erect. And if all that goes in me. And if it'll be good or bad.*

Rupex nuzzled his head into her shoulder and his tongue, soft but slightly rough and bumpy, left a soft scrape against her cheek.

Layla moaned. "That's so nice. That's better than nice."

"Good, because I plan to do more of that."

True to his word, his tongue swiped down her neck, across her newly bare collarbone, then down across her breast. The nubs flicked and flexed over the nipple of her soft globe, and her mind spiraled.

It was like a massage on steroids. There were too many textures, and all of them were divine, from the thick pads of his paws pulling down her panties and cupping her ass to the nubbly wetness of his tongue lathing across her sensitive breasts and the fluffy fullness of his mane as she tugged it in desperation.

"You taste so sweet. But you smell... you smell sweeter. Muskier. You humans—do all of you smell like sex?" He whuffed out warm air against her ribs and growled as one of her legs wrapped around his. With a quick "snick!" his tail wrapped around her ankle like a chain and pulled her leg back, leaving her pussy open.

"Maybe we do. I don't go around sniffing people."

"You're missing out. Scent is a powerful aphrodisiac, Layla."

"So is touch. God, did anyone ever tell you how velvety you are?" She sank her hands into the fur on his muscular sides.

"No. Leonid Queens wouldn't have appreciated it."

"I must seem sort of...bare." Layla realized the one area that should have been bare, according to most human standards, was between her legs. It was a trimmed, curly patch of downy curls, and perhaps it was fuller than she'd like.

Apparently not a problem.

Rupex yanked her leg with his tail again, and then uncoiled it, pulling her with his paws until her hips were level with his massive mouth.

My God. If he sneezes, he could bite off my entire thigh.

"May I?"

"Absolutely." Layla closed her eyes and settled back with a grin. He had manners, this King. More than most human men she'd been with.

With a jolt, her eyes flared open. His tongue smacked into her pussy with a wet slap and proceeded to drag hungrily across her nether lips as Rupex purred and growled in turns. His paws pushed her thighs apart until she was straddling his head.

I must look ridiculous. He's wearing me like a fucking party hat and— "Oh! Ohhh. Oh, wow." That textured tongue that could lick her from pucker to pearl in one swipe went burrowing in.

"More," Rupex demanded.

"More what?" Layla panted as his tongue pushed inside. It went up and in, then flattened and moved in and out like the world's best vibrating sex toy. As the Leonid's mouth was full, all he could do was glare up at her and dig his pads into her thighs. His tongue wriggled inside of her, pushing past the point where any cock had ever traveled.

Until I take his cock in a minute. The first part ought to be a little tight, but do-able. The second part, that spiky, silky looking pink shaft... how the hell will he fit inside me?

The idea of being filled and stretched to the point where she was simply stuffed, letting sensation wash over her, made the steady torrent of slickness turn into a gushing river.

His purring turned up in tempo and ferocity and *Sweet Lord.* His purring body vibrated against her. His tongue vibrated *inside* of her. Her walls clamped down in a way that she had only heard about, and apparently, Rupex adored that. He ripped his golden head away and leaned over her, smiling with a wet muzzle and a mouth full of shining sharp teeth.

"Wh-what?" Layla whimpered.

"Your sheath gets so deliciously tight when you're aroused. I can't imagine what'll happen when you hold me inside of you."

Her body, which had been on the verge of letting go in a powerful orgasm, was ready to find out. "Let's see."

RUPEX HAD HEARD HUMANS were stupid. He had seen evidence on the Sapien planets that humans were too trusting when they should be cautious and too skeptical when they had facts before them. Layla's attitude about their arrangement puzzled him and pleased him. He could see (and feel) how tiny and tight she was. He didn't dare try to push his pads inside of her for fear her contracting walls would accidentally force his claws out into her tender walls. Yet she trusted him to put something much larger and probably fairly intimidating-looking inside of that soft, yielding place.

"You're a very brave woman."

"Why? Do I need to be brave?" she asked breathlessly, a touch of laughter in her voice.

"I simply find that you are, and it's very attractive," he worked the word around in his throat and let it rumble out as they repositioned, her chest-to-chest with him, which would allow the first several inches to penetrate her. She was so small that the vision of grasping her hips in his paws and sliding her up and down over his cock until he came sprang to mind.

But that would be unfulfilling, a mere masturbatory aid. Leonids needed the latch, the moment of interlocking flesh, where the Queen's sheath was bound to him and he could pump cup after cup of hot cream into her.

Layla's leg scooted eagerly over his hip and her fingers darted into her mouth before coming down to circle the sensitive, narrow head of his cock.

The first brush of her fingers made him roar, but she didn't withdraw. Instead, she cupped her palm around him and mimicked the motions she'd seen him use earlier.

"Just show you once, hmm?"

"Fast learner," Layla winked, her breath uneven and high, coming from her nose and not her throat.

Nerves. Adrenaline.

Things a hunter loves to share with his prey or his pride, and at that second, Rupex couldn't tell exactly what his body perceived Layla to be.

No matter. He gripped her soft, gently padded rear and lined her sheath up with the tip of his cock. "I've heard that the texture is particularly enjoyable," Rupex purred, feeling as though he had to say something to ease her nerves.

"I don't know if we're going to make it to the spiky part," Layla warned.

Ooh. Challenge accepted.

The first few inches fairly flew into her, and she rode them with abandon, her spine curving to thrust her breasts up. She squealed when his claws popped out and gouged into her buttocks hard enough to scrape but not to draw blood.

As his mouth descended to capture her breast and suck it completely into his mouth, scraping with his fangs and soothing with his tongue, he felt her walls flutter and pulse hard.

His cock had no choice. The sensation was too similar to a Queen's as she peaked. His body had heard the command, "Come in. Fill me. Stay in me. Give me your seed, your cubs."

With his weight advantage and muscle mass, Rupex knew that if there was a battle of bodies, his would win, but he didn't want it to be a fight. Letting go of her breast, he grit his teeth and pushed his cock up while pushing her hips down, growling and snarling all the way as he worked against the grasping walls.

"Coming! Fuck, I'm coming again." Layla tugged one of his ears (not the brightest move at the moment) and gripped his mane as if she was desperate to show her pleasure to him.

Or maybe desperate to see if he shared it.

"Easy, little human."

"*You* take it easy," she challenged, a groan in her laughter. She arched back again and brought her slender hand between their bodies.

Rupex hadn't experienced this with any of his previous partners. "What's this?"

"Rubbing myself so I come harder. You feel like the best, biggest cock I've ever had, but external stimulation works *reeeeallly* good on humans," she panted, eyes closed.

"Is that so?" It worked well on him, too. He could feel her fingers bumping the slickness of his cock where it was buried in her, frantic little touches. He wanted her to wrap her hands around the remaining inches that were left lonely outside her warm, wet tunnel.

Instead, he trapped her hand under his own much larger paw, and dragged the rough pads over her clit hard and fast, the way her fingers had been circling.

Her scream made him snap his teeth shut and his claw scraped her soft inner thigh. There was a sudden lifting inside of her, like the tightness of her walls had moved something up and out of his way. Not much. Maybe an inch or two?

"Holy fuck!" Layla's scream ended as the tip of his cock sank in further.

His spikes, at least the first few rows, were home. They sank eagerly into her wet warmth, swelling and pressing outward inside of her, lodging him in place while his sack hardened and swelled.

Layla squirmed, but couldn't move up and down. "What's happening now?" she asked, no fear in her voice, just arousal and curiosity.

"This is how I clamp into you. If you were with a Canid, you'd be knotted, his massive knot at the base of his cock wedged into your tight little sheath until he completely emptied his seed into you. Every last drop. Such an inelegant way to do it."

"Sounds okay to me," she teased in a decidedly saucy tone.

A hot rush of jealousy and possessiveness invaded him so fast that he couldn't control himself. Rupex couldn't organize his thoughts into words. He bit at her shoulder, claiming a mouthful of her silky hair, so much softer and finer than a Leonid's. His cock thrust up, wedging in her, spines expanding to hold her open and make her take every last ounce of his sticky seed. As he felt his balls pulsing, his tip jerking, his tail lashed around her leg, then her waist, roping her to him.

A small part of him feared that he would see her recoil or fight his intrusion, and that would make him a monster, a dominant species forcing a weaker one. That would make her prey and him uncivilized.

His heart found joy and relief when she threw her arms around his neck and clung to him.

"Comfortable?" he asked, cock still leaking into her.

"Uh-huh."

Chapter Eight

Layla was surprised that so much of him fit. She'd heard from girls who had sold their contracts to the Pleasure Parks that there were ways to stretch and take bigger cocks. She'd been told that if anything was longer than about a foot, she'd better offer up her backdoor instead.

The whole concept of having sex with multiple strangers in short order freaked her out. Plus, once you stated your Dos and Don'ts on a contract, the buyer could do anything he wanted to you, as long as he didn't technically violate your rules. The horror stories she'd heard had made her certain that she'd never, ever agree to Pleasure Contracts, although she'd slid into several one-night stands.

But this was more.

And the pleasure was mutual and genuine. "You're so slippery."

"I could say the same of you," Rupex purred lazily.

"How long does a Leonid come? Just asking. With humans, it's a few seconds."

"Hmm. Less than an hour, I'd say."

"An hour? We're stuck together for an *hour*? What do your women do when you're stuck like this?" Layla asked, her voice more screechy than she'd like. "Also, my hair is in your mouth." That was a nice, diplomatic way of saying, "Lion-Dude, stop biting my hair." Right?

Rupex shrugged. They were face to face, pressed so close that she could touch her nose to his. "If it was with my Queen, my mate that I married, and we were trying for cubs, I imagine we'd be talking about our future family. If it was merely for pleasure, we would keep going."

"Keep going? Can you thrust like this?"

"No. You do. You squeeze down, then push out." He mimicked the motion he wanted to make, curling and uncurling his wide pads on her breast.

She tried it, squeezing down on his cock, then pushing out, and trying again.

"And I'll try that trick you showed me." His tail left her waist and slid to her spread legs, caressing her pussy and anus as he aimed for her clit, tickling it with every stroke.

Layla felt like her body was melting. Soft, rich fur surrounding her. This tickling, slapping sensation on her clit and her virgin backdoor, paws kneading her breast, and this massive cock inside of her. She couldn't help but think how much the firm, thick tail felt like another cock one second, teasing between her cheeks, and then the little curl of hair at the tip was almost feathery, like a kiss.

I could have my cake and eat it, too with this guy. Not to mention, I'm pretty sure that he has the equivalent of two human cocks in both girth and width.

Double penetration with one lover.

That's what I call a bonus.

"We have to do this every day?" Layla asked, feeling another orgasm build.

"If possible, at least for a month."

It felt like maybe she ought to be paying him. "Hey, whatever it takes."

MARCUS, THE GRAYING Leonid, was witness to their contract. If he suspected or knew they'd already had sex, he didn't say anything. He tactfully ignored her glowing pink face, the fact that she was limping slightly, and the fact that she was bloated from the bucket of cum Rupex had pumped into her. When they'd finally pulled apart on his bed, she'd felt so embarrassed. There had been an absolute lake on the sheets. Rupex had seemed a little worried.

As they went to the medical bay, she smothered a laugh, remembering the way his ears had gone down and his broad, handsome muzzle had drooped in concern. "Oh dear. I thought more would stay in. Maybe I need to latch more fully?"

"I'll adjust to you the more we do this," Layla had said before he could change his mind.

She wanted his cock. And she wanted to see him smile.

Wait. Had she thought he was handsome, too?

That was kind of new. She'd always thought she was strictly homospecian. Maybe she was interspecian?

Or maybe it's just Rupex...

"Shall we start with a basic examination? A reproductive examination, that is?"

"Uh. I—"

"Unnecessary," Rupex growled.

"I mean with a biomed scanner," Marcus said blandly. "To ensure she has the necessary equipment."

"I'm not a used starcraft," Layla grumbled, but she let herself be led to a cushy white table that was much larger than the ones back home (which made sense, considering the patients would be larger, too).

Marcus went to the other side of the table where the screen would project its findings. Rupex stood at the foot of the table, seemingly unsure where he should be.

"She's got all the right parts, as I told you," Marcus addressed his comment to Rupex who made a low growl.

"Layla. She is right here and an equal according to the contract. That is the mother of my cubs you are speaking to."

Marcus raised his shaggy brows and sighed a curious, purring laugh. "Well, it seems she soon will be. Layla, would you be willing to take your first injection of the chromosome booster? It shouldn't impact anything but your eggs and possibly your heat cycle."

"My what? Heat cycle? Do you mean period?" Layla sat up, happy that Leonid technology was so much more advanced than the mandatory free clinic screening she'd had when she turned sixteen. "I know that stops when I'm pregnant, I'm not an idiot."

Marcus looked at Rupex.

Rupex became interested in the blank wall opposite the screen. "He means your period of arousal. Queens have a month-long cycle several times a year. Marcus, you said humans didn't have such a thing."

"I know what I said, and they don't!" Marcus snapped, slender paws preparing a thin syringe. "They have a short fertile period each month, which is hard to detect. Human and mammalian eggs are minuscule and won't show up on this scanner. I'd need an obstetrics rig for that, and this ship doesn't have one. No. I'm referring to the fact that this booster could potentially cause you to experience a cycle similar to that of a Leonid female."

Horny for a month? While Mr. Big Bad Kitty has to fuck me with that massive cock every day?

Layla held out her arm. "Stick me."

"It might raise your body temperature a bit, but that should be short-lived. As for the state of arousal—"

"We'll *handle it*," Rupex snarled, tail lashing.

Layla stared at it and remembered the way it had smacked her pussy like a feathery whip, how it had held her leg captive like a sentient, possessive vine.

I don't even need the booster to go into heat around him, she found herself thinking.

Marcus swabbed her arm with an antiseptic wipe and grinned. "Nothing you two can't manage. Thank you, Layla. Here we go."

She felt a sharp little pinch.

"To the future of our species and the best of luck." Marcus slapped an adhesive patch over the puncture on her arm and turned away. "We might need it."

Chapter Nine

Hours later, Marcus came to her quarters with an embarrassed expression and a white plastic bag, the kind they put medical waste in. Seeing her shocked expression, he held up one paw. "I'm sorry, it's just what I had to paw that would give you a little measure of privacy."

Layla yawned as she stepped back to let him in. "Well, if we're talking about privacy, Leonids seem better at it than some other species I've heard about. But if you think I can get pregnant with any kind of privacy, I have news for you about how this whole human pregnancy thing works." She smirked and whispered, "You can't keep your pants on."

"No, believe me, I realized that based on the Leonid-human compatibility and my limited knowledge. I understand that you will be attempting pregnancy in the 'old-fashioned' way. As far as I know, you two will be the groundbreaking couple. Normally, our two species' chromosomes aren't compatible. Leonid sperm would be seen as a foreign object, rejected by the human immune system. This is a problem that has plagued other interspecies couples. It wasn't until immunology research related to Queen Fever was made public to lowly medical officers like myself that I decided to try making something that would help humans carry Leonid cubs."

"For a guy who says he's not good with reproductive medicine, you sure seem to be doing okay," Layla took the bag and placed it on her bed. It clanked. *Metal?* She turned, one eyebrow arched, back to Marcus.

He seemed ignorant of her confusion, opening the closet and sighing when he saw a mixture of discarded uniforms and simple white robes and slippers. "Science was my first love, Miss Layla, not medicine.

I found carrying out the tasks of guiding the crew through the ravages of a plague completely—if you'll forgive the pun—*alien* to me. A medical officer is supposed to administer the annual physicals for the crew, help with minor ailments between planets, that sort of thing. When I signed on, I was told I'd have plenty of time to pursue my own studies—chromosomal compatibility, interspecies genome sequencing, that sort of thing."

Layla opened the bag while he was talking. Big words tended to make her shut down and tune out. He could have just as easily said, "I'm the science end of baby-making, lady. Good luck getting knocked up and popping out cubs." It wasn't that she lacked intelligence. One particularly harsh matron at the group home had informed her that she had too much of it, seeing as how she'd never do anything with it. "What a waste you are" was the exact phrase, if Layla recalled. (Of course she did. You don't forget the insults people in power heap on you, no matter how many of them there are.)

"I'm sure you can figure out what those are. You seem very intelligent, if uninformed." Marcus stopped perusing the closet and turned back to face her just as she dumped out two long metal cylinders.

Probes. Fucking probes. Every old Pre-Contact Earth urban legend come true. Layla looked at Marcus and put her hands on her hips. "If you tell me you want to probe me for science, I'm calling you a dirty old lion-man."

"Rupex would kill me," he muttered, with a complacent shrug. "In scientific terms, your body is small where Rupex is large. He needs to get inside without difficulty. Leonids won't ejaculate properly unless a portion of the soft spiny protrusions on the base of the penis are snugly gripping your vaginal canal."

Layla blushed. Somehow the blunt, clinical terms made her more squirmy than the actual sex she'd already experienced. "Okay... Don't you guys ever have a little quality time with a Hot Queens video or whatever?"

"Different amounts and qualities of sperm. I believe it's more like what humans produce as an arousal fluid."

Pre-cum. He could write a book on interspecies sexy times.

Marcus considered the small talk portion of their meeting over. "Those are the closest things I have to sexual aids. I thought maybe you could stimulate yourself with them and work on your tolerance to bigger objects—like a Leonid male. I put medical-grade lubricant in there, too. It's what we have. If we weren't headed for a semi-deserted planetoid, I'd say we could stop off at a pleasure shop somewhere."

"Wait? Deserted planetoid?" Rupex hadn't mentioned deserted. Then again, when he said he was the only one with a house there, what had she expected?

"It's near civilization. It's just that we might be grounded for four to six weeks if... Well. History won't repeat itself, I hope to Bastet." Marcus gave a grave shake of his head and vanished through the sliding doors.

LAYLA ATE HER EVENING meal (was it actually evening?) in her room and turned on the media viewer. Almost every station was showing news updates. Every channel was full of panicked cat-people.

I have to stop calling them that.

Tigerites were solitary and worked through networks of relatives in their jungle-like planets. Their spokesman was gruff and unconcerned, mentioning that Tigerite domains had fared the best of all the other planets in the Felix Orbus Galaxy during Queen Fever.

The Servali female reading the news was barely holding her shit together. Layla could tell a look of fake calm when she saw it.

Finally, she found the Leopardine stations were the only ones not showing a bad news marathon. She watched a Leopardine drama that she couldn't follow, but there was some serious romantic tension unfolding.

Instead of a big make out session, the male Leopardine pulled the female to him so that his chest was pressed against her back and bit her neck. The Leopardine female moaned and undulated against him, their paws coasting down her exotic dress and luxurious spotted fur.

Layla's pussy throbbed. *Is that what Rupex wants? Biting? Snarling? Does he want to come up behind me and stick that big cock in me while I'm bending over?*

I'm getting paid to live in luxury and get fucked royally as often as I want.

Well, I damn well want.

Layla sipped the bottled water provided in the cooling unit of her quarters. It didn't seem to help. She felt hot.

Hot and bothered.

Her eyes wandered to the two long, fairly thick probes on the bed.

She'd never really craved sex. It was something that came along with numbing yourself and not getting attached. Sexual pleasure was a hit-or-miss event.

His dense, velvety fur had rubbed her clit when he was deep inside of her, massaging her outside as he filled her inside.

One of Layla's hands went up under her white robe and stroked her slit. Her leaking slit. Just the slightest nudge sent a river out of her swollen sex.

One hand rubbed while the other rolled the shorter of the two steel probes around on the bed, warming it with her hot skin.

"Why am I so hot?"

It didn't matter.

Cool metal on her pussy made her moan. It slid in like it was buttered, eased by a torrent of slick Leonid cum and her own arousal.

Wanton thoughts assailed her as she pumped it in and held it, working her tight cunt muscles around it, pretending it was Rupex's thicker, longer cock she was taking.

I could take this and him. I could have one in each hole. Oh my God, what's wrong with me? Why am I wondering if he wants that? I don't want that!

Do I? I could find out...

The second probe was almost within reach if she just rolled—

"Layla? May I enter?"

Rupex! Rupex was outside her quarters, and his voice through the intercom made her jump.

"Just a minute." Layla shoved the makeshift toys under the sheets and smoothed down her hair.

"If you are at rest, it's not urgent."

"Enter!" Layla perched on the edge of the bed and hoped she looked somewhat presentable.

Rupex appeared as the sliding door opened. He was in a different outfit, still all in one piece, but it looked softer.

Are those his jammies? Or is that a sleeping uniform? Layla smiled. "I Ii."

Rupex opened his mouth—and a low rumbling growl came out.

"What's wrong?" And why did that warning noise make her drip?

"Nothing. Nothing. It's just that scent is a powerful weapon. You remember I mentioned that during our—our good faith encounter." He cleared his throat and put his paws behind his back.

Layla smirked. The King and Captain might try to look reserved, but she'd seen the hungry look in his eyes when he had his tongue buried in her spasming tunnel, had his claws just barely teasing her thighs.

"Is that what we're calling it?" Layla swung one leg restlessly over the other.

His pupils dilated and he licked his lips. "I came to see if you had everything you needed and if you would like a different set of rooms? Also, Marcus informs me that the chromosomal booster should be reaching its full effect in the next forty-eight hours. If you are not expecting cubs after the first cycle, he will try weekly doses of the booster."

"Will it hurt to give me more boosters this month? I mean, might as well use every tool in the arsenal." Layla shrugged. She wanted to earn her money. She wanted that house on Sapien-Three.

But the thought of another month full of daily mating...

No. Be good. Fulfill your contract.

Rupex nodded, his chin to his chest, mane catching the light of her room and making his fur shine like red gold. "Agreed. I will inquire. Finally, he told me there were no clothes appropriate to your small stature."

"Are you calling me short?"

"I'm calling you human-sized. You are easily two feet shorter than most Leonid Queens. However, where we are going, there will be some clothing from adolescent Leonid females. Hrm. My sister, Alana, still has some things are still there."

"Oh, Rupex. I'm so sorry. She died when she was only a—"

"No, she was not a child. She was an adult female. A Queen. Married and living on Leonid-One with her husband. My brother-in-law, Jaxson... He still mourns her, but he saw no need to return to our childhood retreat and collect her old clothes. They will likely fit you with some slight alterations."

"I can sew by hand, the old-fashioned way."

Rupex looked horrified. "You simply need to put it in the AAU. We have one aboard the ship, but I'm afraid it needs a new control module."

Layla nodded. AAU. Automated Alteration Unit. All the rich people had those machines—and never used them. When they needed new clothes, they just bought them. She wondered if Rupex would ever understand her kind of poverty.

No. Probably not, and that's good. That means your kids—I mean, his cubs, will never go through what you went through. They'll never have to sell their bodies and souls to the highest bidder.

"You are sad. You smell like salt and grief. I thank you for mourning my sister," Rupex said gravely, bowing low to her. "Or is it someone else you mourn?"

Feelings. Icky things to discuss. Unless they were the fun kind, the massive-cock-in-tight-little-slit feelings. "I was just thinking about how nice it's going to be for your cubs to have everything they could ever need. I didn't have that. I know a lot of people who didn't. Dax, Wendy, and Elio didn't have that. I couldn't give them that. That's why I'm sad. And I'm sad for all the Queens your galaxy lost. I can't imagine what it's like."

Rupex nodded several times. His tail swung like a worried pendulum behind him. "I am sorry for your fears for your friends."

"Thank you," Layla gave him a half-baked smile. "You're not good at small talk or deep feelings shit, right?"

"That is not a King's way. The King of a pride must remain objective and goal-oriented. The captain of a vessel must do the same."

"You get it with both barrels, huh?"

Rupex squinted at her. "I think so."

She had to laugh. "I bet there are plenty of Leonid expressions I won't get. It's okay."

RUPEX SMILED BACK AT the grinning girl. Naughty girl. No, naughty woman, he corrected himself. Actually, even though she was a human, the more he talked to Layla, the more he was reminded of a Queen.

She has the heart of a queen, he thought to himself. The way she protects. The fearless way she attempts to solve problems.

Rupex could imagine her hunting beside him, even though civilized Leonids did not hunt any longer. They got their meat from the farms and seas where things were bred to be eaten and the animals did not possess a higher intelligence.

Nonetheless, he was struck by the image of Layla stalking beside him on the sandy beaches of Leo Falls Island, entering the humid woodlands and catching the sand chickens and marsh ducks that liked to nest there.

"So. Um. Tell me about the place we're going? You said you used to live there when you were kids?"

"Yes, during the summers, if my father didn't take me with him. It's a beautiful place. Overgrown by this time, I suppose." Rupex frowned. Squatters could have taken over the small island. Outlaws. Smugglers.

Or maybe it would be like stepping back in time and finding a magical world where everything was the same—the two tiny shacks, his and Alana's, under two Tigerwood palms. Two fishing poles left on the stoop.

But Alana wouldn't be there. There was no magic in the cosmos to bring her back.

"If it's such a sad place for you, why go back?" Layla asked gently, her voice soft.

My cubs would be fortunate to hear such a voice soothing them to sleep.
"Because it is a safe place, as far as I know. I want to keep you safe. You and the cubs."

"That's good." Layla waited for him to say more, her expectant little face peering up at him. She was standing so close his tongue was frozen to the roof of his mouth. So close—her scent, her warm, sensual scent, bombarding him whenever she shifted from foot to foot.

"If it's too painful to talk about you don't have to." Layla placed a hand on his arm. The jolt of her touch surprised him. Not so much the touch itself, but the way he instinctively reacted. He purred and moved closer. It was not the light unconscious purring of simple contentment. This was a deep rumbling purr of possession, the kind a King of Knight would make when you possess something you particularly want and no one else can have it.

It was the purr of a mate.

That is such nonsense, Rupex told himself. My body is simply confused because we performed the act of mating. But she is not my mate. Layla is a human and would never want to live life as a Leonid Queen. She wants to go back to her own people and rescue her friends. She wants to set up a house on land. She doesn't want to travel around the galaxy with you, raising cubs on board this vessel.

"I'm sorry," Layla repeated, taking her hand from his arm.

"Oh! No, it is not you. It is not talking about Leo Falls. I love that place and I could spend days talking about it. I was only struck by a few logistical considerations. That is the problem with being the King of a pride as well as the captain of a starcraft. One keeps being molested by sudden concerns."

Layla nodded and spoke up in a voice that was resolute and more positive than he would have expected. "Let me know how I can help. I'm basically going to be an incubator. As long as I'm not vomiting or getting my injections, I ought to be able to do *something* useful on the ship." With a nervous grin, she tucked her hair back behind her ears, her neck bared and catching his predatory eye. "Of course, if it's anything like a specific full-time job, then we could take out a secondary contract."

She is shrewd, but the contract comment was an afterthought. Rupex could tell that her first instinct had been helpfulness and her second had been to keep things professional. *That seems to be the way his mind was working, too. First, personal, second, professional.*

In other words, completely backwards from the way we ought to be carrying on.

"I'm not sure if you can help with this problem. I was only thinking of how different life will be for my cubs. I do not intend to give up my position as captain. The *Comet Stalker* is quite large and has plenty of room for passengers. I will turn several into family quarters when the time comes. But eventually, I will have to procure a nanny." Layla nodded. Her eyes lit up.

Rupex felt a strange fluttering in his chest. *She's going to offer to do it. She is going to offer to stay with me and the cubs. That would be wonderful for them to know their mother, even if she is a human.*

But instead, Layla's smile disappeared. "I wish Wendy was here. Wendy, the one I was telling you about? She wanted to become a teacher or a childcare provider for a wealthy family on Sapien-Two or Sapien-Three. I think that's one reason she took the lab contract, hoping to get money and an education while she was their 'guest.'" Her tone became bitter. "Maybe she made it out. I don't know. Maybe she's teaching now."

I could find her friend. I could hire her friend and find Layla a job aboard the ship. Then she'd want to stay.

What in Bastet's name is wrong with me?

Rupex was beginning to wonder if Marcus had somehow given him a breeding drug.

"Perhaps Wendy would be willing to do so. Perhaps all of your friends would be willing to take on positions? As you can see, we don't have a crew. If we are locked down in this galaxy for a while, it is entirely possible that the crew I was heading to pick up will have found other positions. And if I am to take on a family, I will likely need additional crew members. Obviously, I'm thinking about the few months you're onboard the ship. Before you set up your permanent residence."

"Right. Right. But... You mean you would buy my friends contracts from labs on Sapien-Three?"

"Provided they are reasonable and your friends wish to go. I was thinking they might," Rupex tried to keep his tone nonchalant, "as you are on board." To cover his eagerness and this whim of his, he added, "Naturally, Wendy would have no purpose unless there were cubs to care for. We would want to wait and make sure our attempts had been successful."

"And it takes a few weeks to get back to Sapien-Three anyway. Plus time on Leo Falls." Layla paced in front of him.

Please stop doing that. It's too much like an agitated beast that I should stalk, Rupex found himself pleasing silently.

To his relief, she did stop her pacing.

To his chagrin, she pounced on him, hugging him around the neck, burying her face in his fur. "Thank you! I...I can't imagine why you'd do this for me, but it's the nicest offer I've ever had."

His body reacted without his consent. Rupex felt his cock growing and straining against his clothing, felt his mouth fill with saliva as she rubbed her scent all over him, pressing her warm, squirming body across his.

With a snarl that probably terrified the girl, he pounced, taking her backwards to the bed. Something hard and unyielding rolled under his paw, making him curse.

"I'm sorry, I can't help what you do to me," Rupex hissed, dragging his rough tongue over her neck and down her shoulder.

"Good," Layla panted, grabbing at his collar.

His eyes widened in surprise. "But—"

"Fuck me again," she whimpered, hands buried in his mane.

"Is it to thank me?" he demanded, tearing her clothes off and pushing his own down. *Do I care if it is?* He'd do more for her, as much as she wanted, as long as she let him fill her, rut in her, mark her as his.

"Yeah, but not just that." Layla squealed when he gave up on trying to get the fabric around her waist off and simply ripped it aside.

They shifted and kissed, tongues mating. Hers was a tiny, dancing tease, something he wanted to capture and possess. He stuck his tongue into her mouth and felt her throat closing around it. He pulled back, leaving her gasping. *I fill her mouth completely. I could fill other parts completely.* He put his paws on either side of her shoulders for leverage and found the cursed hard object again.

"What in the cosmos?" He batted the sheets away to reveal long, silver cylinders and a tube of thick lubricating gel.

"Marcus. He told me to practice taking big cocks," Layla snickered.

"Gods, you are naughty." Queens that he'd known were so much more reserved, even in their flirtation.

Layla lacked their grace and elegance, but there was sinful deliciousness about her that no one had ever offered him. His one taste of her had made him hungry for another.

"He didn't say it like that. He told me to get your sensitive nubby spines into my pussy and keep them there so you make gallons of cum and fill me with cubs." She bared her short, blunt teeth at him in an imitation of his own snarling smile.

Fuck, she is adorable. Naughty, insatiable, clever... His early opinions about humans and Layla in particular were being reversed far too fast for his normal reticence to allow. "If Marcus told you to do that, I'll eat the ship's navigation unit."

"He didn't use those *words*, but the meaning was the same," Layla whispered as she struggled under him, fighting his clothes down.

Rupex knew he should tell her to stop squirming. It was too much like prey. The urge to bite was prickling at the back of his mind, but he channeled it into his cock. *Thrust. Attack. Penetrate. Make it so she can't move, stuffed with your cock and pinned by your spines.* Fuck, how he wanted that, wanted to feel her little walls locked around him as she writhed, helpless to shift away.

"You do things to me. Things a Queen has never done," Rupex confessed.

"You do things to me, too. Things I like, things I want more of." One of her hands seized the silver probe by her head. "Think this thing will really help us?"

"I prefer the old-fashioned way, as paradoxical as that sounds." Rupex sneered at the phallic substitute.

"So you don't want to watch me warm up for you?"

He froze above her. Watch? Watch Layla forcing that long silver rod inside, exploring the depths where he wanted to go?

Tempting, but... no.

"No. Your 'pussy', as you call it, is mine. At least for the next seven months or so," he growled.

"Then I guess you'd better help me with my assignment," Layla said with a coy smirk, one hand stroking his cock, the other stroking the metal probe. With a daring grin, she put both together, watching him grunt in surprise as the long, smooth phallus rubbed against his. "It's too cold, isn't it?"

The sudden thought of toying with his prey—his lover, he corrected himself sharply, was far too appealing to pass up. The toy was smaller than him anyway, but only by two or three inches. "Marcus assigned you this? To stretch yourself with these?"

"Mmhmm. But he didn't say I couldn't have help."

LAYLA KNEW THAT SHE was sick. Sick in a wonderful, twisted, kinky way that had to be related to the shot she'd received.

Why else would she be sucking on Rupex's cock while he slowly worked the long metal probe in and out of her leaking pussy? Why else would she be moaning and squealing as he started moving it faster and faster, telling her to open up for him?

She'd never let men boss her around, but she hadn't been a prude. Sex was a cheap drug, it let her escape and get numb on her terms. It didn't give her feelings like this.

"Ohhhh. Oh, *fuck*, Rupex."

"Is it true some human women take lovers of this size?" he demanded, panting, one of his paws working the base of his cock.

She slid under his paw and dragged her nails along his spines, watching his back arch and his massive jaw go slack in pleasure. With a push, she batted his paw away and replaced it with her tongue, licking along the rows of nubs while she watched him shudder.

"Human women don't take human lovers that size because they don't exist on Sapien-Three. But toys exist. Other species exist. Some women take them, or at least in part. I like this better." She pulled on his rigid cock, eliciting a growl as she rubbed it over her stiff nipples. "At least now I can tell Marcus I was a good patient and did as I was told."

"You don't strike me as terribly obedient," Rupex moaned, pulling free of her grasp.

Layla bit her lip as the slippery metal stayed inside her. Rupex grabbed both her ankles easily in one paw and hoisted them up, leaving her speared and full for his lustful eyes.

Not obedient? No, she'd never been one to go along without questioning. But with Rupex... Well, she felt strangely safe. She could see herself obeying his orders in certain situations. He was a captain. She was a guest on his ship and even if she wasn't part of his crew, she hoped she could help him while she was on board. Besides being a captain, Rupex was a King. She felt the power, real, *earned* power emanating from him.

"Wh-what orders do you want me to obey?" Layla asked, feeling gravity and pleasure work against her clamping muscles.

"No commands but to take me inside of that tight, soft little paradise again." Rupex brushed the crown of his cock against her opening, already full.

Holy crap. He wants me to take both? At once?
Not possible.

But she wanted to try. Her common sense was deleted by desire.

Rupex surprised her however, finishing her off with a flurry of hard strokes that bordered on painful, confusing her body as the hard metal jabbed in and the pressure on her g-spot made her hips arch as if begging for more.

More was just what she got.

With a roar, Rupex jerked the metal probe out and flung it behind them. Layla faintly heard it clatter to the floor, the noise hidden under the reverberations of her lover's bellow. And then—blessed relief, excruciating pleasure— his thick cock slid in deep and fast. His clawed paws jerked her thighs forward and his tail locked around her ankles, keeping her in place.

"Let's see what's more effective, shall we?" Rupex laughed, thrusting in and bowing his body down over hers. His tongue traced over her breasts and up over her throat, nuzzling and purring.

The purring created vibrations that filled all of her, not just her pussy, not just her chest.

If I die like this, I'm okay with it, Layla thought in a haze, her insides so full that she felt her pussy leaking, no room left for her juice. Each thrust made her squirt out a sharp, exquisitely pleasurable stream. "Fuck, Rupex... What are you doing to me?"

Making you mine, little queen."

Queen. He called me queen.

"King. My big, beautiful King." Layla looked into his startled eyes, loving the flecks of gold, green, and amber that swirled in them.

Wow. He's just as amazed as I am.

That we fit.

"A little more. Please, a little more." Rupex's voice was softer, more insistent.

She didn't have enough air to make words. She nodded, trying to force herself down and feeling his thick cock head shifting and slipping inside of her—slipping up and under. It was as if he had managed to push past her cervix, not going through it, but under it, in a hot forbidden pocket she didn't know existed.

Right now it didn't matter. Right now, a hundred little spines were pressing into her, swelling until her pussy felt like it might tear—

The world went out of focus. Was this an effect of the drugs? An endorphin rush? The pain wobbled out of sight and was replaced by wave after wave of pleasure, coming in time with spurt after spurt of hot Leonid cum.

Chapter Ten

H is little Queen. His little Queen was asleep, impaled on him, or perhaps rendered unconscious. Rupex hoped not. "My Layla?"

"Mm. My big kitty. Big kitty, little pussy. Ha."

Rupex shook his head in bemusement. He and his human surrogate had been locked together for several hours. He had dozed, but Layla slept hard, curled into his furry hide for warmth.

If there was an emergency aboard, it would be most problematic as his Layla was still melded to him, her swollen pussy refusing to release his spines. Her abdomen was swollen as if she was already in the first fifth of her pregnancy.

Hm. And perhaps she was, even if only by a matter of hours. If the booster worked...

"Layla?" He shook her shoulder.

Nothing but an agitated sigh.

"Quarters, this is Captain Rupex," Rupex called softly.

"Good morning, Captain," the automated voice replied.

Morning? Already?

"Quarters, are we on course?"

"Yes, Captain."

"Quarters, news?"

The voice switched and the media viewer in Layla's room flickered on.

A Leopardine journalist in a lavish purple dress was explaining that Felix Ore, the largest space ore mining company in Felix Orbus, had reduced crews to essential personnel and that it was going to impact profit margins.

"Damn."

"The Servali planets are scrambling to halt all on-world traffic this morning as three further deaths were reported in conjunction with a mutation of the Queen Fever Virus that is tragically impacting our Canid neighbors. Our hearts go out to them at this time. The Leopardine Prime Minister recommends that all females, especially those in high-contact professions, obtain an additional dose of the QF vaccine. Word is expected today from the Felix Orbus High Council on whether all F.O. planets will restrict traffic and place a mandatory six-week quarantine on docking ships. For further—"

"Oww. Ow. Oh, shit." Layla was awake and wincing.

Quickly, before her squirms could arouse him, Rupex ripped his semi-soft organ from its sweet nest. Even soft, he was still a good number of inches in length, probably about the size of a human male's erect genitalia. Layla made a yowl of pain that shot him in the heart and made him grab her back, pulling her against his chest. He purred and licked her bare back and shoulders. "Shh, shh, my Layla. It'll be all right. A hot shower and rest in bed. You can come to my quarters while your quarters are cleaned."

Layla nodded groggily and pulled free of his embrace. Rubbing her eyes, she stretched, yawned, and gasped. "Am I already pregnant?"

Rupex blinked. "I would love that to be the case. Do you feel pregnant?"

"No, I look—" Layla stood up and pointed at her puffy lower abdomen.

A torrent of cum gushed out from her when gravity took hold.

"Ick. Why is cum so sexy in the moment and gross later?" Without waiting for an answer, Layla scurried off to the shower. "I need something to wear, too!"

Clothing and cleaning. That was the least of his worries.

MARCUS WAS IN THE MEDICAL bay, but he didn't even look up when Rupex came in.

Rupex paused. As a captain, the ship was his from stem to stern. Still, he usually didn't invade Marcus' privacy.

Right now, Marcus was speaking to an old Servali Queen, the monitor of his database computer revealing a small, regal female with her head wrapped in the traditional red Servali kerchief.

"My love to you, too, Mama. No, I think the young Queens will be fine without another dose. They only had one last cycle."

"The schools will be closed for six weeks. The Servali High Council already announced it."

"Good, good. Can't be too careful."

"You cannot be too careful, either. Kaya told me you wanted to mess about with viruses and pathogens, blood cells and chromosomes. Tch." She made a snorting noise of disapproval.

"I am not dealing with immunology in terms of the virus, Mama. Only in terms of reproduction."

There was a silence.

"My Kaya would have been proud of you."

"Thank you, Mama."

Mama? Marcus was a Leonid. His mother was not a Servali! Furthermore, that Queen must have been in her mid-fifties or even sixties, just a decade or so older than Marcus. She couldn't possibly be his mother! Not that Rupex would have cared if she was, but he admitted to feeling puzzled. "Hrm. Marcus, a word when you're free?"

Marcus gave him a curt nod. "Mama, I must go. Love to all the little ones. Keep them close to home."

"Bastet go with you, my son."

"And you." Marcus slapped the screen with a huff and it went back to displaying medical data. "Good morning. Or should I say afternoon?"

Rupex's tail lashed. It was still morning—barely. "This was your idea."

"I didn't expect you two to seize on it with such alacrity. Not that I'm judging."

"You must be, to mention it. You're the one who told her to 'stretch.'"

"Why should sexual activities cause the human pain?"

"They don't! I mean, I won't let them! That is, as far as I know, they haven't." The tail went into a full metronome pulse, guilt nipping him on every swing. He had been far too vigorous. His body and mind were confused by Layla. Feral instincts he'd thought long dead came out around her. Not to mention, it had been over six years since he'd made love. "Enough about me! Layla and I have signed a contract and I registered it yesterday. The receipt is already recorded in this morning's communications. Credits are already transferred to her account."

Marcus said nothing, simply stared at him.

Rupex groaned. That made it sound as though it was all right to cause her pain since she was paid for it. "I'm very fond of her. Speak to her yourself if you wish. I... I satisfy her. In many ways."

Marcus raised one eyebrow slowly. "Many ways, hm?"

The leering tone was too much. "All right, if we're prying into one another's private affairs, how is a Servali Queen only a decade older than yourself your mother?"

Marcus didn't answer, and that nettled him. Why should his medical officer be so calm and cool while he was tying himself in knots over the complicated feelings he'd developed for Layla in the space of two days? "Don't tell me. Your father has remarried."

"My mother and father have both passed and you know it."

Did he know it? "Oh. I'm sorry. I... There were so many that..."

The graying Leonid waved his paw. "That was Kaya's mother. Kaya was my wife."

Rupex hoped his surprise was masked. Surely, he should have known that his longest-serving crew member had a wife?

"Don't bother to hide it, Ru. You can be shocked. You didn't know because we didn't tell any of my family. We got married six months before the first outbreak. I took my two-week planet leave and didn't bother to tell anyone I was going to marry a gorgeous Servali waitress half my age. She worked in her mother's cafe. Best salmon en croute I've ever had, rubbed in curry." Marcus kissed the tips of one paw. "A work of art, made by an angel, served by a goddess. She was pregnant with four cubs."

Rupex sat, his stomach falling. Marcus never applied for spousal or dependent pay raises. "Was?"

Marcus busied himself on his computer. "She was in a high-contact position. She got the fever right away. She was still working, only in the second-fifth. They tried the hormone treatment on her. It made her lose the litter. Then she died a week later."

"Why didn't you—" But Rupex knew why he didn't tell him. Alana had died during the first outbreak, too.

"I did tell you that I wanted bereavement leave. You signed the papers. But there wasn't anywhere we could go, confined to the ship. You mourned in your quarters. I wept in mine. You talked to your brother-in-law and parents. I talked to Kaya's mother and her little brothers. Thank God, Kaya's mother was just old enough that the fever didn't kill her, just put her in the hospital for a few months."

"Marcus, I'm sorry. I never asked. I never thought to ask. You didn't say anything, not a word. Why?"

"Because there are a lot of bigots in the Leonid community. Purity of the Pride dungheads and the rest. Of course, they all changed their tune when Leonid Queens became few and far between. No one would look twice at Kaya and me if we walked down the streets of Leonid-One today. But we won't get that chance."

What could he say to that? The world was different six years ago, with species being more selective. His sister and her Canid husband had been a rarity of rarities, but they'd been raised on starcrafts, seeing every combination of couple, thruple, and interspecies mix. Except one.

"That's why you decided to see if humans could have cubs? Because you know that Felix Orbus is—"

"About to have a massive population crisis that even super-sized litters won't fix in time? Yes. And Leonids, with their stupid bigotry, will be the hardest hit unless people like you set an example. A King, a captain... people will listen to you. Especially if you stop taking on all-Leonid crews." Marcus glared at him.

"I didn't do it on purpose!" Rupex protested, but maybe some small part of him had preferred to work with his own species. He knew what to expect from them—sometimes. "Last night, I even suggested that Layla's old littermates come aboard. Well, technically they weren't littermates, but near enough."

"Good. What about Tigerites?"

"They don't like to stay off-world for so long."

"Leopardines?"

"Too used to luxury."

"Servalis?"

"Small."

Marcus growled low in his throat. "Rupex! Listen to yourself. Have you learned nothing from all we've lost?"

"I have. No, Marcus, I have. Those are reasons I would have given in the past. I will change my thinking—for my sons and daughters. But first, we have to make it to the point where I could even take on a full crew again. You heard the news?"

With a heavy sigh, the older Leonid tapped a few keys and a different screen projected an ominous headline. "Dock by Daybreak says Servali Prime Minister."

Rupex pushed himself out of the chair. "Will Layla survive a lightspeed jump?"

"Not comfortably."

"Then I'm going to switch to manual and put the *Comet Stalker* through her paces. We're going to be at Leo Falls by the time the Leonid Prime Minister makes his declaration."

It wasn't a question anymore.

Chapter Eleven

Layla had never been so lonely or so horny in her life. For the past two days, she had only seen fleeting glimpses of Rupex when he'd come to his quarters to eat. She'd waited in the hall near the sliding silvery door to his rooms in the morning and the evening, expecting him to pull her inside and take her to his bed with a passionate lunge.

He hadn't. He'd politely, almost formally invited her to share his meals, but they hadn't been romantic, or even social. The DDS on the ship (Dietary Delivery System, Layla quickly learned) was stocked with healthy, nutritious foods for Leonids. She could eat her fill of meats, veggies, fruits, starchy tubers, and grains. Rupex had ordered for her, insisting she eat meals that were clearly meant for Leonid-sized physiques. Somehow, she'd gotten through them, suddenly ravenous.

But she'd eaten them alone. Every meal for two days, Rupex had drunk two cups of liquid, one steaming and black, the other steaming and reddish-brown. "Protein and caffeine. Optimized energy and nutrition. I've got to get back to work, but you take your time. Nap or watch the media viewer in here if you like." He'd make the same offer every meal as he gulped down both beverages and then raced back to the flight deck.

Finally, after the third morning meal, Layla had protested when Rupex tried to dash away.

"Look, I know you're busy on the ship, but this isn't the deal we made." Layla ran a hand down between her breasts. "I'm not earning my credits."

"We've mated twice in a short span. It's too soon to know if either mating was successful. This satisfies our contract as far as I'm concerned." Rupex put down his mug.

"Fine. Well, what about you?"

"Me?"

"Yes! You have to hold up your half of the bedroom action, too. You can't get me addicted to awesome Leonid breeding sex and then rip it away from me without a warning."

Rupex stared at her for a minute, muzzle twitching, eyes narrowed. Maybe I shouldn't have said anything, Layla thought to herself, chest tightening. She realized she wasn't afraid of the giant, furry man before her. The sensation was more like *expectation*. It wasn't even a wholly unpleasant feeling. Other parts of her tightened as well. The breath vanished from her lungs as Rupex growled and rumbled deep in his chest.

In the next second, the towering Leonid bounded over to her and gripped her shoulders, his claws poking through the soft warm pads of his paws as he kissed her hard. Layla could feel his hardness pressing into her middle as he half-lifted her, half-bent to meet her lips with his own.

"You have no idea how hard it is for me to stay away from you. I'm doing this to get us to safety as fast as I can. I would advise you to watch the news, except I hear stress isn't good for women who are trying to conceive." His chest heaving, Rupex pushed her away and shook himself. He gave her one last burning look through golden eyes as he marched from the room.

NATURALLY, SHE WATCHED the news. It seemed to be the only thing on.

The quarantined Sirius Federation ship that had started all of the trouble was now reporting deaths in the dozens. The new mutation of the Queen Fever didn't just affect Canid females but also males if they were in "rut."

Layla shook her head. Some "primitive" instincts had not gone away, even over the centuries. While the Leonids, Canids, and the like could control their behavior, their hormones and blood levels still told the tale of ancestral mating and breeding patterns. Hormone injections were keeping people alive and battling febrile seizures if administered early enough. Others were too far gone to save. To make matters worse, some of the passengers on the ship had left the ship during the previous week at various excursion points, including Servali moons.

Even the unconcerned Leopardine newscaster that Layla had taken to watching finally seemed rattled by this revelation. Passengers who had disembarked without symptoms had later developed them—and the mutated virus was spreading again. Ships were being grounded, planet-side excursions and events were being canceled, and people were being told to remain at home unless they were in designated "vital" professions.

As usual, Layla saw no mention of Sapien-Three or its sister planets. So many other galaxies tended to avoid them. Interactions were becoming more common, but she supposed they would dry up again.

"Quarters. Turn off the media viewer." Layla sat weakly on the edge of the bed, hands gripping her knees.

Wow. I'm actually glad that I got sent off-world when I did.

What if that jerk Paul hadn't tried to ship her off to some depraved Lynx-man? She shuddered. What if Rupex hadn't been honorable?

Was he though? He wanted something out of her. He could be acting.

Gnawing desperation overcame her. For the first time in years, she didn't feel hopeless and pointless. She had a contract she wanted —helping give someone a family. Rupex was a good man who needed a family.

Her insides got all fluttery and soft. Mushy.

Focus on the other things. Like hope! For the first time in...ever?

With the credits she earned, she could find Wendy, Dax, and Elio. She could buy their freedom herself. They wouldn't have to agree to take a position on Rupex's ship unless they wanted to. Layla knew she could have a safe place of her own, that no one could take from her.

Of course, all that was connected to trusting Rupex and giving him what he wanted, what he'd paid for.

Layla ran her hands through her hair. She felt like her skin was on fire, and it was only getting worse.

With a sudden stomp, she hopped off her bunk and marched in her plain white sheath of fabric down to see Marcus.

"YOU. MEDICAL MAN. WHAT'S wrong with me? You said the injection's side effects would peak and then subside. I'm only getting hotter and hotter. And crankier." Layla didn't mention the other side effects, the side effects that left her feeling as though she was going to go insane if she and Rupex didn't fuck soon.

Marcus looked up from his database computer. His screen was filled with complicated diagrams and calculations that made her eyes glaze over. "Ah."

"'Ah' isn't an answer! Am I sick? Did you poison me?" She chewed her lower lip.

"No. The side effects aren't from the injection itself. It's from... Well, trying to make your chromosomes compatible with a Leonid's has variables."

"What does that mean? In small, simple words." Layla shifted, leaning on the wall, then the exam table, her hips restless and her neck flaming. She stopped chewing on her lip to puff a cooling breath onto her flushed face, but it didn't help.

"My guess would be that the injection has put you in a state of prolonged pre-ovulatory or ovulatory sensitivity."

Layla resisted the urge to march over and pluck out one of Marcus' short, black whiskers. Those words weren't short or easy—but she understood them. Sort of. She was going to be horny for a prolonged period of time while her body decided whether or not it was going to make eggs. "How prolonged?"

"A Leonid Queen remains in a heat cycle for about a month at a time." Marcus frowned. His muzzle twitched and he smoothed a paw through his mane in a nervous gesture.

"What else do you want to tell me that you think I'll freak out about?" Layla demanded sharply.

"I was wondering if I haven't miscalculated a few things. Oh, nothing to do with chromosomes, but the human propensity for only creating one mature egg per cycle. Leonid females produce more." Marcus rubbed his eyes. Layla observed they were more sunken than Rupex's and she hadn't seen the younger Leonid sleep in almost two days.

"Yeah, you said, two to four is common." Layla shrugged. "But won't the booster—"

"The booster makes eggs compatible with Leonid sperm. It doesn't make a bumper crop of eggs."

"They used to make fertility drugs to increase the number of eggs so women could have multiple babies. But that's banned now on Sapien-Three. The planet can't sustain extra bodies."

"No, no, I know. Such medicines are not banned in Felix Orbus. As you can imagine, after Queen Fever, they were encouraged. Now, if you and Rupex wanted..."

Layla waited, but Marcus didn't speak. She imagined he was going to suggest she take those drugs, but she didn't know if that would be safe. For one thing, they wouldn't be formulated for humans. "Marcus? What were you going to say?"

"Hm. Oh, nothing. Nothing, yet. I was just thinking how unfair the fever was to so many people," Marcus said softly, a sad smile crossing his face.

"Oh." There would be a lot of people who would kill for this chance, a chance to have a partner and a family. At least the family part, she corrected herself silently. She knew Rupex had lost loved ones. Marcus must have lost them, too. "I think I'll leave you to your work. I was just wondering how long before these side effects stop."

Marcus cleared his throat. "Well, like I said, it's not the injection. To be fair," Marcus continued, "Queens often remain in a state of heightened arousal during the first two to three-fifths of their pregnancy. Then the focus on nesting and preparing the den for the cubs usually takes over."

"Everyone keeps mentioning fifths, but I'm probably going to go closer to sevenths, right?"

"It may well be. We'll have to see. There's much we have to see. It's as new to me as it is to you."

Being the first one to cross a frontier always sounds so glorious in the history and science lessons. No one mentions it feels like teetering on the edge of the world, waiting to see if that "big step" makes you plummet into an abyss or soar to greatness. "There aren't *any* other cases of human-Leonid couples?" Layla pressed.

"Not offspring-producing ones. As you know, Felix Orbus was closed off to intergalactic travel for the past few years. Now that such trade has opened again within the last year, a number of humans have allowed their contracts to be bought by planets in the Felix Orbus system. I'm sure that we'll soon see some partnerships develop, and this technology could benefit them. Look." Marcus tapped his screen. "I'm keeping records. I'm submitting all the research, successful or otherwise, to the Leonid Ministry of Health. Whatever happens, the cosmos will know if human partnerships could be a new hope for our species. And maybe for your own. Have you ever been to—" Marcus paused. "No, I suppose you haven't."

"Been anywhere off Sapien-Three? Nope."

"You might like it on Leo Falls. You might like it aboard this vessel, or others." Marcus' eyes closed, and when he opened them, he swiped away the data on the screen and brought up an image of a delicate Felid

Queen with giant ears and rich black stripes on bright golden fur. The stripes gave away to a riot of spots, all dots and dashes like someone had tossed paint on her canvas of fur without looking. Her eyes were enormous in a small pointed face. The effect was strikingly beautiful and lively.

"She's beautiful."

"That's my—that was my wife. She was Servali. Before I met her, I could never imagine living anywhere but Leonid-One or Leonid-Two. After I met her and spent just a few days with her family, walking with her on the beaches, eating the food her mother made...I would never want to live anywhere else but with her."

Layla had a feeling that Marcus had intended to make a point, something about how her part in this experiment was going to help people. He could be telling her not to waste chances others would never get. Or maybe he was not-so-subtly telling her happiness wasn't attached to a place or a preconceived notion but a person.

Rupex. Her heart gave a guilty thump. *Just sex. Not a relationship. Shut up and don't let yourself get carried away.*

Whatever Marcus' point had been—he was no longer in any condition to make it. The graying male put his head on one paw and stared longingly at the image of the pretty Servali on the screen.

"Hm. Marcus? I'm going back to my quarters. Thanks for the info. If you think of anything else I ought to know, can you tell me?"

"What? Oh! Go to the Leonid Ministry of Health website and read up on Queen gestation symptoms and the side effects of heat cycles. I didn't know for certain, but based on what you described, it seems likely that you'll have to deal with both."

Chapter Twelve

Rupex breathed out a sigh of relief, his paws shaking with exhaustion. He could put the ship back on autopilot and lock the course. Just ahead, he could see the soft pink and blue rings of planetary atmosphere.

Leonid-One. Home.

More specifically, a speck of rock, sand, and vegetation in the Northeast Sea on Leonid-One. Leo Falls.

"Course locked. Docking in approximately five hours and twenty minutes. Manual docking required. Confirm?"

Rupex nodded at the electronic voice that confirmed his course was locked. "Confirmed."

"Warning. Non-Leonid citizens are not allowed to enter—"

Leo muted the machine. *So. It's happened. We're in a quarantine situation again, if only for a short period.*

A few days ago, that thought would have filled him with wracking, unspeakable grief that he couldn't find words to describe.

Right now, he treasured the idea of hiding Layla away. Keeping her safe. Keeping her to himself.

"I brought you some actual food. The kind you have to chew." Marcus entered the deck with a plate held in front of him. "Game hens in mushroom sauce. I think our guest would like to dine with you, too. Or at the very least, see you for five minutes."

Rupex seized the plate and ate like a savage, uncaring for his manners. Marcus had seen worse. "I need to sleep."

"Good luck. She's going into heat."

Rupex stopped lapping up the rich sauce, eyes looking up over the rim of the plate. "What do you mean? Humans don't—"

"The chromosome booster didn't just make her eggs receptive to Leonid sperm. They seem to be impacting the whole 'monthly cycle' human females endure."

Rupex chomped into the small game hen, crunching bones and grinding them to a powder with his sharp teeth. "Is she at risk of contracting the fever?"

"I don't believe so. She's just going to have similar symptoms to a Queen in heat." Marcus avoided his eye.

Damn him. Marcus knew this would happen—but he hadn't known about the virus rearing its ugly head. No one could have foreseen that, not after so many precautions had been put in place.

While Rupex wished a million curses upon the wretched fever, he had to admit that he didn't mind Layla desiring him as her mate.

Layla's tight, willing body swam before his eyes.

Layla on his bed.

Layla on his island.

Layla on her hands and knees on the floor of his wooden beach shack. Layla stretched out like she was roasted on a spit, his cock in her glistening pink opening, the narrow space between her hips bulging slightly when he filled her, his tail binding her hands above her head so she couldn't stop him from ravaging her. Ravishing her. Adoring her.

"One other thing."

With a growl, Rupex left his fantasy, grateful for the interruption. He had to stop envisioning Layla in all of those lewd positions. "What is it? Out with it."

"Humans don't usually release more than one egg at a time. I was so focused on ensuring compatibility that I neglected to think about efficiency." Marcus spread his paws in an "oops" gesture. "I could work on procuring fertility drugs and altering the dosage or—"

"I don't know. Is that safe for her? I don't want to put her at risk."

"I would have to research, and you would need to hold off on mating this cycle. Otherwise, she could be pregnant by the time I could get any drugs and run a simulation. It would be too late to administer."

Rupex paused, his tongue slurping the final remains of his meal. *Ask her to stay for longer. I could ask her to stay for years. I could sign her on like crew, for a three or four-year term. To enlist, like a soldier, a soldier in this war to rebuild my people.*

I can't ask that of her. She has dreams that she wants to pursue, and those dreams never included an interspecies relationship. By Bastet, my plans never included an interspecies relationship, either. I never expected to spend any time with a human except in passing.

Rupex tried to cast humans back into their former category—little pale hairless blobs that were bumbling through the Galaxy like awestruck tourists. Occasionally, you heard of a particularly bright or fearless one. The first scientists of note within the galaxies had been humans, after all.

He found that his experiment was a failure. Now when he pictured humans, he pictured Layla sitting across from him with her slender pale legs crossed, an impish smile on her face, and a brilliant glitter in her eye. If he let his mind delve deeper, he saw her naked body embracing his and could hear her passionate cries in his ear, feel her fingers tugging his mane fearlessly as she rubbed her sensitive pink petals against his dangerously sharp teeth.

"I had a small visit with the young lady," Marcus was speaking again. "I told her about my wife. I mentioned that sometimes the unexpected things in our life turn out to be the best ones."

"Don't try to matchmake, Marcus."

"Another booming industry," Marcus took his platter away and headed to the door, tail swaying impudently through the slit in his uniform. "Do you know on Leonid one that there are some eligible bachelors offering a billion credits to find a Virgin Queen? Oh you know, purity of the pride and all that. Ha!"

Rupex rested his head on the table, supporting it with his folded arms. Was Marcus jabbing at him? He wasn't so narrow-minded! Was he?

Rupex tried to rise, but his adrenaline had fled once he had seen the horizon aura of his home planet.

I want to see Layla. To tell her that she is... that we could be *more to each other than simple business partners.*

That's a foolish thought, one that will leave you with a new kind of grief, Rupex thought groggily, nestling his weary head deeper into the pillow of his arms.

"MANUAL DOCKING SEQUENCE needs to commence in twenty minutes. If you are not ready to begin the manual docking sequence, please reduce the speed, change destination, or engage the engine idle function. Manual docking sequence needs to—"

"Ugh." Rupex sat up with a groan. An insistent and familiar voice was booming ever louder in his ear. The tinny, annoying voice was juxtaposed with a soft hand on his shoulder, a small weight on his arm.

Layla. She was blinking sleepily against him.

"Layla! What are you doing here?"

"I miss— I didn't want to miss this. You were sound asleep so I let you rest. The ship has other ideas, huh?" Layla stood and stretched.

Rupex swallowed hard. When Layla stretched, the simple white strip of fabric that was currently her only covering slid down. She grabbed for it, but not before letting him catch a glimpse of her breasts—so different from the small, muscular, mounds of Leonid Queens. No golden fur to hide the finer details and puckers of nipples and the peachy-pink ring of flesh around the hard little pebbles that made her squeal.

Rupex admitted that he missed that sleek, seductive tawniness of his own species. But Layla created a different sort of appreciation in him. "Layla. I—"

"Manual docking sequence needs to commence in eighteen minutes."

Rupex grimaced in irritation. "It'll keep doing that every two minutes until I take manual control of the ship."

"Then you'd better do that." Layla moved toward the door.

"Why don't you stay? Have you ever seen footage of Leonid-One? Or the great Northeastern Sea? See that pink tinge turning a deeper red? We're in Leonid-One's atmosphere now. In minutes, you'll see the island."

Layla hurried over and perched next to him in the vacant co-pilot's seat. "It's beautiful. I've never seen it before, but it reminds me of the films I used to see about Sapien-One. You know, the Atlantic, the Pacific, and all those old oceans."

"Yes." Rupex smiled. Calmness filled his soul. They were almost home.

Sadness chased it. Home without his mother or his sister.

But you have Layla to show around—and Marcus. Maybe you haven't appreciated him enough, Ru. "Layla, I'm sorry I've been busy when you wanted to see me."

A strong air current shook the craft slightly, coming right across the nose as a sparkling green and blue sea came into view. Layla put her hands to her mouth, her eyes wide and sparkling. "Oh, Rupex! It's breathtaking."

She is rather breathtaking as well.

"We'll talk when we land. Can I stay with you or do you need to concentrate on docking?" Layla asked, eyes thirstily drinking in the sights of his home world.

"Stay."

Chapter Thirteen

Layla was practically liquifying, turning herself into a gel with her fevered bouncing and jiggling. "Can we get out? Do I need a helmet? I can breathe on this planet, right? Are there other people there, do you think?"

Rupex wished she wouldn't do that. It was deliciously distracting, even functioning on only a few hours of sleep. "Layla, wait. There are docking procedures."

Marcus came up, a portable computer tablet resting in the crook of his elbow. "Rupex, get her off now. If you wait much longer, we're going to break quarantine restrictions that Leonid-One is imposing. She's not a citizen."

"No one checks this island."

"Then today will be the day they start. Manes and whiskers, Rupex, are you going to risk them taking her to some holding facility?"

Layla squeaked and looked at him with wide frightened eyes.

Rupex growled and scowled at his medical officer. "Come, Layla. Do you have baggage?"

Layla's mouth dropped open. "No. I guess I don't. My gosh! That shithead Paul! My room at the Metro Rentals! My clothes, my shoes, all of my stuff! It was mostly junk, but I bet he's sold it by now. My pictures! My—"

With a grunt, Rupex heaved the light human off her feet and up over his shoulder. "The man is human garbage. Justice will find him."

"How?"

Rupex didn't answer at first. "One day, his contract will be bought by someone worse."

Someone like me. I will sell him to a Lynxian prison colony as a latrine attendant.

"That's not—"

"I will buy you whatever you want. Find you whatever you need. You are the mother of my cubs. That makes you... that makes you my Queen. At least for now. I shall treat you like one."

That shut her mouth.

Marcus sighed. "Leave the paperwork to me. I'll see you back onboard tonight?"

Rupex swung around, a huffy Layla swinging over his shoulder and struggling around to get comfortable as she swung halfway down his back. "I thought we'd camp on the island. There is ample room, Marcus."

"Maybe tomorrow. Why don't you two go exploring today?"

Layla stopped struggling. Her sweet round rear was directly next to Rupex's nose and he could smell a salty-juicy current in the air. She had the same thought he did.

Alone? On an island?

"That sounds fun." Layla shoved herself upright and peered into his eyes.

Marcus hurried away, chuckling under his breath.

LAYLA WALKED HAND IN paw with him on deep, soft sand. The *Comet Stalker* rested on its belly in the deep, soft sand that covered what must have been a runway at one point.

The air was warm and heavy. It was a struggle to take a breath at first because of the dense mugginess of the air. "It smells like the botanical gardens, but better. And the salt air. And the sound of the waves! Oh my gosh. I always dreamed about seeing the ocean! Or going on a vacation."

Rupex was silent.

"Sorry. I know this isn't a fun place for you."

"No, no. It is a very happy place. I was only thinking... my cubs will never say such things. I will take them to see every corner of this galaxy. The deserts of Serval-One, the jungles of the Tigerites, the opulent steppes and palaces of the Leopardines... My life was a vacation. This was home."

Now it was Layla's turn to be quiet. *What a great life they would have! What a great life I could have if... if I stayed with them. But maybe Rupex won't even tell the cubs I was human. Will it show in their faces?*

"Here. This way to Alana's hut." The sand thinned and two paths emerged, leading into a forest filled with sandy grass and trees with thick striped trunks.

The hut was painted blue and yellow, weathered by salt, sand, and wind. Shingles were missing off the roof and the door hung slightly off of its wooden frame. "Are you sure I shou—"

"My sister would welcome it. She was much more loving and open than I."

"Hey! You're pretty loving and open."

Loving. Open. The way he split her open around his cock, the way he loved her, licking her all over, sending her skin into an overdrive of delight... Layla forced herself to think logically before hormones overtook her again. "Speaking of open, will you tell the cubs about me? That I was human?"

"I hope you'll tell them yourself. You... you will stay in touch, won't you?"

"Oh, sure. Sure, yes. If you want me to." *Not ready to be a mom. Not ready to be a mother, Layla, don't kid yourself, no pun intended.*

Not ready to be a single, poor, struggling mom on Sapien-Three, living from contract to contract. But living with a Leonid on his floating mansion of a star cruiser? Traveling the galaxy with him?

Maybe...

"I would like it if they knew you. I miss my mother terribly."

"Me, too. Don't remember her, but I miss having one."

She loved the way the gigantic paw wrapped more tightly around her hand, engulfing it well past the wrist. No one had held her hand in... well, she couldn't recall when. She had held Wendy's small, brown hand, and Dax's hand, and Elio's little fingers...

It struck her hard, like a rogue wave.

I loved them like little brothers and sisters... like kids, even. I wanted to protect them and love them. I failed.

"You didn't fail at loving them. I didn't fail at loving Alana, even if I couldn't save her. A virus hasn't killed your friends, one hopes. You still have time."

Her already flushed skin burned a deeper hue. How much had she muttered aloud?

To take her mind off of the constriction in her throat, tears that she had long ago stopped shedding, Layla bounded up the three sagging steps that made up the front of Alana's little hut.

Rupex reached above her and pushed it open.

The air smelled fresh but damp—like the smell she was coming to associate with the oceans around the island. "It's not much, but it could be yours if you like. At least the clothes."

The inside of the house was painted that same aggressively cheerful blue. There was a table with two stools (low for Leonids, but she'd have to climb up to get her bottom on the flat round seat). There was an old-fashioned ore stove and pump sink. It was hard to believe that outside there was a fortress that could travel the galaxy with every modern convenience. Layla couldn't imagine why Rupex would like this place.

Maybe Leonids like things primitive. She shivered.

"Oh, you poor thing. What is that, a spare bedsheet?" Her host took her arousal for a chill.

Layla looked at the thin white material knotted around her. "I think so. I didn't go to the medical bay to get another gown."

The air hung heavy between them. She didn't go get a gown because he had torn her last one to shreds in their passion.

"Here." Rupex suddenly walked into a room that had a painted green bedstead and no mattress. With a grunt, he heaved open a little wardrobe and pulled out three silver packages that had been compressed to the thinness of flat pillows. "Here it is. 'Alana. Pre-Academy.' These are my sister's things before she went to Academy. Children's wear."

"Won't they have a tail hole?"

"We can close it. You can wear her shirts as dresses, I imagine." Rupex pressed a valve on the top of the package and it poofed out, bright fabric bursting from the seams. "They should be fresh and wearable, but we can hang them on some branches for the day to air if you'd like."

Layla held up a striped pink sundress—which was probably a sleeveless top or undershirt for the deceased Queen. "I need panties. Underwear. And bras."

"Ah. That... hm. That may be a job for the AAU when we replace the control module. Leonid females are more muscular and less... buoyant."

Layla watched his eyes zero in on her breasts. "Let me try this on." Feeling a spike of lust that wouldn't be dulled, Layla held his gaze and dropped the sheet-dress to the floor. Under his simmering, unblinking gaze, Layla picked up the sundress, her breasts tightening, the nipples turning to rocks as she watched Rupex's tail lashing the ground. His uniform was noticeably tented in the front.

"Put that on," he growled.

Layla hesitated, the dress up to her chest. "N...No."

His eyes widened. "What?"

"No. You take that off. We're not on the *Comet Stalker* now. You're not the captain. Maybe I wanna claim this little spot of land for

Sapien-Three," she taunted, swinging her naked hips, feeling slickness kiss the space where the tops of her thighs rubbed together.

A low, warning growl rumbled, making the fabric against her chest rustle. "You don't know what sort of game you're playing."

"But I know who I'm playing. *You.* You like this game." She stepped closer, aching to undo the collar and peel him out of his tight-fitting black uniform.

"What game is it?"

"Seduction."

His eyes flickered but didn't show agreement.

"Conquest?"

He panted without speaking.

Closer, but not close enough. "The thrill of the hunt?"

His tail lashed so hard that it sent the other two packages toppling to the ground.

"Rupex?" She dropped the dress and held out her arms, but the Leonid didn't approach. Maybe she was going about this wrong. Layla swallowed, confused signals running between her brain and her body. "I thought—"

With a half-roar that made the hairs on her arms prick up, Rupex yanked his uniform down to the waist, revealing the tightly woven tapestry of hard sinew and muscle under luxurious golden fur. With a growl that made her juices run like a river, Rupex shucked the rest of his clothing off, hard cock swinging at half-mast, bobbing as if undecided about hanging between his thighs or standing at attention against his abdomen.

"Oh, God." Layla bit her lower lip, then gasped. Rupex fell to the ground, crouching on all fours.

"Run, my beautiful little tease. Run and let me catch you. That's how we play this game."

IF YOU RAN NAKED ON the streets of Sapien-Three, you were probably escaping from a gang of thugs who had stopped to switch positions, your home had caught on fire while you were in the shower, or you had gone insane.

Naked and public didn't mix. They were terrifying.

This was liberating and exhilarating. A different sort of fear coated Layla's nerves—the fear that she would wake up and find herself running naked out of a drug lord's den, her mind gone and her body ravaged.

A laughing roar sent her mind back to the present.

Sandy dirt paths. Lush green trees with broad fringed leaves. A violet-blue sky and a teal-blue ocean.

Paradise.

"Laaayyyla!"

A monster's paradise.

Rupex's snorting breaths and slapping paws overtook the wind in her ears as she ran. He was so close that she could feel wisps of fur as she swung herself nimbly in a U-turn around the base of the tree, heading off the path. She was smaller and able to fit easily through the trees while he growled and clawed in frustration.

But in just a few yards, Layla found herself staring at the beach again, a beach farther down from the place where they'd docked, as if the island were curving to give them privacy.

Realizing that she didn't know where to run or turn made her pause.

"Ah ha!" Rupex sprang at her when she turned to look over her shoulder.

Her heart stopped for a second. Maybe there was a glimmer of fear. Seven feet of raging muscle, flying fur, and snarling jaws would give anyone a momentary twinge of unease, right?

Paws connected with her, one seizing her hair, the other grabbing her wrist. Before she could cry out, Layla's mouth was smothered in a frantic kiss and her wrists were pressed together in one of his unyielding paws.

"Oh!" She managed to gasp as Rupex hoisted her in the air as if examining a piece of prey he'd just snared. She dangled above him for a minute, her navel at his nose.

Then the hot, furry muzzle butted her thighs apart, putting her on display for the world to see—but they were the only two in this little part of the world.

His long pink tongue slathered and slapped at her overflowing pussy, purring and growling in turns as he ate her out. Eventually, Rupex let go of her wrists long enough to set her astride his muzzle, his tongue deep in her pussy.

Layla couldn't even make words. She hung onto his mane and let the Leonid devour her, too overcome with pleasure to worry about him slipping and biting into her.

"Knees. On your knees!" Rupex's voice was urgent, desperate, and harsh. Not mean. He didn't want her to beg for mercy.

He wanted to take her from behind.

Layla felt his jaws close around the back of her neck, but he purred contentedly as his paws pressed her palms into the soft sand. Her knees sank under his weight and her thighs were forced apart by his hardness.

She was wet and ready for his size, but not his ferocity. Instead of easing into her to make sure she could handle the vastness of his cock, Rupex seemed lost in a primal haze. His teeth pricked her neck and his paws dug into hers. His cock speared her hard and fast, leaving her breathless with the sudden burning pain, and then shaking in relief as the pleasure followed.

He wouldn't let her thrust back. When she tried, his tail lashed around her waist and held her still.

The message was clear. I'm fucking you. You're taking it.

Should that make her whimper in delight?

Maybe not, but she did it anyway.

"Yes! Yes, I'm yours. Fuck me hard. Fuck me any way you want to," Layla managed to warble.

Rupex let go of her neck to lick it and nuzzle his big, shaggy head to hers. "You are mine?"

"Uh-huh. Just don't stop," she begged.

"Say it, then. Say it each time."

He pounded into her steadily, faster and faster. Her cries of "I'm yours! I'm yours! I'm yours!" became one long, wailing babble. "Yours!"

Layla felt an extra savage push from behind, one that left her cheek in the sand and spitting out grit. Rupex had managed to work his spines into her and she felt them latch, pressing her apart as warm cum started pouring into her, flooding her pussy as she came. The pain was dull, but there. She reached back to rub her clit and found her wrist snatched away and bound by his tail.

"That's my pussy, little Layla. Mine. You said so."

"Yes. It is."

"Then ask me to take care of it."

"Rub my clit. Please. I need—I need to come more. So big."

There was a pause. "Are you hurt? Did I—"

"No! You're just big, sweetie."

Another pause. "Sweetie. You call me sweetie when I fuck you like this?"

Uh-oh. Was that bad? Am I in for a rougher time now?

Why is that okay with me? "You can be rough with me... you're still sweet. And it feels good. But can you please just—"

Before she could finish, his paw was over her pussy, slipping through the juice and dripping cum of their combined essences. He rubbed her hard bead and its hidden shaft of soft, springy tissue with as much fervor as he'd fucked her.

When she wailed her orgasm, the ocean muffled it and the wind swept it away. Rupex roared in response, long and loud, as her pussy gripped his spikes and forced another load of hot, creamy cum from his aching shaft.

"You turn me into so many things, Layla. Beast comes to mind."

Layla answered, still high from pleasure, "I'm going to love island living."

Chapter Fourteen

"Again?" Rupex woke up to find a naked Layla with pouting, swollen nether lips, flushed pink breasts, and sex-mussed hair standing over him.

"Again."

"I thought you were hungry."

"I *was* hungry, but not just for food."

Just like a Queen in heat. He wasn't complaining. "Any sign of Marcus?"

Layla sighed and slipped one of his sister's old green shirts over her head. It came to just a few inches above her knees and hung baggily around her body. "No. I guess we should go check on him and hear any updates?"

"That sounds reasonable." Rupex eased off of his childhood bed (that still held his frame with room to spare. It had even survived Layla's middle-of-the-night cravings, where she braced herself against his thighs and slid her pussy down around his aching cock, bouncing herself on him as deep as she could go, lost in her own sensations like someone scratching a long-unreachable itch. "Where's my uniform?"

Layla looked around vaguely. "Don't you have any casual clothes on this island?"

He did, clothes that would still fit from his teenage years, clothes still packed away. "I haven't worn these things in two decades."

"What about when you came back to the island? You said you used to visit it."

"I did, but I preferred my uniforms, I suppose. My mother was proud that I was captain of my own vessel, and I suppose I liked the adoration." He gave her a bitter smile. "Leonids are a proud people. There are slightly more females than males in our society—well, there used to be. Some families used to adhere to the old archaic pride structure, with one male King and several Queens as his wives. That ended years ago in any civilized part of the galaxy, but the idea of prides still continued. Usually, a married Leonid was considered a King. To be a King because you had risen to a position of power or authority was a big deal. It meant you had other males and females at your command—Knights and Queens." He coughed into his paw. "It also made you more desirable as a mate."

Layla's face closed over. A moment ago, it had been bright and eager. She had been untangling her hair, finger-combing it while she listened to him explain about his culture, a world she knew little about (or had known little about before last week). Now, she looked cold and distant.

"What's wrong? I didn't mean to upset you, Layla. I must have sounded like a pompous fool, caring about such things."

"No. It's cool to reach goals and you're a great captain. A good King." Layla huffed and shook her head. "I'm the one who feels like a fool."

His eyebrows shot up. "Why?"

She didn't answer, shaking her head and leaving his room. "I think your uniform might still be on the floor in my room—I mean, Alana's room. You've been torturing me for twenty-four hours, walking around naked," Layla muttered as she shuffled away.

Rupex caught up to her easily. "Do I need to put it in writing that you will tell me what you are thinking? I don't wish to upset my Queen—that is, my partner. You."

Layla looked over her shoulder, mouth open. "You could never think of me as a real Queen. I'd always be a substitute, wouldn't I?"

He hesitated. He didn't know.

That was enough. "Thought so. You wanted a real Queen and there isn't one. You picked me to do a job, and I get that."

"You must 'get something' that I don't! You're angry."

"I'm jealous! You were talking about being desirable to Queens and getting a mate, and we've been fucking each other's brains out..." She found his black suit halfway under the bed and tossed it to him angrily. "It's dumb. I forgot that it was only business."

Rupex blinked at her, his own mouth falling open. "You want a home on Sapien-Three with your friends. You don't want to raise the cubs with me. I never thought... I didn't think you'd ever consider being a Leonid's Queen."

Layla shrugged. "A week ago, I would have said you were right. Now? I'm wondering. Maybe it's the hormones. The booster. Can possessive jealousy be a side effect?"

"Of feelings for your mate? Yes. Of a Queen in heat? I suppose."

Layla groaned. "I'm mixed up. Is this a sexual chemistry thing?"

Rupex wanted to shout no, it wasn't. It was a dark, forbidden yearning, and no, maybe he would never consider her a Leonid Queen, but he would consider her *his* Queen if she'd like that.

"Your silence is deafening. I'm going back to the ship. Maybe I'm already knocked up and we won't need to keep doing this dance." She pushed past him as he stood half-clothed in the doorway.

His strong paw snagged her elbow and pinned it to the wall, making her eyes shoot wide open. "Stop. This 'dance' is far from over, my Layla. If you have even a spark of interest—I'll fan it into a flame. Once I tasted you for the second time, I wanted to possess you." *Possess her always, claim her as my mate, and keep her.*

He kept silent on those thoughts, afraid to scare her off. "I don't know if I will ever see you as a Leonid—but why should I? You are a human, and beautiful as you are. I think humans and Leonids have more in common than I first thought, than humans believe. And as for you being 'knocked up'? That won't end your craving for me. You'll want your mate worse with every passing day. First, it will be like a breeding heat, and then it will be as your rock, your anchor as the cubs take your strength and your agility. I will look after you, and them, always."

Her elbow went lax under his arm. He released Layla from his paw and sighed inside when she didn't run away. "What if this doesn't work? What if we can't have kids? That's the whole point of having me around, isn't it?"

"It was. But we also have plenty of pleasure in trying. Marcus and other medical professionals will continue to make gains in interspecies fertility. I would be willing to extend your contract."

"For how long?"

"As long as it is mutually desired." *Or to put it another way—until you no longer need one. Until you simply wish to stay of your own accord.* Rupex saw the hunger in her eyes that had nothing to do with sexual delight. *She wants me. She wants a family, always has.* "I know you love Sapien-Three—"

"Ha! That's a big fat no."

"I know you love some of the people there," he corrected gently. "If you wished to use your credits to build a home for the four of you elsewhere... say on Leo Falls—"

It was his turn to be pinned to the wall, the tiny human digging her soft, harmless fingers into the fur and muscle on his chest, driving him backward. "What? Seriously? But this is your place!"

"Well, yes, but you would be part of my family—the mother of my cubs. And therefore we would always be connected. If you think your human friends might like living in such an isolated place—or to travel on the *Comet Stalker* part of the year..." Rupex left the morsel dangling, and she pounced. She pounced on him, kissing him.

He should feel better. Layla was kissing him. Smiling. No longer angry.

But he didn't feel completely at peace. They hadn't sorted the root issues. Did she want him for his own sake? Or the things that he could give her? And was all of it colored by her "heat"?

Rupex wondered if she felt the same way. Uncertain of why he wanted her. If Silvia magically reappeared and he had to choose before the beautiful officer and Queen he had longed to court or this little human who confused him and wasn't fully compatible with him or his culture—who would he choose?

"I don't know," he whispered to Layla's vanishing back.

Chapter Fifteen

"There's no spike in MGH. That's Mammalian Growth Hormone to you non-medical types."

Layla didn't know if she was relieved or disappointed. "I'm not pregnant?"

"Can't tell yet. It needs more time to reach detectable levels in the bloodstream, even with all of our fancy labs. The body is still the boss. And speaking of the body being the boss—there's still the issue of humans only releasing one egg at a time. Or on rare occasions, two."

"Marcus, stop. I do not wish Layla to take something risky and possibly illegal for her species. It's fine if the birth is a litter of one." Rupex stepped between the exam table and his officer.

"Wait, what about three cubs? You mentioned two to four, and three would be ideal."

"That's probably the most a human could safely carry given the size difference." Marcus shrugged.

"But Ru," Layla turned wide eyes to her Leonid lover, "you wanted more than one. There was a per-cub bonus."

"I didn't have all the knowledge at the time, Layla. It's fine."

"You two ought to just put an annual renewal amendment in the contract. Re-up every year for another cub if this first one works," Marcus said, peering over his spectacles at his screen, speaking nonchalantly as if he were telling them to pop a pill or elevate a twisted ankle.

Layla exchanged a glance with Rupex. He turned his eyes toward Marcus, face blank.

Doesn't he like that idea? I know he likes that idea. He doesn't want to pressure me.

She cleared her throat, trying to swallow the sudden dusty feeling inside it. "I'd be okay with that." *Until he decides we don't even need a contract. Until we're not business partners—we're just lovers. Or more. Do Leonids marry humans? Well, they never have before, but would he? Do I want that?*

"You'd be amenable to having more cubs with me? Even if it takes a longer time? Years' longer?" Rupex moved near to her, his eyes soft and hopeful.

"I-If I survive the first one."

"I'm also not ruling out the possibility of two or three. The booster is having other effects that I thought would be only temporary, such as this breeding frenzy you seem to be in. If the yowls I heard coming from the woods yesterday are any indication, your body takes to the booster like a cub to milk."

"Marcus! How dare you eavesdrop." Rupex bared his teeth, his mane puffed up angrily.

Marcus looked away, unconcerned. "Rupex, it's a wonder that ships from the mainland didn't file a noise complaint. I spent the day inside the vessel for my own sanity, not merely your privacy."

"Oh, God." Layla buried her head in her hands.

Marcus seemed (or pretended to be) oblivious to her mortification. "I had no idea humans were so noisy. The ship has far better soundproofing than the island."

Rupex snarled. There was a dark, violent gleam in his eyes that Layla didn't like... but also didn't mind. It was odd. She didn't like violence as a rule, certainly not when she'd seen far too much of it growing up. But this dark hungry look was like a warning.

He wants me.

But is lust the same thing as caring about me?

Maybe it would be better to just get this over with. I don't know...

"Rupex, were you going to contact the crew today? These new flight restrictions are probably going to play havoc with every flight plan and crew in Felix Orbus." Marcus panned through another screen full of documents—crew physical forms by the looks of them.

"Bastet's claws!" Rupex lost his fierce look, replacing it with one of harried distraction. "I forgot. How could I forget? Damn." He stormed out of the medical bay.

Layla didn't. "Marcus. You talked about doing a booster each month, right?"

"Yes."

"Or every week?"

Marcus swiveled in his chair. "Yes. I can't promise it will help speed things up. It would definitely increase the—ahem, amorous feelings you have, as well as raising your body temperature."

"Can we do it anyway?"

Marcus frowned but didn't answer, just walked over to the small cooling unit by his desk. "I'm not going above one a week unless your MGH levels spike with a pregnancy and then drop."

"You're the expert. I just want this to work."

Marcus selected a vial. "The contract you signed? You're being paid for your time, aren't you? Regardless of pregnancy?"

"Oh, yeah. I'm not doing this to try to rush." Layla twisted her fingers nervously in the hem of the oversized shirt serving as her dress. She would have to find a scarf or belt later to make it look less like she was wearing a tent.

"Then why are you doing this?"

"I..."

"I won't tell Rupex. He's my King and my captain, but you're my patient." Marcus fitted a needle top onto the vial.

"I want this to work. I want this to work for him. I want him to have a family. I see how much he misses them."

"Ah. That's very altruistic, Layla."

"Well, the credits in my account don't hurt, either. At least Paul-the-slave-trading-scumbag can't access those." She and Rupex had set up a new account for her and closed her other one after transferring the balance—not that there'd been much to transfer.

"Mhm." Marcus pushed up her sleeve and swabbed alcohol on it. "Would you like to know something?"

"Sure." She shrugged, closing her eyes and waiting for the sharp, steel prick.

"He hasn't been sad since you came aboard. I'm serious, in case you think I'm just being polite. I haven't heard him talk this much in months or seen him smile in years. He has hope because of you."

"Yeah, because I'm going to help jumpstart his family."

"Perhaps. I think it's more than that—and I've known him far longer than you have. There. That didn't hurt a bit, did it?"

Layla looked down at her arm. "Not a bit."

Her brain was another story. "I think I'll go take a nap in my quarters."

LAYLA WOKE UP WITH a gasp. Something huge, hairy, and hulking was standing beside her bed in the pitch black room.

"Layla?"

Her lungs reinflated. "Rupex! You scared the shit out of me!"

"I'm sorry. It's almost morning. I'm sorry I took so long dealing with all the paperwork for the crew. We lost a pawful of Knights and Queens, including the one who was to be Marcus' second officer, two repair technicians, and the Cook." Rupex sat on the edge of the mattress, causing it to sink with his weight. "I came to apologize for abandoning you to Marcus and his medical jargon, and here I am, waking you up before dawn and boring you with staffing problems. None of that matters for six weeks anyway. That's how long all non-urgent ships are grounded."

"Six weeks in paradise with you sounds amazing," Layla yawned, sleepiness leaving her words unguarded.

Rupex chuckled softly and eased down next to her, wrapping his long, heavy arm across her waist to pull her close. "Go back to sleep for a few more hours."

"Hm? I'm up now. No late night—well, early morning—mattress tango?"

"Maybe later," he laughed, nuzzling her hair and sighing into it. "Is it all right if I stay here?"

She swallowed. "Perfectly fine."

LAYLA WAS WOKEN BY an excited shout in the hall. "Marsh ducks! Ru! An entire flock of marsh ducks just landed. Maybe a hundred!"

Ru stopped curling his soft, furry body around hers, sitting up with a snort. Layla gasped as his lashing tail swished across her arm.

"Ow!"

"Sorry." Rupex patted the air behind him, as if he was somehow petting her, and bolted to the door. "Are they in the water?" he called as he ran to open the door of her compartment.

"Some, but most headed inland. They'll be looking to make nests near the marshy areas in the woods." Marcus was bouncing on the balls of his long, arched paws.

"There's a small freshwater inlet that curves around the west side. Should we wait?"

"With that many? I'd say losing four won't harm the species."

"What are you guys talking about?" Layla demanded, blinking herself awake.

"Marsh ducks! Hunting for them."

"What, with guns?"

Rupex and Marcus gave her pitying stares. "No."

"Oh. Oh! Well... Can I come?"

"You'll scare them away," Marcus protested.

"Let her come." Rupex smoothed down his mane and grinned.

"No, no. Marcus is right." Layla shook her head and held up her hand. "It's fine. I don't know what I was thinking. I don't know how to hunt a duck, even with a gun."

"Well, at least come off the ship and go for a swim or walk on the beaches," Rupex smiled at her.

Her heart tugged. He wanted her nearby. Or was he just being considerate? Or cautious? She could probably break something pricey, wandering unsupervised around the *Comet Stalker*. "Sure. I'll meet you outside."

While Rupex and Marcus dashed off, more animated than Layla had ever seen them together, she yawned and eased out of bed. Parts of her were definitely feeling tender and achy. That didn't mean she wanted those parts left alone. No, they were definitely craving attention. A computerized voice chirped, "Main airlock open." Her Leonid companions were already outside.

The thought of being away from Rupex made her feel physically sick. Layla rubbed her stomach where she felt cramps forming. Could that be from the wild bout of sex? Were these premenstrual cramps? If she was going to get her period, it ought to happen within the next few days. She hated to think of the disappointment on Rupex's face.

But a smaller, selfish part of her thought of trying for another month. Another month of that big, thick cock and that soft, velvety body, and the low, possessive growl that made her pussy leak at the mere sound of it.

And another month of credits, her practical voice tried to reason. *That's why you like it. Yeah. That's it. That's all it is.*

No. I'm turning into a nymphomaniac. A Leonid-craving, fur-and-tail-loving nymphomaniac.

LAYLA MADE HER WAY to the bathroom —much bigger than the ones she was used to, which made sense, considering the size difference between humans and Leonids. After she showered, she stood in front of the mirror, working a comb through her hair.

The fog from the steamy shower cleared almost instantly, leaving her staring at her face and naked torso.

Wow. I look healthy. I look happy. I even look stronger.

Living on Sapien-Three as one of the dregs of society wasn't exactly a healthful way of life. Smog and dirt coated most cities. She drank, but not to excess, and hung out in clubs where people from her social class were tolerated—and those places weren't health spas. Layla knew she was thin, pale, and pinched-looking—but still pretty. Pretty because she hadn't succumbed to the security of a Pleasure Park or a lab holding her contract. The ex-labbers and the Pleasure Park girls always looked battered, like life had chewed on them and found them too tough to gnaw through.

"Things are different here. Better." She ran her hands over her hips and cupped her breasts, which felt heavy and aching. Even in the depths of a different galaxy, she was treated to better food (albeit different), better conditions, more safety, and more... her fingers grazed her erect nipples, more satisfaction.

I wonder what it would be like living aboard a ship?

Rupex must spend some *time planetside.*

Could he make Leo Falls his home base? A place we—I mean, he—comes back to every couple of months?

Just a couple of days roaming around the island had given her skin a light bronzing and put some extra highlights in her hair. It was the cleanest, nicest, brightest place she'd ever experienced. It had become her definition of paradise, and she wanted to live the fantasy for longer.

Maybe forever.

*If I earned enough credits to get Dax, Elio, and Wendy's contracts...
would Rupex buy me a house somewhere other than Sapien-Three? He
hinted at it, but men say things when they're high on lust.*

Layla hurried and got dressed, trying to push away the thoughts
nagging her brain.

*Would he let me buy Alana's old shack on Leo Falls, and would he help
me fix it up to accommodate four humans?*

What would we do for work?

Could we be crew members? Could I keep being his surrogate?

I would be his neighbor.

Layla swallowed hard as she ran to the main airlock, eyes full. The
thought of being Rupex's surrogate and nothing more was painful. The
thought of just being his neighbor wasn't much better.

Chapter Sixteen

Rupex handed Marcus his kill with a growl, wiping flecks of blood off his whiskers with his free paw. "Good hunt, old man."

"Better eating. My mother-in-law taught me how to make marsh duck sing with spice. I'm going to the galley."

"It's a gorgeous day! Leave the labs for a bit!"

"Labs, perhaps. Marsh ducks in your clumsy paws? Never." Marcus sauntered off, stripped to the waist, graying gold fur gleaming in the sun until it gave off a platinum sheen.

The salty breeze brought a new scent. Layla. Suddenly, Rupex was glad Marcus was returning to the ship. He wanted to hunt more.

Hunt Layla. Hunt her across the soft marsh grasses until they came to the clear gray pools of fresh water. Chase her in. Grab her by the scruff—no, by the long, shimmering hair so different from Leonids.

Mate her like he did before, only better.

I wish my Layla to roar for me...

"He's over there."

Rupex heard Marcus' voice drift on the cooling breeze, taking Layla's scent directly to his nostrils, which seemed to be connected to his cock at the moment.

"Rupex! Hi!" Layla bounded across the sandy path, breasts bouncing under the top she was wearing. He supposed it was considered a dress on Layla's small human frame, but it had been one of Alana's old swimming tops, the kind a Queen would wear with wetsuit leggings or shorts.

It barely touched her knees. She was beaming as she ran, her hair still damp and holding her fragrance.

A growl started low in his middle. *My mate. My Queen.*

Look at how she glows with health—so different from the scrawny thing in the cargo hold.

His heart stopped for a second, his breath vanished as she reached him and put her hand on his paw. *Imagine how glorious she's going to look when carrying my cubs.*

"What do you want to do today? Marcus showed me the ducks you caught. I've never had duck. Only rich people eat duck on Sapien-Three."

"Marsh Duck is wild game and a Leonid delicacy few enjoy. But..." Rupex shook himself, trying to stop his limbs from moving on their own. He ached to circle her. Stalk her.

Catch her and eat her. Not in the way he'd devour a duck. She'd be screaming, his Layla, but not in pain.

"But what?" Layla moved closer to him. "Are you okay?"

"But we have it fresh in our part of the world. There's also silverfin in the saltwater and marshfin in the fresh. Would you like to see the pools we used to fish in?"

"I'd love to. I never went fishing, either. The only fishing was on the big industrial trawlers. I did put my contract up for a six-month term on one, but the day I went to sign, I saw the crew that came off. The men looked tired and the women looked scared." Layla moved closer to him, eyes moving. "There must have been 600 men to ten women. I... I decided it wasn't a good idea to be out in the middle of the ocean with no place to get off."

Rupex's tail gave one violent lash, making the air sing behind him. He could understand Layla's unspoken fears and in a heartbeat, he shared them. What if his Layla had been on that vessel at the mercy of the sea and outnumbered by men who had no concern for her life? What if he'd deposited her on Lynx-Nineteen, that tiny backwater pebble of a planet? The rumble in his chest made the leaves overhead vibrate.

"Queens would never be treated that way aboard a Leonid vessel, you know. Queens are revered, modeled after Bastet, and givers of life. A King is nothing without his pride, and the pride only grows if there is a Queen." His reassuring speech was getting shorter and sharper. "We protect Queens... but we do not place them on a pedestal. We view them as gifts. Gifts and equals. With needs and desires."

Layla looked up at him with her mouth slightly open. "I like the sound of that. I like this island. Rupex, I was wondering—"

But he didn't get to hear what she was wondering. He seized her and kissed her hard before pushing her ahead of him. "You have needs. You want to be caught. Tasted. Savored. Am I wrong?"

She didn't answer. She just ran.

HE WAS HERDING HER. Layla ran one way, and Rupex appeared on her left, a flash of fur and fiery eyes. She swerved right, skidding on pebbles and crushing springy grass with her bare feet. Rupex was on her right, fangs snarling.

He's going to eat me. Bite me.
But not in a bad way.

She wanted him in her again, in that rough, pain-kissed way that made the edges of her vision go fuzzy.

Layla knew her Leonid lover could easily overtake her, but he never did. Instead, if she slowed, his pace slowed. He stayed behind her, stalking, making her uneasy with anticipation until she couldn't stand it anymore. Then she'd turn and find him silently watching her, hunger seeping from his pores.

This last sprint put her face to face with a perfectly clear, silent pond that was the color of the old Moon that circled Sapien-One. Its gray, shimmering surface was too beautiful to disturb.

She felt the air rush out of her lungs and her feet leave the ground. She was flying, soaring, and any minute there would be a horrible impact, either from the coil of muscles that had just slammed into her, or the depths of the water. "Ru!" she managed to scream as she clutched him, waiting for water to fill her lungs.

The water came up to her calves as they dangled over Rupex's arm. He snarled out a laugh. "It's deeper in the middle. I wouldn't let anything hurt you."

Layla nodded, shuddering out a relieved breath against him. It was only then that she noticed that he was naked. Earlier he had been in pants, but they were missing. His cock rubbed her bare bottom as he held her to his chest.

"Caught you, pretty prey," he whispered, stripping her shirt off and throwing it onto the sandy soil ringing the pond. "Now, I devour you."

LAYLA WHIMPERED AS Rupex pinned her in the sand, using the shirt she'd been wearing as a thin blanket between her skin and the ground. This wasn't the gentle lapping of a lover's tongue. He had said devour, and that's what he was doing.

Teeth and claws scraped over her skin, making her gasp without drawing blood. His jaws closed over her ankle, dragging her down until she was prone, cheek to the earth. With her belly down, he planted his paws on her shoulders, then the small of her back, roaring before his tongue lathed down her spine and between her legs.

Rupex was in control, there was no denying it. When she shifted, he growled. He wants to be in charge of the positioning? Fine by me, Layla thought as he headbutted her legs apart and began tonguing her hard little pearl.

"Scream for me. I want you to roar."

"Roar?" Layla asked, confused and high on pleasure. "I don't—"

"You will be the time I'm done with you," Rupex warned, snarling against her ear as he flattened his velvety chest over back, pulling one thigh far to the side with his tail.

Layla bucked under him, desperate to be filled. She felt a wave of heat that she was beginning to associate with the booster she'd received. Her hormones spiking, demanding the touch of her King.

Rupex growled in satisfaction when her wet slit rubbed against his crown.

"You want me to roar? I want you to purr. What makes you purr, bad kitty?" Layla taunted, a playful laugh under her breathless words. Her hips wiggled back feeling him stretch her, pain shimmering for a second before he filled her and the pleasure won out.

"You. You make me purr. You make me feel... ways I haven't felt before."

That silenced her, the thoughts crowding her brain too complex for the sensations overwhelming her body. What kind of things? Mere physical things? Leonid pussies wouldn't be this tight, their larger, muscular bodies weren't playthings that appealed to his predatory spirit.

So, did the Leonid mean physical things or heart things?

Layla struggled under him. At first, he held her in place, his growl turning to one of warning until she whimpered, "I wanna see your face."

Instantly, his grip loosened, and she whirled with him in a tangle of limbs, cock, and tail until she found herself staring at his panting face, still flecked with blood around the whiskers from his earlier kill.

"My Layla. My Queen."

"My King. Oh, God, yes, my King." Layla felt her body loosen and relax as she could pull her knees up over his back. His cock slid in deep, stretching and filling her, pounding her to the edge of pain and pleasure. Layla groaned low and primal, a sound that came from the belly.

"That's your roar, isn't it, little Layla? A sound of longing. When words won't come..." Rupex rutted in her and she made the sound again. "Now make it my name."

"Ruuu." Layla dug her fingers into his mane, impressed anew at the sheer size of her lover, not just his cock, but his head, his shoulders—"Huge."

Now, he purred. "Well, yes. Comparatively."

She shook her head, feeling the sand scratching at her scalp and slipping through her hair. Pleasure melted her defenses. "Do you like being the big, bad kitty? The huge Leonid railing the tiny little human?"

His purr intensified, but his lips parted in a snarl.

Guilty pleasure, Layla thought with a smirk. *The same guilty pleasure that admits I love fucking this non-human. I like the fur, the spiky base, and the tail that goes naughty places. Some Leonids would be turned off, some humans would be scared. We're not. We fit.*

"You make me... feel safe." Layla gasped as his paws came to rest on her upper arms, using her for leverage so he could work the final inches inside her. She winced and moaned at the fullness as the spiny nubs found her walls and swelled, clamping them together. Rupex's tail slid around and started playing across her clit.

No words left. Just shattering pleasure as his cum started to flow inside her, unable to escape past his swollen spiky base.

Nothing but pleasure, and Rupex's voice. "Safe?"

She nodded. As a child, she'd wished for someone to keep her safe from the harsh world around her, from the bullies that were just part of the system of growing up parentless and poor. Unable to find one, she had become that bigger, safer friend for her younger housemates.

Layla had an image of strolling Sapien-Three with her lover by her side. No one would dare mess with him. As her orgasm bubbled over, she twisted her arms enough to embed her fingers in the soft fur of his forearms. "Rupex." The only word that she could make.

His answering roar in the late afternoon sun made her shiver. "Layla!"

Chapter Seventeen

She feels safe with me. She called me her King.

I have a pride again, a Queen again. My heart knows it.

That little human doesn't know what she's done, calling me that while my essence is pumping into her. There is no greater act of love, loyalty, and submission to my rule.

Rupex purred, just as Layla wanted. His thoughts would allow nothing else as he held his sweet, soft female in his arms as his member was still buried inside her, still spurting and filling her. The pressure was driving her mad, and he could feel her pussy trembling and convulsing as a chain of orgasms continued inside her like a series of explosions.

Finally, he popped free, leaving most of him inside, and a creamy mess flowed over both of them.

"Wow," Layla whispered, nuzzling her face to his cheek.

"Indeed."

Time seemed sweet and easy, holding her on the lake shore, naked in paradise, like the first creation stories. Lions and humans had been friends then, too.

Things fell.

Like history, always falling and rising again. "I'm glad your kind and mine are friends," Rupex sighed against her neck.

FRIENDS.

Is that all we are?

Layla hid her disappointment. Friends with one helluva a lot of benefits. I can live with that. "Can we sleep under the stars tonight?"

That wasn't a safe thing to do on Sapien-Three, not in the cities. You couldn't see the stars through the haze of smog, anyway.

"After we get clothes on and eat Marcus' duck. It's his mother-in-law's recipe."

"I'll make a fuss."

"You're quite perfect," Rupex purred and kissed her.

Layla yawned. "I never used to feel sleepy after sex."

"I doubt your prior partners treated you like the sexual athlete you are."

"I don't think I was any kind of athlete before you."

"Hm? Oh, well, then I accept the compliment for enhancing you. I doubt I was quite as insatiable before you, either. My Layla." His paw stroked over her side, riding the hills of her hips and bust, cupping one breast on the upstroke. "What sort of contract work did you do before that trafficker caught you?"

Layla snorted sleepily. "That trafficker. You know, I saw him all the time in my neighborhood. I never knew. I thought he was just some slouchy dude who didn't have to work nights. Now I know. He worked nights, all right. He was always working."

"Shh. We'll find him, Layla. He will pay."

Layla smiled as she dozed off. Rupex will find him. And eat him. She giggled. "I'm going insane."

"You are not, you are just overtired. And perhaps relaxed."

"Very relaxed." Guilt poked her and woke her up. "This is an easy job. I shouldn't get paid for this."

"Yes, you should." Rupex gave her a long, soothing lick that ran from shoulder to cheek. "This is very important work, and I can't do it by myself."

"But so far all I'm doing is having sex and sleeping."

Rupex was silent. This time, he asked a different question. "What did you want to do? Contract-wise?"

Layla was silent for a moment. Her body was shutting off, but a memory burned in a single bright spot as sleep stole over her. "Travel out of the cities, to the safe places. The beautiful places. I knew I couldn't. I was allowed to take one course on database computers. It was my favorite. You know? These weren't just the personal access computers that anyone could have to manage their credits and submit their health and work information. These computers let you *see* things. Other places. Even media from other galaxies."

Rupex leaned over her, propped up on his elbow. "Database computers are common in Felix Orbus. Most households have at least one. Hm. I had no idea information exchange and computing was so limited on your homeworld."

She nodded, eyes distant.

"Layla?"

"Hm?"

His voice was gentle. "You had training on one?"

"Long time ago. Little bit."

"We have nothing to do for a few weeks but look for crew members and try to line up our next shipments. Database computers are vital in researching that sort of thing and taking on jobs. Would you like to help? I could show you what to do."

Layla felt a warm wash of happiness coat her—and it wasn't the sticky Leonid cum from their lovemaking. "You're perfect, too."

RUPEX SHUT OFF THE media viewer before heading down to the lab.

Yes. The galaxy was in a low-level crisis, a waiting period. But here on the island, it felt like harsh realities couldn't harm them.

Three days had passed since Layla had called him perfect and fallen asleep in the late afternoon sun by a silver pool.

Marcus was cooking his whiskers off. It honored his late wife's legacy while allowing him to pontificate on the "science" part of culinary science.

Layla was learning to use one of the older database computers.
Layla was insatiable.
Life was somehow...idyllic.

Out here, with just the three of them, the terrors of reality seemed like bad dreams he could switch off.

Especially when Layla had taken to sleeping next to him, her own quarters on the ship and the island largely ignored. Especially when she smelled so... tempting.

The salty air blew through the open windows of the little beach shack that morning, ruffling his mane, making him raise his head just enough to smile down on his petite little Queen.

Petite, yes. Little, yes. But not weak. By Bastet, she made him roar. It was no wonder Marcus had tersely rejected the offer of assembling a portable shelter near their huts. He didn't need to hear the constant mating roars—from both of them.

Rupex snuffled and chuckled, his muzzle pressed to her sleep-tangled hair. He was teaching Layla to roar, too. He was teaching her so many things, like how to ride him, taking him deeper, her pussy stretching around his cock and making room to squeeze him past that hard, firm nub that was the entrance to her womb. He couldn't penetrate it, but there was a pocket of space just under it at the right angle. Last night, she'd slid him in that direction, her eyes wide, her mouth wide, silent.

And then her gasping mewl had turned into roars of pleasure as his spines swirled and clung, vibrating inside her as he purred his satisfaction.

Good little Queen, he'd called her. Good, beautiful, delicious Queen.

"My sweet, delectable Layla, my—" Rupex stopped murmuring a waking endearment into her ear as Layla shifted feebly against him.

Blood. Blood on her thighs.

Leonid reflexes were nothing to mock, even if the Cheetahs insisted they were the fastest. Within a blink of his predator eyes, Rupex had scooped up the sleeping girl and was racing toward the ship, uncaring for their nudity.

I speared her. Oh, my beautiful Layla! How did I fail to realize? I am a fool!

And what if I've ruined our chances of having cubs now? What if I've taken away this contract before it's been a whole month?

I'll ask her to stay on, anyway. It's my fault. It's only right. It's—

"Why are we running?" Layla's panicked voice reached his ear as he careened to a halt in front of the entrance to the ship. "Why are we naked!?"

"You need medical attention! You are bleeding out."

"Ru, stop!" Layla tugged his ear. "Bleeding where? Why?"

"From your insides! There, on your thighs! I injured you last night. I am so sorry, my Layla. I never—"

"I think I got my period. I'm sure your medical bay will have feminine hygiene supplies—or don't Queens—"

"They do! But they don't if they're..."

"Pregnant? Yeah. I know. I guess I'm not."

If she was, I probably injured her with such roughness. We'll be more careful. I can be gentle. She never complained. Rupex opened the bay door and held Layla tightly to him, keeping her pressed to his chest and encircled in his broad arms. If Marcus stumbled out, he would see a few inches of skin, but nothing private. "I'll get you to your quarters to clean up and find you supplies."

"Thanks." Layla looked up at him, her eyes free of their normal fire. "I'm sorry."

"I'm sorry. I was a thoughtless partner. Rough mating and—"

"Whoa, whoa there." Layla shook her head emphatically, features scrunching in indignation. "You're not too rough with me. Nothing is ever painful with you. Well—stretchy, but then it's okay. This isn't injury-related bleeding. This is 'body getting ready to try again' bleeding. If you still want to?"

"Oh, I do. I do! Even if you could never— That is to say, if I caused you some injury and you were unable to pursue other careers or fulfill this contract, I would—I would make amends. I would..." Rupex put her down outside her quarters, his paw pressing the keypad.

She covered her chest with her arms as she left his side, hurrying to the bathroom. "You would what?"

"I would... buy your contract. In perpetuity. It would be my fault that you couldn't work as a surrogate."

Layla emerged, wrapped in a towel. Rupex could hear the tapping of the water on the hard antimicrobial surfaces of the shower walls.

"You what?" Her face was blank, held halfway away from him.

He found a similar problem. Suddenly, he could hardly bear to meet her eyes. *This is not how a King behaves.*

Yet, he kept his face averted, hiding in the forest of his mane. "I said I would buy your contract. In perpetuity. It would be my fault if you couldn't work any longer."

"As a surrogate, maybe. But not all jobs."

"But I would have ruined your chances of having a family. And..." His chest was tight. *I would be your family.*

"And what, Ru? What were you going to say?" She stepped closer to him, her hand coming to rest on his furry bicep. Her fingers sank in, completely buried in the plush pelt. She massaged him with her fingers as her soft voice and her pleading eyes captured his.

POSSESSED BY THE LEONID KING

I would possess her so fully—and she already owns me. She doesn't even know how much I would devote myself to her... Words stuck in his throat and he growled softly.

Layla didn't retreat. "You can tell me things, you know? If you would be willing to—to let me live on your ship for the rest of my life, you ought to be able to tell me anything that's on your mind."

Words were a snarl, an angry rush.

How can you risk losing another woman? Another woman you love?

His eyes glaring and his voice furious, he hissed, "I would be your family. Not much of one, but still."

Her hand fell away. Layla stumbled back, face as white as the towel, and eyes perfectly round.

Rupex sniffed at her, his ears swiveling forward. Layla's breath was coming out in short jumps, and her blood was racing. Blood... blood mixed with sweet womanly juices... Rupex knew he wasn't supposed to be tempted by her scent, especially not *that* scent.

We do not hunt our mates.

But I have been hunting for her for so long without knowing it.

Now I've scared her away.

"I'm sorry. I know that was unprofessional. I withdraw that last remark," he murmured, turning from her and preparing to leave her quarters.

"Don't you dare!" Layla sprang after him, her towel dropping as she flung herself onto his chest.

He caught her, giant paws completely spanning her back, gasping as her legs wrapped around his waist. "Layla!" He'd thought humans, with their tiny, almost hairless bodies, their clawless hands, their lack of tails, and their blunt teeth, would be weakened during this time of blood loss.

Not his Layla. She was gripping him on the sides of his face, pulling herself up so that her eyes were level with his as she stared him down. "Did you say it because you felt like you owed it to me? Was it guilt?

Just a payoff so you don't have to go to the Courts of Contract Arbitration?" Layla demanded.

"What? No! It's an honorable action on my part."

"The family part! Did you mean the *family* part? Why did you say *that part*?" Her fingers tugged, making him snarl.

"Because I wish it were so! That you would stay and raise cubs with me, or just be with me. And... I wish you would stay, even after the contract is up and you have all the credits you could desire to build a house on Sapien-Three." His guilty, angry words rushed out. This was a whim—well, no, not a whim, but a foolish wish.

If it was so foolish—then why was Layla kissing him?

Why was she rubbing herself against him, pressing her juicy womanhood against him, soaking her blood into his fur?

Marking him.

"Layla." A single word. He didn't know what ought to follow it.

She pulled him with her, little gasps against his muzzle as she peppered him with kisses. These were beyond carnal kisses—they were affectionate.

"You need to bathe. Privacy."

"I know, I know. I'm sorry, am I grossing you out?" Layla began to regretfully let go.

"No. The opposite. Your scent is far too tempting right now."

"It... is? Like you'd bite me?"

Rupex liked that she asked her question with a smile, still gazing into his eyes. "No, little Queen. Like I want to spread you across my table and have you for the first course, lapping you up, licking every drop of nectar from you."

Layla's eyes widened, going dark as the pupil expanded in desire. "Wh-what? Really?"

"Blood is wine to predators, you know."

Chapter Eighteen

Layla's eyes widened as Rupex licked his lips. "I... I still should shower."

"I could join you. There's one part of you that I'd love to clean myself."

Before she could protest, the Leonid hoisted her back into his arms and marched her back to the steamy shower.

"This was obviously built for Felids." Rupex fit comfortably under the shower head, while Layla had to reach her arms as far above her head as possible and stretch on her tippy toes to adjust the nozzle. On the other hand, once she was in the shower, Layla had to admit it gave her delusions of luxury, letting her imagine herself standing in one of the Beauty and Health Spas she could never afford.

And now she was there with her very own scrubbing buddy. A scrubbing buddy with a mane that was slicked down with water, turning a dark reddish brown as the spray drenched him.

Rupex continued to cradle her, but he kept lifting her higher until the apex of her thighs was even with his muzzle.

No way human guys could do this. Or would want to, Layla marveled as her back hit the shower wall, her calves dangling over Rupex's shoulders. She felt his paws kneading and treading in soothing push-pull motions on her rear as his big, nubbly tongue went to work on her swollen, sensitive pussy.

His touch was soothing. Layla found herself laying her head against the wall and mimicking the motions of his paws with her hands, kneading his scalp and the back of his neck. He began to purr, and his tongue vibrated against her.

"Ohhh," she moaned out softly. Her body went limp with pleasure.

Not just with pleasure, Laula realized, blinking into the steam.

He wants me to stay with him.

He said... it wasn't just about money or cubs.

Someone likes me. He *likes me. Wants me. Maybe even loves me.*

A hard nip on her clit refocused her. She watched as Rupex nuzzled in deeper, then pulled back to grin at her, his tawny fur bearing crimson streaks across the muzzle.

"Pretty prey. Sweetest thing I've ever hunted," he whispered, licking his lips.

The words shouldn't make her pussy jump with excitement, but they did. "Only time I've ever wanted to be hunted. Stalked. Pounced on and devoured. Oh, God! God, Ru, deeper. Fuck me with your tongue!" Her cries crescendoed as he dove back in, snarling and growling in between licks.

I should feel panicked, shouldn't I? He could bite me in half...

But he won't.

Layla felt an orgasm beginning to build in her middle, a tight knot of pressure forming each time his long, rough tongue invaded and buzzed inside her.

He wants you. Likes you. Maybe even loves you.

You trust him, Layla. When was the last time you can say that happened?

Faces of vanished friends swept past her closed eyes and then vanished as she focused on the Leonid lavishing her with his tongue.

"You're all clean, sweet Layla. Sweet, juicy Layla."

"But we're not done. And since you know I'm not expecting yet... we can go a little wild. Do you know that's what they call the non-evolved species on Sapien-Three? All the lions, tigers, and panthers? Wildcats?"

Rupex dropped his shoulders from under her legs and deftly caught her, a lion batting a mouse. In seconds, she was bending under him, his cock invading as she pressed the wall for support—not that she would have needed to. One of his massive paws was wrapped around her throat, the other tugging back her hair, and something—oh yes, his tail—was busy stroking her clit while he pounded her.

"Wild like this, Layla?" he growled.

She felt the fleshy spines at his base invade her much more smoothly than they'd done in previous encounters.

He's stretched me out already.

Not that I'm complaining.

"Wild like this," she agreed, squeezing down on his cock and waiting.

It came. The tidal wave of cum, arriving in long, shivering jets.

"This really is the spa. Luxury treatments, inside and out." She nuzzled into his arm as he released her throat. "You make an exceptional loofah."

The once-taciturn Leonid laughed against her skin. "I aim to please."

"IT ONLY LASTS THREE days or so. Then it's time to start baby-making sex so we don't miss the fertile window. I've always avoided getting knocked up, so I have no idea when the heck that is."

Layla toweled off and waddled out of the bathroom in bulging underwear. "Leonid Queen pads are not human-sized. And I don't even want to know about their tampons."

"Nor do I." Rupex looked mystified and alarmed. "Are you sore?"

"No. I'll just have to cut these down to size or something. Do you guys have scissors, or do you just use claws?"

"I'm sure we have scissors," Rupex said drily. "Now, come. We should eat."

"Not full?" Layla winked at him and pulled on a black sleeveless top that was a baggy dress on her.

"No, but curiously sated. Still, Marcus will wonder if we don't appear at some point. He was planning to catch and fry a brace of roundfish for lunch."

"Roundfish?"

"I think they are a cousin to the flounder on Sapien planets. I understand flounder are a rare species, however. Roundfish are plentiful here, but only in terrestrial waters."

Layla stopped braiding her long, damp hair.

Food in abundance. Healthy places to live and love.

I love him, I think. This sweet, sincere man.

"Layla?"

"If I... If I wanted to stay with you and have cubs with you—"

"Yes?" Rupex stood up and put an arm around her shoulders.

"Would you still pay me enough credits to buy a house someplace? Someplace closer to your flight path. Someplace like... Leo Falls?"

"Layla, if you were to stay with me, I wouldn't charge you. You could have any land on this island that my family owns, free. You'd be in the family, wouldn't you?" His voice held a wistful note that made her chest ache.

"I can't abandon Dax, Elio, and Wendy, not if I have a chance to save them. I have to have a place where they can rest." *And get better. Be free.*

Layla pictured her friends pale, sickly, and thin, worse than the other residents of the impoverished cities. She knew it wasn't necessarily true. The labs could pay good money, and they probably had plenty of food.

Maybe they'd sold their contracts to other places by now. Maybe they were all together, on some sunny farm growing carrots or milking goats.

Maybe they forgot me. Or they didn't want me after I couldn't keep us together.

"Layla? Layla, you are far away even though you're in the same room. You don't... You are under no obligation to stay, you know."

Layla let herself lean back into his strong, furry arms. "I love this place. Love... love so many things about this 'new life.' Especially the people in it," she murmured, studying the whorls and curls in his fur, hoping he understood the words she *didn't* say. "It was one of the best feelings in my life when you said I could stay with you. But I want that safe place on solid ground to come back to. I want a home where I can bring the other family I had. The family I *should* have kept together. At first, I thought any safe place on Sapien-Three would be enough." She looked up at him and found another new thing she loved—the way his eyes crossed like a curious kitten's when he looked down at her from this angle. "Then you brought me here."

"There's nothing here! This is a fishing shack at best. There are no stores, no medical centers, no entertainment..."

Layla shook her head and squirmed until she was facing him, still wrapped in his arms. "We're in terrestrial waters. We can travel to Leonid-One's nearest city. We can travel with you—I mean, if they could work as crew. The *Comest Stalker* is a floating city."

He snorted. "Hardly."

Layla stepped back and fixed him with a hard, unblinking gaze. "There are books, food, clothing, and medical supplies on this ship. That's more than you could say about my room on Sapien-Three most days. Oh, I might have two out of four, but not always the same two, and not on all the days."

Rupex was silent for a long moment, stroking one paw absently down her hair, smoothing and combing it with the very tips of his claws. When he spoke, his voice was far away, even though he was holding her close.

"A few years ago, it would have been unheard of for a Leonid to consider a human part of his pride. Friends or business associates—possibly. Partners? No. It just wasn't done. Now, well—much has changed, but some things... Any human who becomes part of a Leonid family would by extension become part of a pride. Pride rules. Pride laws. Pride discipline."

Ru's claws flowed through her hair now, the most effective combing out Layla had experienced in days.

Layla rested her hand on the back of his much larger paw, stilling him on her shoulder.

He can bend—but not that far. A half-Leonid child he could overlook. Me, he could overlook, just for the sake of his big heart... and maybe my little pussy.

"I get it." She swallowed and tried to look like it didn't matter. "You don't have to explain." *My family can't be his family. It's too much of an affront to his culture. I don't even know if Wendy, Elio, and Dax would want to live this life.*

"Then... You are willing to take the risk?" Ru's voice was less distant. A flicker of interest shone in the depths of his golden eyes.

"Risk?" *Wait. What did I miss?* "What risk?"

"Leonids and other Felids—Tigerites, Cheetahs, Servalis, Leopardines, and the rest...they might always view us as outcasts. Your friends would be far from most other humans. They would be outcasts, too, and they would have to let me lead them. There is no challenging the King of a pride, or the captain of a starcraft."

"You mean, you're willing to give it a try?"

"It doesn't just impact me, my Layla."

"Oh, hell." She waved his words away, "My friends and I were *already* outcasts. The nobodies. The orphans. The... The whatevers. Prejudice and side-long looks never went extinct, even if so many other things did." Layla's laugh masked tears. How could his world, a world of furry, fanged predators suddenly seem so much more civilized than her human life? "If you'll take the risk with us, I'm willing to ask them."

Rupex smiled at her. He opened his mouth a few times, then licked his muzzle. Layla watched his tongue with harlot eyes, lusting after him in whole new ways. Before, he had given her pleasure and credits. Now, he might give her a new life.

Her heart somersaulted around in her chest and socked her in the stomach. For the first time ever, she thought about living with Rupex and seeing his cubs—and they weren't just products of a job well done.

I hope they're as honorable and big-hearted as their father. And I hope they love me. I hope... I hope I'm a good mom. I hope I get the chance to try again with the first family I ever had.

Maybe one day... he'll love me, too.

"What is it?" she asked as he stood, his tail tapping against her leg, a sign she'd come to associate with nerves.

Rupex's padded paws flexed on her shoulders.

"If—if they love you as much as I've come to, then they'll accept your offer, no matter who else is in your family. That's all. I—"

"Who wants to have a fish fry?" Marcus' voice suddenly boomed from the intercom next to the door of Layla's quarters. "I've caught six roundfish and they're all beauties! *Nourishing* beauties! Good for the mother-to-be!"

"Marcus!" Rupex released her and began to stride toward the door—before realizing he was naked.

"Oh, you're in there. No surprise. When you're done with your 'business activities', come on out! I'll teach you the Servali way to fry fish over an open beach fire."

"Privacy in this corridor! Go outside, Marcus. That's an *order*."

"Sorry to interrupt!" The intercom beeped to silence.

"Where were we?" Rupex turned back to her, his smile apologetic. "Oh, yes. Your friends. After we eat, let's begin to trace their contracts and see if we can get in contact with them. Hopefully, they have usable skills, but even if not, they can be trained."

Layla nodded, lips pressed together. He said it. 'If they love you as much as I've come to.'

Tell him. Tell him you're falling for him.

Years of fear kept her silent—for now.

Well. Show him, then.

"That's a very generous offer you've made. I can't tell you how much it means to me. How much I love—that you're so thoughtful and big-hearted—while still being a tough kitty."

Rupex growled, but he smirked in acknowledgement of her teasing.

"It's a lot of trouble you're taking on for me." Layla bit her lip and fluttered her lashes seductively. "I think you deserve a special thank you. Is there something... you'd like?" She ran her hand over the curve of her achy breasts and down one hip.

With an audible gulp, Rupex swallowed and licked his whiskers. "I can think of a hundred things I'd love."

That word again. Her stomach fluttered. "You'll have to tell me all about them."

Chapter Nineteen

Rupex could barely eat. He'd practically proposed marriage. He wasn't changing his mind, but his mind was boggled. His poor father would have had a fit if were alive. First, his sister married a Canid, and now he wanted to mate with a human and add humans to his pride?

The gnawing shame was washed away with desire and something bigger. Love. He was smitten with his little queen, and her submission to him was more of an aphrodisiac than he could have imagined.

He'd feasted upon her monthly blood, he'd hunted her in the woods, and devoured her screams of pleasure as he took her in the wilds of his island.

Layla is mine. She is my Queen, the mother of my future cubs, however they come to be.

He watched her toss the fish bones into the sea and laugh with Marcus, who was shirtless and wearing a pair of loose cotton *shendyt* in red cloth, probably a gift from his Servali mother-in-law or late wife.

She is a good addition to our pride.

Layla turned to look over her shoulder, catching his eye and holding it.

His heart pounded, and he could practically hear her soft, seductive voice in his ear, repeating her earlier question. "I think you deserve a special thank you. Is there something... you'd like?"

I want to make love. To try the romancing end of mating. Soft lights, soft beds, sweet words.

Would she laugh at me for such a suggestion?

There was only one way to find out. First, he'd go and lay the groundwork. "Marcus, Layla! I am going to attend to some things I shouldn't put off."

"Want help?" Layla shouted back.

"Don't touch the lab!" Marcus warned.

"I'll manage. Amuse yourselves."

"IT DIDN'T WORK." LAYLA blushed and looked at the sea instead of the graying Leonid beside her. She figured if his predatory nose was as good as Ru's, Marcus would have smelled blood on her.

"That might be my fault," Marcus said, patting her bare knee with a quick swipe of his paw. "Human cycles respond better to medical intervention during certain times. I have been looking back at some older fertility manuals I found in the Online Medical Preservationist Archive. Knowing the first day of your menstrual cycle can help you time your mating better. And now that I know, I can also time your boosters better. It might help. It might not. All we can do is—"

"Layla!" Rupex's voice was a harsh snap. "Come inside. There's a communication for you. A live one."

Layla hopped off the rock she'd been sunning herself on. "Me? I... I don't have anyone who—" Her eyes lit up. "Is it Wendy?"

But how would she have found me? It's ridiculous to hope.

Rupex confirmed her fears. "It isn't a human. The call isn't from Sapien-Three or any of the Sapien planets. It's a call from Lynx-Nineteen. They've received word that their 'shipment' wasn't coming and they can't get hold of the man who brokered your contract. They want to make you an offer."

Layla's legs turned to stone. She seemed to sink in the sand, only realizing that she was swaying when Marcus hoisted her upright. "Wh-what?"

"They are threatening to send enforcement officers here to search my ship and arrest me for theft."

"But—I thought everything was straightened out?"

"In terms of a refund, yes. In terms of finding out about their 'property,' no. I told you, Lynxians are primal, backwater, barely-evolved..." Rupex struggled for a word.

"Beasts?" Marcus supplied helpfully.

"Beasts! Uncivilized."

"What the hell kind of offer did they make?" Layla hissed as she reached her furry lover, leaning on him as soon as he was within reach. His broad chest under her cheek calmed her. Her heart calmed and her stomach settled—a little.

"They haven't made it to me. Come. They are waiting."

"Ru. They can't—they can't take me from you, can they? Our contract is in place." Would he let them buy her contract for a higher price? Like she hoped to do with her friends to free them from their contracts with the labs?

Honor was one thing. Friendship was nice. But for all of her life—survival and a bigger pile of credits had always won out.

Rupex growled, a sound so deep and gravelly that she felt it reverberating in her own body. "No one can take you from me."

His words comforted her—and left her reeling back into the past, a night when she'd been twelve and the others had all been nine or ten, and they'd huddled in her arms, under the thin sheet on her bed in a makeshift fort, while a thunderstorm rocked the city and blew out the lights.

Will we be blown away, Layla?

One of the few trees outside crashed into their window, but it didn't shatter, just cracked.

Nothing can take you from me.

That had been a lie.

Layla marched into the ship, unable to talk around the stabbing pain in her throat.

"WE WANT TO SPEAK TO the human alone. Without you, Leonid."

Layla cast a panicked look between the screen and her lover. Rupex bowed. "I will be outside the door. They cannot harm you through this screen, Layla." He put a paw on her head and backed away, locking eyes with the Lynxian on the screen.

Layla turned her attention back to the screen as well. The being on it was a dirty gray-gold color with jutting pointed ears that ended in a shock of black fur. He didn't have a mane, more like the equivalent of muttonchop whiskers that made his head look bushy. His cold, yellow eyes looked her over.

"I didn't sign the contract. I was trafficked." Layla choked out words, her throat seemingly filled with sand.

"Is the Leonid gone?" the Lynx-man demanded.

"Uh... Well, he's right outside if I need him." Despite Rupex's assurance that they couldn't hurt her through the screen, Layla didn't know if her nerves believed that.

"Cherie, come here." The Lynxian waved a massive, fluffy paw and Layla's eyes widened.

Cherie was an absolutely stunning black human female, with waist-length hair and a chic dress that looked like it was made of woven furs and hides.

"What is it, Lover? Oh!" Cherie and Layla regarded each other through the screen.

"That Leonid canceled her contract and has her on his ship. Cherie, darlin', talk to her. Tell her we can help her if he's holdin' her prisoner."

Layla tilted her head. "What? Prisoner!? Rupex didn't traffick me! A human scumbag named Paul Bermauger did that. But Ru said... uh..." She froze again, blinking at the couple on the screen. How could she tell "Lover" that Marcus and Ru had said they were primitive hicks who would hurt humans? It was pretty obvious that the Felid and the woman were more than employer and employee. Cherie was absently stroking the tufts of fur on "Lover's" ear and was settling herself on his knee. He was nuzzling his thick, cloud-like muzzle into her side.

"Were you told they were dangerous? They are." Cherie answered. Her voice had a lilting, rolling accent that Layla couldn't place. Everyone in her area of Sapien-Three sounded the same—flat and toneless.

"You don't seem to think so."

"Oh, he is gentle with me, but to bad men? Traffickers? He rips them apart." Cherie kissed his paw. "I think that's why they stayed home and sent you by a third party."

"But... why do you want women? Er, people?"

"Mainly women. We weren't lyin' when we sent the job listings. We wanted women to help raise our cubs and make us mates again. You may not have heard, Miss Layla, but there was a virus that impacted our whole galaxy. The Lynx planets were some of the hardest hit, not by the numbers, but by percentages 'cause we're so damn small."

Layla had wondered why there were so many of those planets and yet they were considered so "backwoods." The Lynxian speaking to her had a drawl that reminded her of old-time terraforming movies, the kind where the men square off in the center of the arable land and fight to the death for rights to farm and graze their livestock.

"Small and rocky. Tough country. Some of the planets are balls of ice and air, and not much else. Few Lynxian Queens live on the outer fringes of our system. Because they were mostly clustered on Lynx-One and Lynx-Two, we lost a drastic number to the virus."

"I'm so sorry. I know it was similar with the Leonids," Layla offered her condolences sincerely.

Cherie put her hand to his muzzle and stopped his speech. "Dane, sweet one, let me explain more. Layla, the contracts offered are honorable... but not to all humans' liking. There was a group of Lynxians who decided to resort to dealing with traffickers. When Dane found out, he dealt with the men, both Felids and humans involved.

But when the women who arrived were waiting for transport back to Sapien-Two or Sapien-Three, many of them found the lifestyle out here invigorating. For one thing, they are treated like prized gems. Even though they cannot provide offspring, they provide companionship for the cubs that survived and the widows and unattached males. You are one of the last contracts still floating about. We thought—"

The Lynxian called Dane took a turn silencing his mate, rising from his chair and thus pushing her off his lap. He pounded his paw on whatever flat surface was next to him. "Thought, nothin'! Leonids are uppity purebred lovers. They'd sooner eat a human than mate 'em. Miss Layla, by Bastet's whiskers, I don't care if there *is* a quarantine on. I think you're in danger, and you'd better lay low until we can get there. We'll bring you here and you can take a shot at the rugged outdoor type of life. If it don't wind up workin' for you, we can arrange a transport to Sapien-Three when this damned quarantine lifts."

Layla smiled, bemused by the twang in his voice and the sweet offer from the people she had been afraid of. "Leonids have changed a lot. Not all of them, maybe, but Rupex, the Leonid King of this pride, is a wonderful person. Being. Whatever, he is wonderful. I want to stay with him."

"But he refunded the contract price to our contract agent. He's gonna expect you to pay him back. Has he said how? Girl, you're two licks away from bein' his main course!"

Layla's smirk broadened. Her eyes left the irate Dane and turned to Cherie. The other human saw the blush on her cheek and the sparkle of mischief in her eyes.

"Ahh. Lover? I think Layla has already been his dinner *and* dessert."

"I'm paying off my debt and then some as his partner. *Business* partner. I'm his surrogate Queen. That is... I'm hoping to have his cubs."

Dane crashed back into a chair, mouth open, revealing small, cone-shaped teeth and two big fangs. Cherie leaned forward, getting into a crouch so she could look directly at Layla.

"How? Please, can you tell us how? We've been together for nearly a year and everyone says it cannot be done."

"Not naturally, no. But there's a very talented medical officer and researcher on board. Dr. Marcus—Well, I'm sure he has a last name and he probably told me at some point, but that's not important. Can they come back in now?" Layla gestured behind her. "Rupex can set your mind at ease, Dane, and Marcus might have something your human-Lynxian couples will value. It hasn't worked yet, but at least we have hope. When this quarantine lifts, maybe one of our first stops can be a rendezvous with your medical officers to explain how the chromosomal compatibility works. I mean, you're going to have to let Marcus explain it because I have no idea. I'm just hoping." Layla found herself looking into Cherie's eyes and seeing the same longing mirrored there.

That gorgeous woman loves that rough and wild Lynxian. I can see why. He's cute, in a scruffy way. And he might not be too sophisticated, but I like his style. Layla didn't have to guess too hard what had happened to the traffickers and the Felids who worked with them. She couldn't say she was saddened by the thought.

"Please, Dane. Let's ask them. If it's too dangerous, we won't try."

"Hell, woman. You know I can't say no to you. Miss Layla, if they're forcing you to say anything under threat of harm, blink at me now."

Layla rolled her eyes. "Would you like me to give you an up close and personal demonstration of just how much I'm enjoying my contract? I'm pretty sure it's something cubs shouldn't see."

Cherie smiled wickedly. "I wouldn't mind."

"Hush, Cher!" Dane pulled on his whiskers nervously. "All right. Bring 'em in."

Chapter Twenty

Rupex felt like a fool. A fool outsmarted by a paunchy old Lynxian with nubby teeth and a Queen who absolutely adored him.

Adored him for free. No contracts between them. During their long conversation, it transpired that Cherie now taught at the community school and shared a home with Dane and his three nephews and one niece, his widowed sister having been killed by the virus. All the cubs were trotted out and displayed with pride. They crawled over "Auntie Cher and Uncle Dane" with obvious love.

He held Layla to his side and felt her melt against him. Tears trembled on the surface of her eyes, catching the light.

She wants my cubs. Wants me.

Marcus and a local Lynxian doctor who had been patched in split off onto a separate call. Rupex and Dane made awkward farewells and half-apologies for suspecting each other of horrible crimes against civility—and tacitly agreeing not to mention that they would both murder human traffickers in warm, delicious blood.

"Are you and Dane official? You know?" Layla bit her lip.

"A marriage?" Cherie sounded surprised.

"Only rich people get married, I know," Layla laughed off her foolishness.

"Say what? It don't cost a single damn credit to get married. Well... the license fee is a little pricey, but you don't have to throw a big do." Dane proudly hauled up Cherie's arm and pointed to a circle of golden bangles on her small wrist. "You better bet I asked for her to wear my ring!"

"That's a ring?"

Rupex elbowed Layla. "Very lovely. There was no trouble with others in your community?"

"We ain't too proud. Love of a good woman is love of a good woman. Don't matter the thickness of her fur."

Cherie laughed at Layla's confused expression. "It is an old Lynxian expression from back when the first inter-species marriages occurred between Servalis and Lynxians. It just means that no, there is very little prejudice. Many Lynxian males seem to find their human Queens have most desirable attributes. Isn't that so, Dane?"

Dane leaned forward and addressed the screen. "She ain't got a tail, but she's got a mighty fine—"

"That's wonderful!" Rupex declared in a strangled voice. "Uh. Bastet's blessings to you both. We'll be in touch. We must have dinner sometime."

He smacked the monitor and ended the call. "Interesting people."

"Very. But you interest me more." Layla yawned and leaned against him, giggling into his side. "It's funny how you and Dane both thought the worst of each other. Turns out, you have plenty in common. You both like women who have no tails but mighty fine asses."

Rupex gave her a grudging smile. "Yours is far superior. And I am nothing like that old rock dweller with gravel in his fur."

"Is that an insult to cat-people?" Layla asked, trying and failing to hold in a yawn. "I get sleepy during my cycle. There's so much to do and to talk about...but I can barely keep my eyes open."

"Then don't. Rest them."

"But I don't want to sleep. I want to—" Layla stopped speaking as a huge yawn threatened to dislocate her jaw. "Do research," she concluded.

"You can research after you rest. Right now, all you'd find out is that resting your head on a database computer is useless. It doesn't have a neural link to read thoughts. They tried that back in the early 2100s. Massive failure and fatal within a short time."

Rupex stopped his lecture as he realized Layla's eyes were fluttering shut. "Enough talk. Bed."

LAYLA WOKE UP TO AN empty room, ensconced in her big, soft bed aboard the *Comet Stalker*. Rupex was nowhere to be found, and the digitized numbers next to the bed showed it was early the next morning.

"Ru?"

Nothing.

Well. You can't have him with you every second.

Even if it feels like you want to. What's going to happen when this quarantine situation lifts? He'll be zipping all around the galaxy—far, far into the Felix Orbus galaxy if Marcus and Dane have anything to say about it.

But hopefully to Sapien-Three or the Milky Way Intergalactic Port first. Her stomach knotted. *Gotta find Wendy, Dax, and Elio.*

Gotta get cleaned up and act like a member of this crew!

Layla bathed, dressed, and took care of her hygienic needs, missing Rupex more than she would like to admit. Having a period had made her feel dirty and inconvenient on Sapien-Three. Rupex regarded it as a monthly treat, a feast, and his tongue tracing over her achy body made her feel wonderful.

She switched on the media viewer as she sorted through the clothing she'd bought from Alana's hut.

A stoic Tigerite male in a dark suit was speaking with a Leonid male, also in an immaculate suit.

"Containment measures are proving effective. Our booster programs have been rolled out. Now, it does take about three weeks to reach a state of higher I-cells, which help evade the Queen Fever," the Leonid explained, gesturing to footage behind him of young Leonid females getting shots at a clinic in a sparkling white clinic.

"That's excellent news, Minister Swanet. What about planets on the outer rim of the galaxy?"

"Convoys have reached them with emergency supplies. So far, there have been no deaths reported from the virus on most of the outer planets."

The Tigerite leaned forward and the screen filled with his face. "Excellent news for the Felix Orbus Galaxy. Sadly, the Sirius Federation has reported six hundred deaths and over three thousand hospitalizations. The best scientists in the Intergalactic Health Alliance are working on formulating boosters specific to Canid immune systems. Let's go via Comm-Link to Dr. Anwar from Sirius-One."

Layla gawped at the screen as a dog-dude in green medical garb appeared, looking exhausted. He reminded her of the seedy dancers at the Anthro-Club, the ones who wore collars and had jackal masks. Only this guy was truly a handsome being with glistening black fur, bright blue-gray eyes, and a muscular build.

"I wonder if that's what Ru's brother-in-law looks like?" she murmured.

"No, he's more like a brown wolf, and he styles his fur to look like one of those hotshot pilots." Rupex's voice made her leap up from the edge of the bed.

"Rupex!" She ran toward him. "I didn't mean to sleep all night."

"You must have needed it. I wasn't too concerned—although I did check on you several times." Rupex came to her side and stroked her hair. "The other day, you said I could pick out a special thanks or gift." He coughed into his paw. "Would... what would a human female assume if a male she'd been intimate with requested her company alone for several hours? The whole night?"

"That he wants to do some naughty mattress dancing?" Layla quirked one eyebrow up.

"Yes." Rupex coughed into his paw. "Yes."

"Why? Is that what you want? You only have to purr and I come running." Layla lightly tapped his elbow, hoping he'd lose the strange grimace gracing his muzzle. "I'm yours pretty much every night—at least until we achieve conception."

The grimace deepened, pain smashing across his features so deeply that even the proud Leonid King couldn't conceal it. "If I were to return the contract to you—"

"What?" Layla felt her stomach drop out of her, and yet she still felt queasy. "We had a deal! No. No, I don't agree! Not without a whole lot of explaining and—"

"Shh! Shh, my Layla, no. I didn't mean I wish to return your contract. I wish... I wish that I could have a brief cessation of the contract, just for one night."

Why? Why does he want that? Does he want to do something with someone else? Who? Where would he find someone else? The contract isn't exclusive when it comes to dating. Not that it had to be. I wasn't a hired bride. I was an incubator.

"You want out?" she whispered.

"Yes, even with a swift verbal agreement. May I have a pause on our contract for tonight? Or tomorrow? When is convenient for you?" Rupex's smile returned, brimming with relief.

Layla couldn't understand it. She kept her answers brief. "Tonight, tomorrow, whenever." She shrugged.

Rupex squinted at her. "You're upset."

"I might be. Don't have a right to be." Another sharp shrug.

Rupex's tail lashed suddenly, then stilled to a mild twitching as he stared at her. "I don't want you to be upset. I want you to be happy."

"You screwed up on that one, which is funny considering you're a pretty smart guy. And I thought you liked me." *I know he likes me. This doesn't seem right.* Layla locked eyes with him. "Can you tell me why you want to take a night off?"

The embarrassed look returned to his face. "I would like to have a special evening together. I would like it to be just the two of us, Rupex and Layla, courting. Dating. Not Rupex and Layla being intimate because we are stuck together or have a mission to achieve." His eyes traveled to her still flat stomach and back to her face. "It has been over six years since I wanted to romance a Queen in hopes that she would be my mate. I cannot romance someone contractually obligated to mate with me for the sake of breeding. Therefore," he gulped, "therefore I had this idea. I'm regretting it now."

"You want a night off so we can have a date?"

"A date that is not part of your contract. You could reject it, you see. This isn't about reproduction—it's about romance." He gulped again.

Layla put a hand over her mouth to stifle the sudden hysterical giggles threatening to erupt. "You look adorable when you're nervous."

"I'm glad you think so. I find it demeaning."

"I find it delightful. Um. But, you said romance. And romance implies... stuff beyond just getting pregnant."

"I know." His voice was a soft scrape against her skin as he stepped closer, his massive form enveloping her.

"Maybe we're not on the same page?" Layla asked cautiously. *Don't get too excited. Don't get your hopes up.*

But he already makes me so high. I'm floating.

Is that what love is like?

"Maybe not. But I could try to show you the page I'm on tonight." Rupex nuzzled the top of her head.

"Sounds good." She snuggled back into him. "What do you need help with around the ship today? Or is there something you need me to do on the island?"

"Leo Falls is off-limits to you today and tonight. Today, because I'm going to be gathering supplies to woo my Queen. Tonight, because I'm planning a romantic evening in my quarters—where the soundproof doors seal and the bed is much larger and softer." he gave her a wink that curled her toes and sent juices rushing south.

"Okay," her voice came out as a breathless gasp. She swallowed and tried again. "What can I do here?"

"Find your friends. I've got the Sapien-Three Contract Registry page loaded and waiting in the Information Officer's station. You'll need their last names, and then you'll need to narrow it down by birth year and region. Do you know those pieces of information?"

Layla nodded. "I remember everything about them."

WENDY MULLIGAN
Dax Sanz
Elio Ma

She started with Wendy first. Wendy had been younger, but more caring, more nurturing, and more gentle than she was. Wendy was a born caregiver.

Wendy taught me how to be a big sister or something like a mom. God, I need her here now. I'm not ready to be a mom without my family.

Rupex's voice and the memory of his fur on her skin erased her rising panic.

I guess I have something like a family. But I want the rest of it back.

With a few taps, Layla added Wendy's birthdate and home region to the screen and choked down a gasp when she saw her beautiful friend's picture appear on the screen.

Wendy had black, glossy curls that a bad diet and pollution couldn't harm, and a spray of freckles across her nose that trailed over onto her round, beige cheeks.

The girl in the picture was older. A woman, now.

There were dark circles under her eyes. Her cheeks were thin. That hair was still the crowning glory of her beauty.

She was alive. She wasn't stick-thin or obviously ill.

Layla touched the screen with longing fingertips and yelped when it switched to show Wendy's profile.

Her smile was gone. There was nothing left of the laughing brunette Layla had always tried to protect.

Guilt seared her. "Don't worry. I'm going to get you and the boys back, Wendy."

The contract price wasn't disclosed on her page, but the identification number across the bottom of the photo informed Layla where she could inquire about bidding on the contract and speaking to Wendy Mulligan.

Her fingers hesitated, torn between finding the boys and opening up a call channel that second.

Impulse was winning, but then she steadied herself. *Think more like a mom. You have to make sure all the cubs, or kids, are safe.*

Dax and Elio's pictures appeared one after the other. Dax had grown a mustache. Elio was tall and squinty. Neither of them were smiling. Both of them were pale.

Whether it was true or not, the labs resembled a prison camp in Layla's mind, where the inhabitants were tortured with medicines and their side effects, fed bland food, kept away from others, and given a minimal amount of sunshine.

All three of them had the same contact number at the bottom of their photos.

Layla opened the channel with trembling fingers, fully expecting to get no response or an A.I. menu that would frustrate the hell out of her.

In moments, an A.I. human female appeared on the screen. She looked identical to a living human being, but the faint blue glow at the edges of her eyes and skin revealed her artificial nature.

"Hello. This is the Metro Labs Contract Registry, one of Sapien-Three's largest employers with branches in over 900 locations and growing! We're always looking for young, healthy individuals who want to help the medical community grow by offering us their contract for an extended registration! We offer terms of one, two, three, five, and seven years, based on age and medical history. Successful applicants are often offered re-signing bonuses to extend their term for an additional year! Are you interested in offering your contract for approval?"

"No." Layla shook the frost out of her voice. If she sounded too eager or too angry, maybe that would screw things up.

"Are you inquiring about a previous contract registration start date?"

"No."

"Are you inquiring about a contract already registered to Metro Labs?"

"Yes!"

"Please state the contract number."

Layla winced. She was going to have to do this three times. But it would be worth it. She recited Wendy's number.

"The number you've provided is a match for one of our employees. This contract is currently unavailable but will be coming up for bidding in—" there was a pause and the lights flashed in the woman's eyes, "thirty days. Do you wish to make an offer on this contract?"

"Yes!"

"Your terms must be presented to the individual. Please wait while I see if Mulligan, Wendy, is available. Please confirm that this is the individual you wish to speak to regarding a contract bid?"

Throat tight, Layla whispered, "Yes."

"I'm sorry, I couldn't detect a response."

"Yes!"

The screen abruptly went black. Layla's heart froze. "What? Wait! What did I do?"

The black screen made a series of clicks. Then, a weak voice asked, "Dax? You're back?"

Layla's eyes overflowed the second Wendy's voice hit her ear. "Wendy. It's not Dax. It's Layla."

Silence.

"Layla? We grew up together?"

"Elio? This isn't funny."

"Layla, Wendy! Please say you remember me." Her fingers bit into her knees. Why couldn't she see her face? Why did she sound so weak? Maybe it was late at night there on Sapien-Three and she'd woken her up.

Sure enough, a small yellow light appeared and Wendy's shadowy face peered close to the screen. Only a small square of Layla's large screen was filled with a poor quality visual. The lab "inmates" must only have small portable comms, Layla realized.

"Layla?"

"Wendy! It's me! Are you okay?"

"I'm... I'm okay." Wendy seemed confused. "What's happening?" Her dull eyes widened. "Did you sell your contract to the lab, too?" Her voice teetered between excitement and something else. Joy? Fear?

"No. Look, I don't know how long they give you to talk, so I'm going to spit out a lot at once. I should have fought harder for us. I should have gone with you. Once you left, I tried to visit, and they said you couldn't see outsiders because of the testing protocols you currently had. I tried a few more times. I dropped off letters, but never heard back."

"Letters?" Wendy shook her head.

"Not important now. We can have lots of time to talk later. Wendy, please let Rupex, the captain of a Leonid craft called the *Comet Stalker*, buy your contract to be crew on his ship. *Please*. Please, and once you're here, we'll be together and if you don't want to be crew, I can find something else for you to do, but we can be together. The boys, too. I want to bid on all of your contracts. Well, Rupex, officially, but me, too." Layla hoped that her rushed tangle of words made sense.

Wendy was silent. "I have to ask Dax. And Elio. We took the five-year placement and signed the one-year with the bonus. The labs take part of your pay to rent you a room. And your comm. Your clothes. They give you six outfits a year, but if you wear them out, you have to pay for the new ones."

Layla nodded, unease growing. Wendy sounded disoriented and depressed, beyond mere lack of sleep. "Your contract is up soon, Wen."

"Thirty days. We're all getting out. Not going back this time."

Unease, hell. Pure panic gripped Layla's chest and wouldn't let go. "Did you try to leave?"

"Once. Our contract wasn't up, and we couldn't buy off the time. We don't go without each other."

"Baby, I'm so sorry. I should have been there."

Wendy looked at her for a long, silent second. "No. We should have been with you. If we had trusted you, we would have been okay."

"Are you—are you not okay now?" Layla pressed.

More silent staring. "In thirty days we'll be better. We saved up. We're going to get a place, the three of us. We'll do different work. Cleaning. Babysitting. I always wanted to be a nanny. Or a teacher."

They don't need me. They survived without me. They made a plan without me. They'll be okay without me.

But I'll never be okay without them.

"I know you don't need me, but... what does the lab pay per year? Whatever they do, we can double it. And housing is included, no paying it back. The clothes—well, right now the clothes are a little baggy, but... But Wendy, it's safe here. No one would hurt you. No one would make you stay. I'm trying to get a place for us. Um. Wait."

Wendy stared, mute and wide-eyed as Layla tried to display her screen. She opened a second display window to show Leo Falls. There was only a brief aerial view and a coastal view as it wasn't a popular location, but it was beautiful in any picture. "Here. We can have a safe place here. Or we can travel. Wendy... I hope to be a mom soon. There might be other families who need help with their cubs—I mean, babies, too." She thought of Dane and Cherie.

Her voice was tiny and flickering, like her screen. "This isn't real."

"Huh?"

"Not real. Hallucination. A dream. Side effects. Psychotropic. Antipsychotic. Had it all before. Never this clear."

Layla's heart cracked further. *My poor beautiful Wendy!* "They gave you all that stuff?"

"Lots of stuff. It's safe. They have to see how it affects people before they can prescribe it." Her eyes didn't meet Layla's and instead looked around the dark room.

"I'll send the offer for all three of you, including transportation to the Milky Way Intergalactic Port." Layla bit her lip. She was making rash promises with Rupex's credits.

Well, I could belong to him for the rest of my life to work it off—and that's the job I wanted most, anyway. With the exchange rate, maybe it won't seem too bad.

When Wendy remained quiet and confused, Layla pressed, "How about if it's only a month-long contract? A vacation? And if you don't like it, you can always leave. If you love it, you can stay."

"If I see the offer for real, I'll consider it. If... If this is really Layla, I've missed you. We all have."

The call ended.

Layla dissolved into sobs as her fingers sprang into action. She had to hope Dax and Elio were better able to differentiate reality from illusion. Maybe they would help persuade Wendy.

If not, I still have Rupex.

Rupex and romance. I wonder what he wants to do tonight?

Layla used the distraction to help her calm down and prepare for the next emotional upheaval.

Chapter Twenty-One

Rupex gathered the heavenly-scented blossoms of the Pulsewood Bush, dark yellow and red. Some said they were aphrodisiacs. He remembered taking the large, cone-shaped flowers and putting them on Alana's ears, and calling her the Beach Witch.

Alana would have liked Layla. She has fire. She has compassion.

Rupex left the flowers in a bucket of water, along with the fat black and blue shrimp. He would roast them on skewers and serve them with plump duck breast steeped in Marcus' Servali Spice Blend.

Marcus was a willing ally in his plan to romance Layla.

"Good. Glad your heart and your genitalia are working as a team. About time." Marcus remarked with a grim chuckle, taking a break from freezing the serum he intended to pass onto Lynxian and human couples. "What would you like me to do? Be your second? Talk you up? Or just play kitchen boy?"

"Help me make dinner and then spend a night under the stars—or in my shack on the island. Please? I want to feel like we have privacy. Romancing shouldn't feel clinical—or like we have to have an audience and report back on our mating."

"Call it making love, you fool." Marcus spat a pen cap back into his paw as he finished the last label. "Put on some Leopardine mood music. Silk sheets. Red wine."

"Wine? Silk sheets? Are you coming down with something?"

"No, I'm coming up with something!" Marcus left the lab and headed to the kitchen. "Humans need fruit and vegetables more often, too. And dessert. They like sweet things. Do you bake?"

"Do I *look* like I bake?"

"You look like someone who ought to learn. You've already shown success in the sexual arena. You need to prove you can meet other needs."

"I'm gainfully employed and a King."

"I think it's a good thing the girl is easily pleased with simplistic gifts like shelter and a sturdy craft."

"The *Comet Stalker* isn't simple! It's not a pleasure craft, but it is certainly efficient, top-of-the-line, sleek—"

"That isn't romantic."

Rupex groaned. Marcus was right. Layla liked him because he made survival easier. That wasn't love.

RUPEX PREPARED HIS quarters carefully. He put the lights on low, put the heavily perfumed flowers on the table, and lined up the courses of their meal under makeshift cloches made from spare mixing bowls. Marcus pronounced him "ready to try" and took an overnight bag as he left the ship at sunset.

Rupex flicked his paw and the smooth, exotic vocals of Leopardine mood music (said to be sung originally by the harems of Leopardine Sultans when they were in heat) wailed through the speakers and filled the chamber.

His senses were overloaded. Now, all he needed was Layla.

In his best uniform, holding a single deep red and gold flower before him, he strolled to her quarters.

Layla opened the door in what had once been a red beach wrap. It made a knot at her bust and flowed past her calves, leaving a long slit up her thigh. Her hair was in a twist—and her face was tight and tired.

"Hi, handsome." She greeted him with a sad smile that was trying to be brave.

"Layla! My Queen! What?"

"I love the way you call me Queen," Layla laughed and collapsed against his chest, sobbing. "God, Ru, I'm sorry. Tonight was supposed to be so perfect and I'm so upset. I found my friends. Their contracts are up in thirty days."

"Wonderful!"

"Not wonderful. I talked to Wendy and Elio. Dax wouldn't answer, but it was nighttime there. "Elio was a shivering wreck and barely lucid. Wendy thought I was a bad dream or a hallucination. They've been tortured in that place, legally tortured, their healthy bodies put through endless trials of drugs and I-don't-know-what." Layla pounded her small fist into his shoulder. "I'm sorry. I'm just so fucking mad at myself. I hate myself for letting this happen."

"You were a scared young girl! You couldn't protect them if they didn't choose to let you. You couldn't force them, or they wouldn't trust you."

"They sure as hell don't trust me now."

Rupex held her, lost. What to say? How to comfort her?

Love is messy.

"I trust you. I know you will fight tooth and nail, or as we say, fang and claw, for your young. The young you birth or the young you wish to help. You have been working on a way to save them for years—and now you can. I'll help you, Layla."

LAYLA LOOKED UP AT Rupex, her eyes still trickling. He gently said her name as he cupped her face in his massive paws, one under her chin to bring it to his lips.

"Why? Not on a contract tonight," she whispered, anger and self-pity souring her finer feelings. She didn't deserve his trust or his kindness. Certainly not his love.

"I trust you. I care about you. I... I know it's very quick for Leonids and humans to choose a person they want to keep in their lives in a matter of a few weeks." Rupex puffed out his chest and his mane puffed with it, making him look larger and more impressive.

Magnificent, Layla thought. "Most humans where I come from never choose."

"Then I am lucky you are. Because I want to choose you. I want to love you. I want you to love me. I do not say that lightly. After losing so many Queens, I was sure I would *never* say it, not just because there were so few left, but because the pain of losing someone you love hurts too deeply." Rupex pressed her back into the wall of the corridor, warm breath on her face, hard, lean body molding to hers as his paws pulled her hips forward. "But I've discovered love is something you can't help. And you will do it, even if it hurts." He swallowed against her as she buried her hands in his mane. "I love you. I thought I had to make a night of perfect romance to show that I love you and hope you will give me your love in return."

"But you don't." She hated to interrupt his perfect speech, but she couldn't contain herself. "You don't need to do anything but be here when I need you—and I need you so much. I never want to be without you. I was afraid of finding someone I wanted like that, because... well, the same reasons as you. It hurts when they're gone."

"Don't leave."

"I won't."

There was a sudden breathlessness between them. "You-you won't?"

"No. If you let me stay."

"Stay! Oh, Bastet and Sekhmet, *stay!*" Rupex erupted into an excited purr, nuzzling her cleavage and neck as he picked her up and worshiped her with his muzzle. "Always stay. Be my Queen, Layla."

"Only if you promise to be my King—and you still have to let me work on this ship and have your cubs. I'm not giving that up." The woes of the afternoon melted and mellowed in his arms. They would find a course of action, together.

"Stubborn, fiery Queen. Yes, my love. And only if you let me romance you as I had intended. First comes a meal—" Rupex stooped and retrieved the flower that he'd dropped in favor of holding her, "and a token of my affection."

Layla took the flower and sniffed it, her brain temporarily hazy with its rich, sultry scent. "I'll tell you what happened over dinner?"

"And I'll make you feel better over dessert."

"SO, THE LAB FOLLOWS proper protocols it seems. They weren't held against their will."

"They were," Layla spat, glaring at him. Her anger softened as Rupex lifted the mixing bowl and revealed a feast.

"But they said they were planning to leave together?"

Layla sank back in her chair and absorbed the surroundings for a moment. A deep blackish-red wine tempted her beside a decadent meal. More of the heady flowers that seemed to make her thighs pulse just from their scent. Languorous music in a strange vowel-centric language she didn't understand. Her cheeks flushed. Some parts of the song sounded very orgasmic.

"At some point, I'm not sure how long ago, the side effects or the situation prompted them to consider leaving. Wendy said they couldn't buy out their contract. So, while they weren't held captive, they were held for ransom. A ransom of wages they hadn't yet earned. I'm pretty sure that's the shady end of legal."

"Horrid." Rupex took her hand. "Yet they stayed on?"

She shrugged, stabbing her fork into the tender pink duck breast. "I've seen it before. A jerky boss treats you well until you're committed to staying on. They all signed on again, probably because they didn't know where to go or thought they hadn't saved enough to get safe housing and survive while looking for work. Their original contracts were auctioned off when they were fourteen. They were a burden on an overtaxed system and they weren't chosen for adoption. They might have had some options, but not a lot of knowledge on how to use it. I didn't teach them..." Layla stopped, the flowers and the food no longer working their magic.

"You were how much older?"

"Two years."

"Why weren't you in the same predicament?"

"My contract *was* auctioned at fourteen—and bought by the Sapien-Three Public Childcare System. I was allowed to remain in group housing because I worked twenty hours a week doing cleaning and laundry for the facility." Layla gave him a tired smile. "I didn't mind. I could do it, and I stayed with my family." She swallowed a gulp of wine. Family. The word hurt so bad to say. "When I realized they weren't going to be adopted and their contracts were being put up for auction, I snuck to the library and used a database computer to look at vacancies in our region. There weren't any for the Public Childcare System. I knew their contracts would go to someone else and we'd be separated. I quit my contract and found a basement flat that had been abandoned. I tried to get them to run away, but they wouldn't come. They didn't think I could support them. They didn't know who would hire them." Layla drained the glass. "And that's the story of Layla's Awesome Failure."

Rupex growled. His claws indented the edge of the table. "That is the story of Layla's Heroic Heart. By Bastet, you tried! They're still alive. We'll get their contracts. They can clean the ship. Didn't you say Wendy wished to work with children? She'll help us with our cubs. If we have none, then perhaps she'll help with someone else's cubs!" Rupex's tail curled around her ankle and stroked her calf gently as his paw closed over hers. "I'll place the bids now."

"I already did, just to hold a spot. I had enough, thanks to the big deposit you gave me. If you can advance my next month's salary..."

"I can, and I will. But I will make the next bid. We need staff and you need your family. I need you to be happy." Ru smiled at her. "I haven't had anyone to be happy with in so long, my Layla. It isn't very romantic, but would you care to sit on my lap while I double your bid for the contracts?"

"I think it's incredibly romantic. Let's eat first. Then we can digest over contract work before we do anything that might be...jarring to the meal."

His eyes widened, the pupils round with lust. "Excellent planning."

THESE CONTRACT BIDS are ridiculously low—by Leonid standards, Rupex thought as he doubled the amount Layla had already entered. Still, he heard her suck in a tense breath.

"How serious were you earlier? About not leaving?" Layla gripped his shoulder as she stood beside him, too nervous to sit.

"Very serious." A formal proposal tickled his tongue, but he pressed it to the roof of his mouth instead.

"Could we... could we renegotiate my contract? I'd say get rid of it but in case... I don't know. I trust you, but I don't trust life so much." Layla gave him a guilty look, her eyes only able to hold his for a second.

"You'd like to renegotiate it? Why?"

"People in love who want to stay together and have a family together don't need to be paid to try to have a baby. I want... I want that for you. For us." Layla's smile was wavery but didn't vanish. "And the money you just spent trying to get my friends aboard your ship—"

Control had always been very important to Rupex, as a King and the captain of the *Comet Stalker*. Having a contract in place and handling this delicate situation as a business had been his preference—and his shield.

Layla pierced his armor more effectively with her heart and her bravery than any laser artillery ever could.

The proposal almost tumbled out—but instead, he kissed her, stalling. Rupex knew the perfect time to ask her, and it wasn't quite yet. "Layla, you can see we desperately need crew, down to the most menial of tasks. What I bid is an offer slightly below what I would normally offer inexperienced Leonids on their first tour of duty. If I left it any lower, I might get a bad reputation amongst other Long Flight Class ships and their crews."

"But that's a fat amount of credits for Sapien-Three," Layla protested, stroking her hand through his mane, tugging it lightly at the ends. Her touch woke him up, making his nostrils flare. A faint hint of blood and arousal put a painful bulge between them.

"Then let us hope that between your love and my money we entice them. There's nothing else we can do for now. Once they give us their answers, we can make transportation arrangements."

Layla nodded, wiping her eyes. "But still. As your... as your Queen-friend—do you call them girlfriends? Mates? Never mind. As your partner, this isn't just business anymore. We can alter my contract."

"We'll take care of your friends first. Then," Rupex suddenly squeezed her hands in his own, "then you can take a course. Paid training."

"Oh? Am I not busting out enough moves for you?" Layla teased, swiveling her hips against him, a playful gleam in her eye.

"Not a course in sexual satisfaction. I believe you're naturally talented in that respect." Rupex closed his eyes as one of her hands pressed firmly down his chest and ended on the crown of his engorged cock. "A course in Information Systems. You have an affinity for database computers, patience for negotiating contracts, and ingenuity to find resources I've requested. With a few courses, you could become a licensed Starcraft Information Officer. And in case you didn't know, that is a well-paying job. You'd be in demand, especially in Felix Orbus. Especially on my crew, my little Queen."

And you could leave me and take your friends with you.

But you'd never be forced to fear hunger and homelessness again.

"Ru..." Layla blinked up at him, her pretty little mouth half open.

"Don't argue with me. It's what we both want, isn't it? You would be happy doing that sort of work, and I'd be happy if you were happy." He smiled and pressed his muzzle to her forehead.

But I never want you to leave. Have I just shot myself in the paw?

Chapter Twenty-Two

Layla stroked Rupex steadily up and down as they kissed on the Command Deck, their stumbling steps made more unbalanced by his hulking frame over her small one and his growing arousal.

"You think I don't realize what you did, don't you?" Layla panted between kisses, climbing him.

He carried her hurriedly, moaning as she bit down on the tight wedge of muscle where his shoulder met his chest. "What did I do?"

"A career. An education. You just offered me everything I could never get for myself—and you told me it would open all kinds of doors. Did you think I wouldn't get it?"

He froze, holding her still against him as he paused in the corridor between the Command Deck's entrance and the elevator that would take them to his quarters. "You're brilliant, pricey education or not, Layla."

His wide chest was still under hers. He's holding his breath, Layla realized.

"You're setting me free."

Still unmoving, his words were almost inaudible. "That's what you do when you love someone."

"I don't want to go. Everything you pour into me, I'll pour back out for you. Don't you get that? When you love, you don't leave, either. When you love, you give everything you've got. I never had much to give, that's all."

His breathing restarted with a deep chuckle that melted all of her into a pool of molten honey. "Oh, never say that. You've had plenty to give from the second I saw you. I never thought I'd be the lucky one to share it."

With a whirl, they were spinning into the opening doors of the elevator. Ru slammed a key with his paw and then went back to mauling her with his sheathed claws, nuzzling her, marking her by rubbing his jaw all across her skin.

It was heaven, being claimed by this beautiful golden beast.

"No one else is on the ship? Marcus is safely camping out?" Layla demanded between frenzied kisses.

"Mhm."

"Good." Her hands attacked his collar. "I need this off of you. Now. It's not fair that you're wearing so many more clothes than me!"

"I'll take you shopping. We can order things in a few more weeks. In the meantime, I would gladly keep you naked." Rupex tugged her red wrap off and left her in panties. His nostrils twitched and his tail followed suit. "Mm. More wine for me?"

"You make me feel dangerous when you talk like that." Layla rubbed her arms as goosebumps sprang up. Her nipples were hard, hungry pebbles and her monthly blood was mixing with slick arousal. The glint in Ru's eyes clearly stated that he'd like to devour her—and she wanted to be his after dinner drink.

HUMAN MEN WOULD AVOID her during this time, Layla thought as Ru pushed her onto the bed, bottom up, belly down. His paws gently raked her panties and absorbent pad off. A thrill of naughtiness and taboo made her thighs jump as his nose pressed against the curve of her ass. "Want me to—" The rest of her offer was swallowed by a harsh, hungry swipe of her lover's tongue.

"Clean up? Don't you dare." Rupex buried his head between her cheeks, pushing her up so his long, textured tongue nicked her curls and then flattened out on her clit and up between her folds.

Her eyes rolled back. Too much stimulation, too fast, but she didn't want to stop him. She wanted to have the high, hard wave of orgasm and then get back to their night of romance, the soft lights, warm temps, and languid music.

There was nothing languid about the way Ru was devouring her, though. He slurped and smacked, eating her pussy while growling and purring in turns. She could feel the vibrations in her body as he feasted on her.

"Come for me, sweet Queen, and then I can take my time with you," Rupex rumbled against her thigh.

She didn't need to be told twice. In seconds, she felt his tongue invading her tunnel and fucking her while his sharp teeth pressed her clit and plump outer lips.

"Fuck," she hissed a single harsh cry as her hands gave out and she came on his mouth, sending another gush of his desired wine splashing across his tongue.

Holy shit. Layla shook her head and tried to swim up from the orgasmic fog that Rupex had sent her into. "All right, mister. Your turn."

EVEN THOUGH LAYLA INTENDED to turn around and gobble as much of the Leonid's cock as she could, Rupex slowed the pace, holding her close and nuzzling her, his tongue cleaning any traces of blood from his face.

Layla wondered if she should feel repulsed by the idea of kissing a creature who wanted to taste her blood—who was turned on by it.

As he purred against her, gently rubbing his thick, wide pads over her skin and making it sing, she decided, no. It didn't repulse her or disgust her. So many human males and probably other types of men were grossed out by a necessary and basic bodily function, treating her as unclean and inconvenient. Some men had made it clear that it was an occasion to sulk and go without sex.

Rupex loved her during these moments. His taste for prey was controlled and definitely used to her advantage. She had no idea how soothing his oral ministrations could be to her, and the intense orgasms he gave her made her achy muscles dance in relief.

"I love that you love every inch of me. Every drop." She pulled away, getting to her knees. She was going to prove that she felt the same.

"You don't mind that I enjoy it so much?" Rupex's tail did a jittery tremble on the bed, like a guilty child fidgeting.

"I do not." She shifted herself over his thighs, straddling them. Rupex moaned and reached for her plump, swollen lips. "Ah-ah. Your turn, I said."

"But this is supposed to be my night to woo and romance you. I have to show you my constant attention," he argued, mischief in his eyes.

"But I'm making love to you, too. I've never done that before." Layla clasped her hands around the base of his cock as she looked into his eyes. "Lots of sex. The best has been with you. But making love? Nope." Yes, she had used the term sometimes to soften the way she felt about sex, and she thought it often when she was in Rupex's arms, but this was different. This time she could tell him.

"I love you." Her tongue slowly circled the tip of his cock. "I love your taste. I love the little extras you have." She ran her fingers lightly over the spines at his base and watched his head flop back to the pillow as if he'd gone boneless. "I love the way this feels inside me, filling me up and stretching me out."

"I don't know if I've mentioned this," he half-snarled, "but Queens are typically passionate but not overly talkative in these situations. A lot of moaning sounds." Ru gestured to the noises above them, the moaning, chanting mood music.

"You want me to shut up?"

"No. I want to thank Bastet that you are my Queen, blessed with an incredibly wicked mouth."

"You just wait." Layla wrapped her lips around him and pushed down, the wide crown filling her mouth completely, snagging on her teeth with a little catch that made him shiver and purr like a transport motor. Her hands wrapped around the base, tickling his spines as she stroked him steadily, sometimes twisting her hand around the base to swirl the spines horizontally instead of stroking them vertically. Rupex whimpered, and salty, slightly sweet pre-cum began trickling down her throat.

He's going to keep doing that until he's buried inside me, so deep inside me.

Her pussy throbbed hungrily. Layla pulled her mouth off to glare at him playfully, still stroking, her lips pecking his shaft between words. "You. Bad. Kitty. You spoiled me. My pussy will never take another cock now. It only wants yours. Human men won't do it for me."

"Don't talk about them. Don't want to think about anyone else touching you."

"Was that the point? To make me fall in love with your cock first and you second?"

"Did it work?" Ru shut his eyes, hips squirming, claws bunching in the sheets as she started sucking on him again, this time not forcing his jaw-stretching girth in her mouth, but using her open mouth to adore him.

"I think it might have been a tie." Layla worked both hands around him now and ran her tongue over his slit. His whimper turned into a roar.

"No one... ever... so thorough."

"It's us naughty human types. We're not austere. Well, not me."

"I love you like you are. You're meant for a Leonid, Layla. You are more wild than half the Queens with Felid blood. I like you like this, love you like this, so perfectly delicate and yet so fierce-hearted."

"I think you're a lot better than most human men... but to be fair, I didn't let myself get close to any of them."

As Layla began working her mouth and hands around him in unison, she heard Rupex moan, "You were meant for me."

LAYLA LANGUIDLY SLID her tongue lower, finding his spines. Her mouth caused an intense reaction, her tongue licking the little nubs that swelled against her lips as if trying to fill the space and lock her to him.

"So that's how these little guys work," Layla mused softly between licks, watching his spines puff up and create a thick ring of flesh around his base. "That's why you get 'stuck' in my little pussy, hm?"

Rupex's paw suddenly clamped down on the top of her head, lightly scraping her scalp and entangling in her hair. "Come here, you. You can't drive me to the brink of madness with your naughty mouth and ruin my carefully planned evening."

Layla left her perch between his thighs with a pout, fingers trailing over his furry, muscular abdominal muscles and giving a longing whimper at the perfect pair of balls hanging tight and full under the base of his cock.

"It was an amazing evening, and you're amazing for not minding the way I tilted it on its axis." Layla allowed herself to be drawn into his arms, giggling as she nestled onto his chest. With a twist, he put her on her back, his long, lean form over her, his thick tip brushing her pouting, slick pussy.

Before, their encounters had been full of pleasure, heat, and even a little danger as he stalked her and chased her through their private island paradise.

This was different. His head settled over hers and he pressed his forehead to hers, wide triangular nose against her lips. He nudged her with his cheek, over and over, purring over her in a new way. This was a steady, low possessive sound that never shut off. It even caused his voice to thicken and distort as he murmured, "My Layla. My love. You were meant for me. I have been looking for you for so much longer than I thought."

"Ru..." She wrapped her arms around his neck and her calves around his thighs, feeling the now-familiar stretch that stung her opening for a split second before it swallowed his cock. She felt him holding back, moving slow. Each inch was sweet torture, pushing her wider, filling her deeper, making her wish that he was buried in her to the point where she strained to take him.

Tonight, her pool of juice and extra lubrication seemed to make it easier. Pleasure came faster and harder, even though he moved slower.

"I just want to be filled by you," she hissed, clamping her pussy on him for a second, her muscles barely able to flex.

His thrusts were slow and steady, his purring increasing as they kissed, hands stroking through manes and hair. "Filled you will be. Heart and soul. Body's just a bonus. You had so many sad days, yes?"

Layla nodded, unable to speak as the hard flutters that melted her brain and turned her pussy into a puddle took over.

"So have I." Rupex thrust his hips forward and Layla moaned as her insides stretched to accommodate him. "No more emptiness for either of us, my Queen."

"I love when you call me that." Layla let her mind slip as endorphins surged, pushing past the discomfort of his size to the place where she found herself coming endlessly on his cock. She waited for the final thick push that would force his spines inside her, and they would press into her walls, meshing them together until he was spent.

Her limbs seemed to grow limp under his growling, arching thrusts, her body spiraling into a blackness where there were only bright lights of pleasure in her brain. Her clit sent up a surge to join the party as Rupex's tail tip began stroking it. The fur, slick with her pussy juices and his leaking pre-cum swirled over it like a second tongue.

"My Layla. So giving. Look how you give me every inch of yourself."

"My Ru. So talented. Not many guys could fuck me, 'lick me', and melt me with sweet nothings all at once," she panted, eyes still closed, body wrapped around him like a second layer of fur.

"Sweet nothings? No, precious. You are my everything."

Layla's eyes widened as he finished his sweet words in a hiss. As his words died, his roar replaced them, building as he suddenly shook on top of her, pushing a torrent of hot, creamy cum inside her, pressing her full pussy even further past its limits.

"It's a good thing I like being so full of you," Layla whimpered.

"I like being full of you, too. I must not be doing my job."

"Huh? This was the best, sweetest, most wonderful love-making I've ever had." *Also, the* only *love-making I've ever had.*

"You come like I do when I push you over the edge." Rupex worried her shoulder gently with his lips, teeth hidden under them.

A few weeks ago, Layla might have blushed. Having squirting orgasms seemed too intimate, too private, and maybe even wrong to talk about. Rupex was her lover and he made her come that hard. He owned every inch of her. Layla realized with a feeling of delight that she owned him, too—at least, if he meant some of the things he'd said earlier about always being together, cubs or no cubs, contract or no contract.

"You did your job, babe. Believe me."

"But I could do better." Rupex slowly moved their bodies until he was spooned behind her, his rigid cock still impaling her, her belly puffed out with his thickness and his cum.

"What are you—" Layla didn't get to finish her question. Suddenly, her arms were caught up in one paw over her head while his other paw plundered her hyperstimulated clit, rough pads, and smooth fur taking turns to rub it in hard circles while his cock put so much pressure on her aching pussy from the inside.

"I'm worshiping you. I'll not let you go until I've received your... blessing."

"You are adorably kinky."

"Hmm. I prefer to think of it as ridiculously in love."

Layla felt his tail slip between her cheeks, teasing her soaking wet second entrance, lubricated by the slickness they'd been making. "Ru..."

"Whatever it takes to push my Queen to the heights of her pleasure," he promised.

Layla closed her eyes and let him have her, feeling the pressure build, the hot, burning urge to squirt that she couldn't deny or control. "I love you."

"Mm. I'm so very glad. I love you, too."

LAYLA SLEPT IN HIS arms while he slowly softened and slid from her. Later, he'd spoil her and scrub her gently in the luxurious bath his captain's quarters possessed.

But not yet.

I told her I loved her. I told her she was mine.

Am I a fool? So many will question, doubt, or outright reject us.

Rupex briefly thought of Silvia. His mother. Alana.

Would I let any King or Knight call me out for loving them? Alana did not let the age-old tales about "cats and dogs" stop her from loving Jaxson. Why should I let others rule my heart?

He felt a grudging admiration for the grizzled old Lynxian he'd talked to. That gruff and gray backwater-dwelling hadn't hesitated to show off his human lover.

Times have changed. Worlds have changed.

"Layla?" He kissed her shoulder and then used his mane to tickle her cheek and ear. Her eyes fluttered open. "Layla?"

"What's wrong, baby?" she whispered groggily.

"I love you."

"That's not wrong. Love you, too. Even if you are slowly wrecking my ability to walk." Layla winced as she tried to roll to face him.

He cuddled her, keeping her still. "That's not wrong. I love you. Wanted to tell you. I wanted to ask you something."

"Look, I'll try it, but I don't think your cock is going to fit back there. We should start with some toys. Or a good tail-fucking."

Rupex felt his cock surge back to alertness. His sexy, naughty, beautiful Queen. He could easily imagine fucking her tight back passage, something he'd never attempted with previous partners. The act of fully giving herself to him, every single opening, made his eyes darken with lust.

He shook his head to clear it. "Not that. Not yet, at any rate. Layla? Would you be my wife? Officially?"

Layla went stiff in his arms. "You want— what? Really?"

Rupex couldn't keep her still this time. She spun on his best sheets with a splash of spilled juices. "Oh, f—"

"Shh. That doesn't matter. I want an answer. Please. Will you marry me?" Rupex grabbed her face gently to force her eyes away from her thighs and up to his face.

"Yes! Yes, of course, I will. But... but no one was ever... I mean, I never thought I'd ever get asked that question!"

Rupex blinked at her, trying not to laugh at her squeaking protest and her shocked expression. "Well, I've asked you now. That *was* a yes you babbled at me, wasn't it?"

"It was." Layla blinked up at him. "Now what?"

Rupex thought. "We take a warm shower, and I go wake up Marcus?"

"We can get our own breakfast!"

"I want to tell him the good news. We may butt heads—more in the past than we do now—but he is the closest thing I have to family. Well," Rupex kissed her forehead, "he used to be."

Chapter Twenty-Three

Rupex woke up one morning several days after his proposal to find his new bride-to-be shrieking outside the hut they were sharing, his hut to be precise. Dragging pants over his slightly sore limbs, Rupex stumbled out the door.

"Layla!"

"Contracts accepted! Contracts accepted! A whole bunch! Look!" Layla was running through the sand in a loose white dress that only came to the top of her thighs (it had probably been one of Alana's undershirts), her breasts bobbing up and down, blonde hair streaming back from her sun-kissed face. She looked like a goddess. The only imperfections were the bruised starburst on her arm from her most recent shot and the tablet in her hand.

"Which ones?" Rupex held his paw out, his heart slowly returning to normal speed. Each day they had checked for word of contracts being accepted and for news of the quarantine procedures and flight restrictions. They already had their first post-grounding flight plan scheduled—out to Lynx-Nineteen. That would be a long-haul flight, lasting around five weeks, and that was provided they had enough crew.

Layla was thrilled to be with Rupex and to have accepted his offer of marriage, but her joy seemed incomplete. Every day she would spend a happy hour or two learning about Leonid wedding customs on her database computer, an hour or so studying for her entrance exam to the Information Officer Course, and an hour pacing, wondering why her three friends had not been in contact.

By the look on her face, Rupex thought that wait was over.

"They're coming! They're all coming! Look, look!" Layla scrolled frantically, too fast for him to see the words. "They've all accepted the position of 'Crew, Maintenance.' Oh, and we've got some others. There is a Tigerite, Talos, who accepted the offer for Security Systems Officer. A Servali chef—you know Marcus was rooting for him to accept, and a Leopardine freight coordinator, and an Engine Systems Mechanic..." Layla's face twisted suddenly, something bright in her eyes.

"An Engine Systems Mechanic? Thank Bastet! We haven't had one in three years. My brother-in-law, Jaxson, was the head ESM for Sirius Flight—What? What are you giggling about?"

Layla couldn't speak. She put a hand to her bright pink cheeks, eyes sparkling at him.

"Oh, love! I'm sorry. Of course, it's so wonderful about your friends! That's the main thing. I—"

Layla tapped on the screen and showed Rupex a familiar face—a rangy wolf-like face with bright, laughing eyes, a ready smile, and dark reddish-brown fur. "Jax!"

"He applied. I—um. I knew it was a post we needed and I figured... well. Nepotism. There were other candidates that offered contracts, but I wrote back this morning and told him he had the job. He's family. I hope... I hope I did the right thing." Layla's eyes dimmed. "I was so excited about my family coming home, I thought... Maybe you'd feel the same?"

Rupex nodded slowly. Jaxson would remind him of Alana.

And why was that a bad thing? His cubs deserved to meet their uncle. "I am so glad that our cubs will grow up with family all around them. Like it should be in a pride." He shook his head again, snorting out a soft laugh. "My pride will be an odd one, won't it? With a Canid, a quartet of humans, and every sort of Felid imaginable."

"It sounds like paradise to me." Layla leaned on his arm—then dropped the tablet down to her hip, letting her hand slide across his furry chest. "I think I like the shirtless look on you, Ru."

"Layla. Again?"

"Just had my shot. My temperature's rising." Layla's fingers slipped across the neckline of her dress, pushing it off her shoulders. "Gotta get out of these clothes."

Rupex's mouth dropped open. He found himself with the tablet shoved into his paw as his fiancée stripped naked on the beach, her beautiful body bared against the sand and sky.

"You are going to ruin me," he whispered. "I can't get any work done!"

"I've done most of the work for an hour or two." Layla pouted. She stretched, showing off the arch of her spine and the curve of her bottom, bending to reveal the pink slit between her thighs and the tight pucker they'd started pleasuring more consistently. They hadn't actually attempted the full sex act there, but Layla's devilish smile told him that he wasn't the only one thinking about it.

Operative word... thinking.

"Your work is brilliant on the contracts, but where are all these crew members expecting to come aboard? What about Jaxson? He's a Canid, and there will probably be extra restrictions on taking him aboard as the Sirius Federation is in a much more difficult situation with the Queen Fever mutation. Crew coordination and new flight plan addendums have to be filed...and then I'll ravish that sweet pussy of yours."

Layla's pout returned, this one even sadder and harder to ignore. "Can I just sit on your lap while you're working? I don't want to be away from my mate."

Mate. Oooh. She had him by the tail, she did. He could never refuse her anything when she called him that most feral of names. "Yes, my Queen. But *sitting* on my lap—not riding it."

Layla retrieved her gown from the sand, pausing to let her fingers dip between her legs and spread her pinkness for his eyes. "Okay. You're the King. You're the captain. I'll just sit on you like a good girl. I'll be very still. I won't squirm or anything."

Rupex sighed. She'd won before he even got to the deck. "That remains to be seen."

FOUR DAYS LATER...

"My eyes! Bastet, Sekhmet, and my grandfather's mane! Don't you two have *rooms*?" Marcus stumbled away from the command deck, a paw over his eyes and tail lashing. "You can't do this when you have other crew members, you know!"

Layla didn't even care. Nothing mattered to her except that Rupex was hers, and he was mating with her constantly to prove it—and to sate the urges that even daily love-making wouldn't quiet. It had to be multiple times a day. If there wasn't actual mating, there at least had to be touching. His scent was a comfort to her.

Working hours meant hours where Layla needed to sit on his lap, preferably with his cock inside her and his tail wrapped around her leg or her waist.

Rupex pulled out of her with a groan. "I told you. Your luck only holds so far."

"Three days without getting caught was a good run. Come on, back to your room, it is the closest." She tugged him from the chair, ignoring the wet puddle she'd left in his trousers.

"Talos, the new Security Systems Officer, wants to have a conference. He's going to help me update our cyber defense systems, even before he's aboard. I can't refuse that kind of initiative without seeming like a lazy King and an unfit captain."

Layla nodded. That was definitely important, and rationally, she understood that. But the idea of being away from Rupex for several hours, unable to feel his fur or breathe in his warm scent, made her eyes prickle.

Rupex didn't notice, busy cleaning himself up. "I'm surprised he offered up his contract for this. Tigerites are loners."

Purely to distract herself, Layla argued with him. "Really? Isn't that a stereotype?"

"Not if it's true. Tigerites don't live in prides. They don't have packs, either. The Tigerite planets are pretty rugged and devoted to a lot of different things... but none of them are big on metropolitan life. Nothing like you'd find on Leonid-One."

"Is this Leonid superiority talking?"

"No! Honestly, one day, we'll go to Tigerite-One if you'd like to see it. Beautiful place! Jungles. Temples. So much lush, green land. It's one of the system's chief agricultural belts. I have had a Tigerite crewmate before, back when I was young and my father was alive. I think his name was Burton—yes, Burton, from Tigerite-Three. Burton told me most Tigerite males make a sort of pilgrimage into the main city on their planet to get their higher education, and then return to their homestead, take a mate, and live a few miles from anyone else. Their cities would be like Leonid-One's districts or Sapien-Three's provinces or states because they're so spread out."

"Huh. Wonder why he wants to be aboard a ship then?" Layla wound her arms around her future husband, burying her nose in his back, wiping her eyes on his uniform.

"Well. Times are changing. Maybe he wants to break with tradition. Maybe there's not much work for a security systems expert out in his part of the world. We certainly had to change after the Queen Fever. Had there not been a shortage of females, Marcus would not have experimented with the idea of chromosome compatibility. Then you wouldn't have been asked to partake in this damn foolish experiment, and I would never have found the love of my life!"

Layla felt anger surge and spike in her. Seconds ago, she thought she would die without Ru's touch and now she wanted to smack him. Foolish experiment? Is that how he thought of their attempt to produce a family?

Calm down. You didn't even want a family. You wanted to get knocked up, get paid, and get gone.

Yeah, well... Now, I don't feel like that and I don't like him saying that.

It didn't matter that Ru didn't know her feelings. Irrational as it was, Layla couldn't let go of her anger, even knowing how precious family was to Rupex and aware that his words had been poorly chosen.

Layla grabbed the small handheld tablet she'd been using. "I'll let you get on with the Tiger-guy."

"Layla?"

"Gotta go."

"Layla, my love, what's—"

"It's nothing. Just... something *foolish*." Layla banged her palm against the panel that opened the command deck's doors.

Ru's paw crashed over hers. "You're angry with me." He blinked in surprise as he turned her face toward his.

"I'm just... I feel like crap. I love you. I don't know if it'll ever work out for us, but I hope one day we have kids. Cubs. Babies! Maybe it'll work out for other couples, healthier couples. I'm polluted." Layla rubbed her eyes. "Let me go. I wanna lay down."

"I'll be there soon to check on you, my Queen." Ru kissed her with concern in his eyes, paw lingering on her shoulder until she was completely out of the room.

LAYLA BYPASSED HER own quarters, a feeling of sadness and misery that she couldn't describe hanging over her. It was worse the further she got from Rupex. Her anger faded into a confused ball.

"Maybe I have something wrong. Intergalactic flu." Layla stepped into the elevator and leaned against its steel wall.

This was where she'd first been pressed to Rupex. He'd been angry then. A lot had changed in a month.

Wow. Had it been a month?

Six weeks, technically, since she'd been trafficked and ended up in this cargo bay. Four since she'd made a bargain with the handsome Leonid who has won her heart.

The elevator doors opened to reveal Marcus pushing a cart toward the medical bay.

"Marcus?"

"If you've come to apologize, it's all right. I'm an old Leonid. I've seen enough body parts from various species to last me a lifetime. Never expected to see my handiwork displayed with such... hrm. Enthusiasm." The older Leonid cleared his throat.

"I don't want to apologize. I ... I want to sit down." Layla staggered past him and made her way unevenly to the bed where she'd had her first exam.

"Layla?" Marcus' voice took on a note of alarm.

"I feel... hot. Really hot. And sad. And angry."

"I think we just found out that humans can not tolerate a twice-weekly booster," Marcus said as he hurried to stand beside her, one hand on her head. "It was noble of you to try it this week, but no more."

"I'm going to be okay, right?"

"I think you'll be fine, but feverish for a few days. Why don't I take you back to your room so you can rest there? It's got a lot more ambiance."

"But not the great doctor." Layla smiled at him.

"I promise to be your personal bedside physician." Marcus scooped her up in his arms, nostrils twitching. "Hm."

"What?"

"I hope Ru doesn't punch me for touching his mate. You are inundated with his scent. He marked you very thoroughly."

Layla wanted to make a retort, but Marcus whisked her onto the elevator, the paw holding his small medical bang poking the button for her deck. The elevator whirred and zipped to life, and Layla felt everything fade to a misty black.

Chapter Twenty-Four

Layla woke up lying on her side with a cool towel on her head and a tiny pink basin next to her. "Ru?"

"I'm here, My Queen." Rupex hurried over and knelt next to her bed. "Are you feeling better?"

Layla took stock of herself. She felt hot. Horny. And like she wanted to sob into Ru's chest, burying her nose in the softest planes of fur that met over his chiseled pecs.

"I feel hot." That was enough information. "And thirsty."

Rupex put a glass of water in her hand.

"What about your meeting with Talos? Is it over?"

Ru's whiskers twitched. "That was yesterday, Layla. You slept all afternoon and all night. Marcus and I have been keeping an eye on you. It's morning now."

No wonder she felt like she had to pee.

Layla sat up and swung her legs over the edge of the bed—and fell into Ru's arms like someone had pushed her over. "What the hell?"

"Layla, you're not just having a reaction to the booster."

"Help me to the bathroom. Tell me more on the way," Layla insisted.

"Yes, of course. Let me get Marcus while you're otherwise occupied. He made me promise I would call him the second you woke up."

Layla nodded grimly, trying to regain her balance. The room swam, but at least she landed with her bottom on the toilet and not her head.

As she sat, the world slowly settled and her temperature seemed to settle, too. She still wanted to be near Rupex. Her anger at an offhand comment seemed ridiculous now.

Ru said I'm not having a reaction to the shot. Am I sick? What if I'm sick-sick? Don't get well-sick? Layla's stomach churned. *I don't want to waste time being mad about some comment he didn't even think about. He's my Ru. He's the only man I've ever loved—and I don't care if he's covered in fur and has a tail.*

I'm very fond of that tail...

Layla steadied herself and cleaned up before rejoining Rupex in the bedroom, where she was confronted by two worried Leonids. At least, she suspected they were worried. Both had a suppressed anxiousness in their eyes. "Tell me. Just tell me. I've had a lifetime of horrible news, I can take a little more."

Marcus shrugged. "I don't think it's horrible. I took blood while you were sleeping, just to rule out anything serious. You have a very sharp spike in MHC."

MHC. Layla racked her brains. She'd heard that word before. It had some medical connotation obviously. Was it in conjunction with the virus? Had she been exposed somehow, maybe when she was drugged and shipped like a piece of hardware?

Fear for herself vanished. "I don't know how I was exposed to it. And it must be mild to be dormant for so long—but what about you two? Ru? Are you going to be okay? You said the virus wasn't fatal to males."

"Virus?" Rupex came and sat next to her, pulling her gently into his lap. In fact, he handled her like she was beyond breakable, like she was already coming apart. "That isn't the virus, is it, Marcus?" His voice had a tremble that Layla instantly loved and had never heard.

"I wanted to tell you when you were together. It's early days yet, but you know how advanced lab tests for simple things like pregnancy have become."

"But... my period was just a week and a half—wait! Did you say pregnant? Did he say pregnant?" Layla put a hand to her heart and felt it racing.

"He said pregnant, little Queen." Rupex nuzzled into her neck, leaving wetness on her shoulder.

"But I can't be very far along. Maybe just a few days!"

"Maybe. But your surge is very definite and noticeable, and you've felt some strong side effects." Marcus gave her a bright smile. "Shall we see what a blood draw next week brings?"

"What do you think is making the surge so high if it's so early?" Layla whispered, unable to put her thoughts in order.

We did it. Pregnant. Us!

Ru's crying on my shoulder. Happy tears. I love him so much.

Thank God I'm not sick.

Oh, holy shit, I'm pregnant.

I'm so horny. How are we going to have sex when I'm all puffed up like an inflatable ball?

Marcus is a genius! Oh, all those happy couples in the Lynxian community!

Pregnant!

Marcus' voice seemed to come from far away. "Multiples. Given human capabilities, I'm not expecting a *litter* by the traditional Leonid definition. Twins seem possible. You two have had a streak of luck a light year long—even finding one another was a one-in-the-galaxy chance. I see no reason why your streak shouldn't continue." Marcus' stoic speech ended with a shrug, and then his expression softened.

"Twins!" Rupex made as if to squeeze her, and then stopped, lightly nuzzling her cheek. "Do you think so, Marcus? Truly?"

"I'm a medical professional. I only lie off-duty, and I'm very much on the clock." His smile widened. "I'm getting paid for making you two so happy. By Bastet! Rupex, do you know what this means?"

"You're a genius," Layla answered, standing up and walking into his open arms. "Your research, your little 'study' in your free time might save your species. Or at least give it a big boost."

"It's too soon to say. I'll feel better when I hear heartbeats."

"My God. Heartbeats. They have hearts! And tails. Will they have tails?"

"All in good time, I imagine." Marcus patted her arm softly.

"Hey, you made it happen—no matter what happens next," Layla said firmly, squeezing the graying paw. *Please let everything be okay.* "I bet you have some big science-y reports to write, right?"

Marcus' eyes glazed over. "Ooh. I suppose I do. Oh, I do! I have evidence. Layla, we need to—"

"In a little bit, Marcus. In a bit." Rupex took hold of the other Leonid's shoulder and steered him out of the room. "What should Layla do? Remain resting? Fluids? What should I bring her?"

"Can we have sex?" Layla piped up.

Marcus frowned. "I honestly don't know. Leonid Queens certainly experience a surge in libido after conception. And you seem to share that trait if yesterday's impromptu love fest on the command deck was anything to go by."

Layla's cheeks flushed, and she fanned herself. "But will it hurt the baby? Or babies?"

"I don't think so. To be on the safe side, you might want to avoid anything with penetration or vigorous...uh... actions. Just for a month or two."

Layla sat down heavily on the edge of the table in her quarters. "A month or two?" Her voice was an agonized whine.

"We'll be fine, my Layla. There are so many things we can do to pass the time." Rupex winked at her and his tail snaked around his own ankle in a silent reminder of just how much fun they'd had exploring each other.

"Rest, good nutrition, and avoid stress. You've been taking prenatal supplements, Layla. Keep it up." With a little wave, Marcus vanished through the sliding door.

Left alone, Layla walked slowly into Rupex's arms. "Hey. That was fast."

"It didn't seem fast. It seemed like a lifetime of waiting for you." Rupex pressed his head to hers.

"Couldn't agree more. But... I am a horny, shaky, dehydrated mess. Want to cuddle me and get me some juice?"

"I intend to have you within arm's reach at all times for the next seven-to-nine months."

"I intend to have you in reach of the bed at all times for the next seven-to-nine months. I feel like celebrating," Layla whispered, climbing up him until his paws gripped her cheeks and pressed her into him.

Rupex snickered, a soft huffing chortle that she loved. It made his teeth gleam and his eyes squint like little golden half moons.

"You'll be busy studying for your course entrance exam, and then the course, which is a six-month program. With a bit of our one-in-a-galaxy luck, you ought to be taking your finals just before the cubs arrive. Or cub. You know I'll be happy with just one, don't you?"

"I do know. And I'm happy I get to take my exam. I'm not just going to sit around and study though. If I'm not allowed to get my Leonid lovefest fix, then I'd better distract myself. Are the flight plan amendments all set up?"

"Oh, no. I've completely neglected them. I was so worried about you." Rupex took her hand between his paws. "You've ruined me, Layla."

She hung her head. Layla knew she had changed him, but she hoped he wasn't secretly regretting it. "I'm sorry."

"Don't be. I wouldn't change a thing."

Chapter Twenty-Five

Rupex looked over the course plotted in front of him. Astral Navigation was one of his strengths, but he hadn't had to use it in over a month.

The ship's electronic voice spoke the commands as he entered them, asking for confirmation at each step.

"Flight Plan 486-*Comet Stalker*, initiated. Coordinates set for Destination A: Milky Way Intergalactic Port. Purpose: Collection of Crew Personnel and supplies. Confirm with Captain's bio-identification or code, please."

Rupex put his right paw flat on the sensor. A few days before their arrival, Wendy, Dax, and Elio would be free agents. A travel allowance addendum had been included in their contracts, stating Rupex would pay their fares on shuttle craft that would take them from Sapien-Three to the Milky Way Intergalactic Port at the outer reaches of their galaxy. They were slated to arrive there several hours before the *Comet Stalker* was due to dock in its designated temporary berth. In addition to finding the trio and getting them through the Galactic Port Authority, they would also need to collect food, medical supplies Marcus had requisitioned, and an entire wardrobe for Layla, both maternity wear and regular clothing.

"Confirmed. Destination B: Leonid-One, Bastet Bay Space Port. Purpose: Collection of Crew Personnel and collection of supplies. Confirm with Captain's bio-identification or code, please."

Rupex studied the coordinates and reread the contracts on another screen before lowering his paw. Yes, he had enough time. He had arranged to meet the various Felid members at Bastet Bay Space Port in three weeks' time. With luck, Jaxson would be able to join them there.

but it was possible that the Sirius Federation would keep their citizens grounded for longer and they'd have to rendezvous at another point.

A ten-day flight in hyperthrust to the MWIP, then ten days back to Leonid-One... it would be tight, but they would have a day to spare.

"Destination C: Lynx-Nineteen. Purpose: Cargo run and disbursement of freight and supplies. Confirm with Captain's bio-identification or code, please."

Rupex smiled as he pushed his paw down for the third and final time and felt the engines hum to life.

"Five more minutes?" Layla's soft voice entreated.

"Layla, you've had all day on the beach," Ru protested, even though he wanted to give in.

"Five minutes won't ruin the flight plan. I know that. I'm an Information Officer trainee, remember?"

His petite partner strode in, mid-section looking slightly prominent in the black strapless dress she wore.

"If we make good time, we get a day at Leo Falls with Wendy, Elio, and Dax," Rupex countered.

That sold her. "Put this baby in hyperthrust."

"Already engaged. Are you sure you're not angling for First Mate?" Rupex teased.

"I'm already the first mate. Your *first* mate."

"My *only* mate." Rupex remained in his seat to ease the *Comet Stalker* off the ground. "We have to move, my Queen. We need to get your friends. Our family. I know you want them to be here for our wedding." He closed his mouth after that. He wanted to get married at once! But Layla had become good friends with Cherie, the beautiful, feisty woman who was married to the Lynxian on Lynx-Nineteen and was now friends with several other women in human-Felid couples. Layla was holding off on a wedding until her old friends from Sapien-Three and her new friends from Lynx-Nineteen could join them in a simple ceremony on Leo Falls. The huts would be bridal suites. The *Comet Stalker* would be a makeshift hotel.

It was all very... *emotional*. Very human. Very unnecessary.

So why did he keep smiling?

"You used the W-word. That's becoming your secret weapon." Layla pouted, sitting on his knee, rubbing her delectable cheeks against him.

Before he could blink, she was leaning far forward, rubbing the mound of her pussy to his knee in tight circles, seeking stimulation. A waft of warm, aroused womanhood almost made Rupex exceed initial altitude and send the *Comet Stalker* nose up into the sky. "Layla!" He took the craft back in hand, leveling it out and lining it up for a gradual increase and eventual break through of the planetary atmosphere.

"I can't help it. Do you know what I read? At 22 days gestation, they can detect a heartbeat in most cases. And my MCH levels are way above a single pregnancy, Marcus said so. He showed me three graphs and they all say the same things. Going off the gestation date, my numbers mean healthy twins... or something is wrong."

"Nothing is wrong." Rupex put an arm around her middle and spoke in a stern voice that belied his nerves. "Well, it has been... hmm. It's only been two weeks since you had the second blood draw. It's too early for that, isn't it?"

"He's making me wait two more days since he can't be sure. But... But, I was looking up things—"

"Do you do anything else?" Ru teased her.

"Shush. I think we should be able to see the amniotic sacs on the scanner. I want to know. Can you please ask Marcus if we can do it once we're at cruising altitude?"

"Why can't we wait a few more days?" Rupex stroked her loose hair and tried to ignore the soft gyrations of her hips.

"Marcus said sex is safer after you detect the sacs and the heartbeat. Two weeks without you inside me is killing me." Layla moved the crotch of her panties aside and showed Rupex her plump, swollen slit.

"I—"

"Backdoor today... pussy by next week. I hope." Layla was practically whimpering.

Poor thing. Rupex knew Layla still had to take the boosters once a week to help the cubs develop normally and without any health issues. That combined with her hormones was turning her into a sex fiend. Worse—an unsatiated sex fiend.

"I'll be on the deck for most of the day, Layla. Why don't we compromise and see if you can have your scan first thing tomorrow once we're locked on our first course? Have you been able to talk to Wendy again yet?"

Wendy was a surefire distraction. Layla had been able to talk to each of her friends briefly, but all of them had seemed ill and slow to respond.

"No. I hope they're okay. I did see that their passage was processed yesterday and their tickets were picked up. We have their contracts pending." Layla removed herself from his grasp and paced around his chair. "The second time I spoke to Wendy—after she and the others had accepted our offer—she said that the labs knew she wasn't going to come back next year and were treating all three of them worse than usual." Layla bit her lip. "Ru, what if the doctors or scientists gave them something horrific for their last test because they knew they wouldn't get any more use out of them as test subjects?" Layla fretted.

"They still have to keep within the bounds of legality. Whatever it was—if it was anything at all—will be out of their system soon. Besides, they're on a slower transport and we paid for the best berths. Perhaps they've all taken advantage of the suspended sleep option to make the time pass quicker, or because they're not feeling well."

"Yeah. Yeah, that might be it. Elio looked like he hadn't slept in a year."

"Why don't you see if you can get a message to the registrar of their transport and see if they have any news? If they're seriously sick, they might inform you since we're traveling all that way to pick them up."

"Hm. Let me try that." Layla bent down and kissed his muzzle before heading out of the command deck. "Oh. Don't think I've forgotten what I wanted to do. Mama needs attention... and those steel probe toys that Marcus gave me just aren't doing it." With a sultry wink, she was gone.

Rupex sat transfixed, paws on the controls.

Layla.

Layla moaning on her bed, their bed, plundering her virgin ass with cold steel implements.

His groin immediately lodged a complaint.

Great. I'm stuck here for hours with nothing but fantasies and a stiff cock that I can't attend to.

Rupex felt a surge of sympathy for his horny bride-to-be.

The fantasy shifted, and he was suddenly envisioning her splayed on her back, bump tight and high between them while he fucked her slowly and gently, letting her pleasure build. He wouldn't be slipping all the way into her until after the cubs were born, but still... plenty of inches to wrap in her juicy paradise.

Rupex groaned. *No. Don't give in. No masturbating while you're on duty! I will not be the first Leonid King and captain to crash a vessel just because I can't stop thinking about my mate!*

"YOUR MATE IS VERY IMPATIENT. You might want to work on that, or your cubs will be spoiled." Marcus' dry voice was flat, but his eyes sparkled with humor as he eased Layla behind the scanner and lowered it to her middle. "I'm thinking this will work even better with your human anatomy. Less tissue to go through before we can see what's —ooh. There they are!"

Rupex looked at the image projected beside the scanner on a large black screen. Two round black ovals in a larger black oval. The two smaller ovals shifted and pulsed, something gray flickering inside. "What is that?"

"Those are the babies. Two. Cub A and Cub B."

"Why are they moving like that? Are they having seizures?" Layla's awestruck voice held a note of panic.

"Seizures?"

"They're twitching!"

"That's the heart. The cardiac muscle flexes incredibly fast at this young age. On humans, I believe you can't detect it until the fifth or sixth week, but Leonids are on a shorter timetable. Five months. Hm."

"We figured on seven. An average of seven." Layla's voice was faint.

"Oh, I know. We figured on lots of things. Hm."

"Stop saying 'hm', Marcus. You're making us nervous," Rupex growled, pacing behind Marcus while trying to send reassuring smiles to Layla. He had a feeling his face was not cooperating.

"I'm going to guess we skew closer to the Leonid side based on gestational comparison. To put it in simple terms, if this were a human pregnancy, I wouldn't have much more than a dot in a sea of darkness. Instead, I've got about what I'd expect for a healthy Leonid litter. Still, I'm not certain of the date of conception, so I'm going to say you might expect two bundles of joy between five and six months, not seven to nine."

Rupex hurried over to support Layla, who suddenly seemed to sag against the scanner. "Layla!"

"That's so soon. That's really soon."

"Did I mention that since you're already well into the first month, it's more like four-and-a-half to five?"

Layla squeaked.

"I would very much like you to stop speaking," Rupex snarled, all of his teeth on display.

Marcus ignored him. "The good news is that the chance of pregnancy loss after a visible heartbeat goes down to 10%. Now, you do have a few dozen wildcards thrown in, but still... I'd give these two a great chance of arriving safely—even if their parents decide to do some bedroom activities. Mind you, I said bedroom. Not command deck. Not my lab. Not in public places, for Bastet's sake!"

Layla recovered in his arms, a wilted plant receiving life-giving water. "Sex? It's safe?"

"Just don't go wild. Here." Marcus moved to the side of the scanner and retrieved two sheets of glossy paper. "Cub A. Cub B. There you go, Mommy and Daddy."

I'm a father. I'm a father. My cubs. Rupex stared at the indistinct photo. He blinked and two wet splashes marred the border of the photo. "Look, Layla," he whispered reverently, a paw tracing the blobby shapes.

"They'll get prettier," Layla whispered, taking his elbow.

RUPEX WATCHED LAYLA with hungry eyes, marveling silently. *She is my mate. My temple. The home of my unborn young. My goddess.*

And then his madonna, this pure beacon of light and life, turned to him with a sinful smile and tossed him medical-grade lubricant. "Swiped it while Marcus was lecturing you about having sex in public places. This seems to be pretty private." Layla dropped her dress on the floor and kicked it away.

"You minx."

"You're not going to turn into one of those guys who won't sleep with his wife because she's also someone's mother, are you?" Layla stopped mid-sashay, worry in her eyes.

With a bound, Rupex sprang at her and picked up her naked form, holding her tight, but not too tight, mindful of her growing bulge. "Have I not been giving you enough attention of another variety, my

Layla?" he asked in a low ripple that made her tremble in his arms, her nipples turning into dark, tight marbles of flesh begging for him to suck on them.

Since the discovery of her condition, they had never stopped pleasuring each other, using hands, lips, mouths, and even his tail.

"I just need *more* attention. I thought Queen heats lasted for weeks." Layla launched one eyebrow at him as she hooked her heels together in the small of her back.

"I'm beginning to think 'pregnant human heat' lasts for months. Not that I'm complaining."

"Hmm. Maybe it's not the boosters or the hormones. Maybe it's just you." Layla gripped his mane just behind his ears and kissed him hard, her little human tongue dancing around his sharp teeth, teasing the sensitive lines of his lips. Her wet mound pressed to his middle, overwhelming his senses. The feel, the taste, the scent of her... topped off with the soft, needy noises she was making.

"I'm aching to be inside you, too, don't you know that? If I didn't care so much about hurting you or the little ones, there's nothing in this world that would stop me from burying myself in your glorious little slit," he moaned in return, carrying her to the bed.

"Pregnant Queens have sex, don't they?"

"Yes, but—"

"Butt. Operative word." Layla rolled from his paws and positioned herself on her hands and knees, looking back over her shoulder at him. She pointedly pushed her rear out and spread her knees far apart, revealing a sweet little pucker of flesh above her puffy pink folds.

Rupex's cock seemed to blot out any more words. He thought in snaps and flashes.

Virgin.

Mine.

Tight.

He'd pushed part of his first digit into her backdoor a night or two ago while licking her needy pussy. He'd almost come simply from feeling her ring of flesh clamp down on him. Her breathy, curious moans as he gave her new sensations made him leak puddles of pre-cum.

"If it's too much, we can stop. We can at least try. I've been practicing." Layla ran her fingers through her wetness as he stood drooling at her and unable to articulate his thoughts.

Rupex dropped his clothes to the ground as Layla spread wetness over her anus and slipped one, then two fingers in easily.

"Is it good?" he was finally able to growl, even though his voice sounded more like a primal beast's noise than his own voice.

"It's not bad. It's new. I like it. I'd like it better if my husband were doing it."

They weren't officially married yet, but Rupex loved when she slipped and simply called him husband. Or King. What's more, she knew it. She knew all of his weaknesses, and she used them to their mutual advantage.

"I love you, you know. The way you're sweet while you think you're being so bad." Rupex came behind her and gripped her cheeks, kneading them.

"I'm being both."

"Because you're the perfect Queen." He leaned down and let his long tongue swipe her pussy and then swirl on her unexplored backdoor. Layla immediately shivered and shuddered, arching back into him.

"You're the perfect King."

Ooh, she took the bait. He bit down softly on one cheek, making her giggle and squirm. His paw flipped open the top of the lubricant and squeezed a liberal amount across his paw and between her cheeks.

"First, I'm going to fuck you with my digits. Then something bigger," he warned.

"Oh, yes. Yes, something bigger." Layla put her head down on a pillow and kept her ass elevated.

Rupex slid one thick, wide digit of his paw into her bottom with only a little resistance. His other paw mimicked the action, pushing into her pussy.

"Wow. Oh, wow. My God." Layla squirmed and moaned as both holes were filled with several thick inches.

"Does my naughty little Queen like having both holes filled?"

"Y-yes," Layla stammered out, breath catching.

"Hmm. Would you like two cocks in you at once?"

There was a pause. Rupex felt a gush of wetness on his paw. Clearly, she *did* like that idea.

"Only if they were both yours. I don't want anyone else in me," she whimpered. "But one tail and one cock..."

"That's the right answer," he purred, nuzzling the small of her back and pressing kisses across her hips. "But for now, we can pretend I have two cocks, two small, human-sized ones." he began fucking her pussy and ass in tandem, one in, one out, watching her turn into a groaning, squirming, quivering pile of sweetness.

"Please. Please, let's try your cock," she begged by the time he had driven her to orgasm.

Rupex felt the exquisite pleasure of two holes clamping and trapping him, one much tighter than the other. He applied the lube again, this time to the head of his cock.

"Layla, I don't think..."

"It'll fit. People put big things there all the time."

Rupex raised his eyebrows. "Do they?"

"Whole hands."

"Humans are slaves to their pleasures, aren't they?" He closed his eyes. The idea of Layla lying on her back, his whole hand inside of her, wearing her like a glove and feeling so much of her wrapped around so much of him... "Nothing seems off-limits with you, my love," he finally conceded.

"Well, I'm not up for that anytime soon, but I definitely want something else big and yummy in me. *Now*." Layla thrust her hips backward impatiently.

Rupex lined himself up and pushed forward.

Nothing happened at first. "Layla..."

"Push, silly."

"Silly!" He growled and pushed with Leonid strength, a temporary surge before his common sense kicked back in.

Layla's sudden shriek told him that he'd moved too quickly, but the long, passion-drunk moan that followed told him he'd been forgiven.

Which was good, because the thick crown of his cock was stuffed inside her exquisitely tight, hot tunnel and there was no way they were going to get out of this position yet.

LAYLA HAD HEARD FROM the women who worked in Pleasure Parks that they got used to a point where pain released some sort of chemical in their brains. Layla found Rupex's sudden intrusion seared at her opening, but the pain faded as the combination of his cock in her ass and his fingers in her pussy put incredible pressure on some deep, hidden spot where her nerve endings were waiting to ambush her. Trapped. Sandwiched. Squished and milked between two hard forces, Layla felt her climax approaching in waves that left her shaking. Ru wasn't even moving, just standing behind her, letting out low, rumbling purrs. Lost in pleasure.

But she wanted more. Layla worked her hips back, gasping at the bulk of him inside of her. His hips gave an answering push.

Together, they see-sawed, slowly adding an inch or two before Layla felt sharp, hot currents of pleasure take aim.

And then... then her glorious, wonderful, possessive King gripped her pussy with his other hand, massaging her whole mound while cradling the slight bulge of her middle.

"I'm going to make you come for me. Come for me, Layla, while I'm in every part of you. Even growing in you. Little pieces of me, everywhere in you," he whispered against her ear as he pulled her back against him, forcing his cock in deeper.

Layla whimpered as he bit down on her neck, teeth soft, but jaws strong.

Too much.

Claimed and loved in every way. His paw circled furiously on her clit as he started moving in and out of her, actually fucking her ass now, taking her last virginity.

So glad it's him. "Love you." Her voice was strangled and uneven as she felt the final surrender in her body. With a banshee-like wail, she started coming on his hand, on his cock, on his tail that was teasing a nipple.

Within seconds of her hot, hard release, she felt his erupt, filling her tunnel and making her already full insides cramp with the addition.

Since Rupex hadn't been far in, his spines were not in play. He eased out of her, still sending long streams of cum across her cheeks and the backs of her thighs.

Layla didn't mind. She wouldn't have minded anyway, but she especially didn't mind right now as the afterglow bathed her.

"Finally. Finally fucked like I needed to be fucked all week," she sighed.

"You are my torment, my Queen." Rupex collapsed next to her, ignoring the mess they'd made.

"You are my everything, my King." Layla smiled and drifted off to sleep, mumbling, "We get a shower next."

Chapter Twenty-Six

"I'm going to be so glad when we get the Automated Alteration Unit module at the MWIP." Layla sat at her desk on the command deck, several screens open as she studied.

"Why?" Rupex put a plate of sandwiches beside his ever-ravenous Queen, who looked beautiful and brilliant sitting in her commandeered Information Officer's station.

"The twins have kicked it into high gear. My undies snapped their elastic." Layla stood up and revealed a wad of fabric barely clinging to her exposed middle before retying one of Alana's old beach robes that was serving as her wardrobe for the day.

Rupex stood and stared. Pink lines had appeared on his beloved's waist. "Is this customary? So sudden a change?"

Layla gave him a puzzled frown. "We're officially in month two of five to six. In humans, the baby bump doesn't really show much until the second trimester. I guess I'm entering that, but with twins." Layla's eyes raked his form, so much broader and taller than hers. Her eyes widened and stayed that way, big and round. "Do you know how big Leonid cubs are at birth?"

"Let me think... I seem to recall my mother saying Alana was a biggish cub at twenty pounds."

Layla toppled back into her chair. "Twenty?"

"Well, she was big!"

"*Biggish*! *Ish*! Humans almost never push anything out that's bigger than ten pounds. I'm going to die."

"No, you won't. If necessary, you'll have a transabdominal delivery. Laser scalpel with precision tuning, in and out in twenty minutes. Safe. Minimal risk of complications. Very little recovery time. I've done a dozen as basic med-surg rotation back on Leonid-One when I was just a scrawny young resident at Bastet Mercy." Marcus patted her shoulder and stared out the window. "Just a few hours more. I'll go get my kits ready for your friends."

"Kits?"

"Nothing to worry about. Standard procedure before entering the Felix Orbus Galaxy after the Queen Fever and the elevated quarantine levels caused by the Canif Mutation, as they're now calling it. A quick blood draw and scan, then a decontamination shower. You can be with them during it—just in protective gear."

Rupex grumbled softly in his chest. "The gear won't fit her properly. She can talk to them on the coms until the decontamination is complete."

Layla huffed, but then put a hand on her middle. "All right. I guess. If not for me, for the babies."

"Thank you, my love."

The Milky Way traffic loomed ahead. Rupex wouldn't be able to leave the controls for more than a few minutes for the next day. Sleep would be snatched in the Hover Lane, just a scant two or three hours. He'd feel better when they took a secondary pilot aboard at Leonid-One.

He'd feel better when everyone was on board, when he was headed out to Lyxian-Nineteen, back on track—and better than ever. He smiled at Layla as Marcus bustled back to his lab.

LAYLA STOPPED WORRYING about her clothing to stare at the swirling starry mass and the long line of ships ahead of them. In the vastness of space, they were all spread out, but noticeable because of the bright trails left behind them. "The only time I ever went off world, I was asleep and I missed this," she breathed, coming to stand next to Ru as he reclaimed the controls. "It's beautiful. It's so... big."

Rupex stood to put his arm around her shoulders. "I had forgotten how beautiful this world could be." He bent and kissed her on the forehead. "Thank you, my Queen. My eyes are open again."

"You big poetic purr-baby." She rubbed his chest, wishing she could feel the soft thick fur under his tight black uniform.

They stood in silence for a moment before she asked, "Are we there yet?"

"Layla..."

"I'm helping you practice for fatherhood!"

"No. We are not there yet. And if you ask me again, I'll have to teach you not to *irritate* your captain." His paw slid down her lower back and rested on her rear as his tail trailed up over her calf.

A teasing retort died on her lips, replaced with a sharp gasp. "Ru!"

"I'm sorry!" Ru's paw fled from her behind.

"Not that!" Layla seized his paws and pressed them to her middle. "Wait for it."

"What's the matter? Should I call for Mar—" The stream of words shut off. Rupex's eyes closed. His paws gently moved over her belly and then froze.

Layla's hands wedged under his. "They're moving."

They were. It was a beautiful, mystical sensation, like something slowly bubbling along, then turning. Layla imagined she could feel it sooner and perhaps better than Felids, being so much smaller.

"Does it hurt?" Ru asked, eyes opening, wet around the edges.

"Not at all. It's amazing."

"You are amazing. I can't believe... Weeks ago, I didn't even know you. Now I have a family by my side."

Now she was tearing up. "Weeks ago, I had nothing. I have a future because of you."

Rupex leaned down to kiss her, one paw still on her middle, one paw massaging her neck as he pulled close. "We have a future, my Queen."

She smiled into his embrace. "A future, my King."

Did you enjoy Rupex and Layla's story? Are you eager for more of the Felix Orbus Galaxy? Read Taken by the Tigerite to discover Wendy and Talos' story and see how Rupex and Layla are adjusting to family life!

Taken by the Tigerite[1]

Talos is unhappy working aboard the *Comet Stalker* with a mixed crew of Leonids, Felids, and humans. Leonids and other Felids live in prides and packs, but Tigerites are solitary creatures who long to find just one soul to share their lives with. The problem? The female he's fallen in love with is terrified of him—and she's a human.

Wendy survived a horrible ordeal back on Sapien-Three. Nightmares still haunt her, even though her adopted family aboard the *Comet Stalker* promises she's safe.

When Wendy's troubled past invades her mind, she can't believe aloof, taciturn Talos, the Tigerite who can barely stand to be in the same room with her, is the one who offers her a way out.

Can a journey to the remote jungles of Tigerite-Seven heal Wendy's broken mind—and Talos' broken heart?

---

1. https://books2read.com/takenbythetigerite

About the Author

Bestselling and award-winning author S.C. Principale believes in writing stories she wants to read, which is why she writes thrillers, mysteries, and steamy paranormal romances. Her stories are filled with strong, sassy heroines and the unique, often otherworldly men who love them. S.C. lives in historic Chester County, Pennsylvania, where haunted battlegrounds serve as never-ending inspiration. S.C. is a self-proclaimed history nerd, following old mysteries, baking, and leading theater and musical groups. Her home life consists of scrounging space for her laptop without tripping over two kids, two dogs, a mischievous chinchilla, and the most patient, sexy husband in the world.**Join her mailing list for a free gift![1]**

scprincipaleauthor@gmail.com

Author Website and Newsletter [2]
Twitter[3]
Instagram[4]
Facebook[5]
S.C.'s Sultry Sweethearts Facebook Readers Group[6]

---

1. https://bookhip.com/HWDVHHH

2. https://scprincipale.wixsite.com/website

3. https://twitter.com/SCPrincipale

4. https://www.instagram.com/s.c.principale/

5. https://www.facebook.com/WritesandBites

6. https://www.facebook.com/groups/668289727695362

Monster Brides Monster Fans[7]
Tiktok[8]
Goodreads[9]
Amazon [10]

7. https://www.facebook.com/groups/764631992003020

8. https://www.tiktok.com/@scprincipaleauthor

9. https://www.goodreads.com/author/show/14847508.S_C_Principale

0. https://www.amazon.com/S.C.-Principale/e/

   B01FZZL28I%3Fref=dbs_a_mng_rwt_scns_share

Also By S.C. Principale

Paranormal Romance
CrossRealms Universe
CrossRealms: You an' Me Against the World[1]
CrossRealms: Healing Hope[2]
CrossRealms: Gestures[3]
CrossRealms: A Helpful Gentleman[4]
CrossRealms: Wicked Woods[5]
CrossRealms: Shattered[6]
CrossRealms: Mended[7]
CrossRealms: Whole[8]
Pine Ridge Universe
Pale Girl[9]
Mountain Bound: A Monstrous Love Story[10]
Vampire in Vegas: The Complete Trilogy[11]
The Minotaur's Valentine[12]
Pumpkin Spice and Speed Dating[13]

---

1. http://books2read.com/u/bwKrvP

2. http://books2read.com/u/4ApQoK

3. https://books2read.com/u/mlAJJA

4. https://books2read.com/u/3kPnER

5. http://books2read.com/u/m0B8GA

6. https://books2read.com/u/mBwEev

7. https://books2read.com/u/baDAPa

8. https://books2read.com/u/mKpo9d

9. http://books2read.com/u/bPQ0aJ

10. http://books2read.com/u/bPQp6A

11. http://books2read.com/u/3RLqXY

12. https://books2read.com/minotaursvalentine

All I Never Wished For[14]
My Name on Your Lips
The Orc's Christmas Romance[15]
Haunted Hearts: A Monster Brides Romance [16]
Stone-Cold Groom: A Monster Brides Romance
B-Deviled: A Monster Brides Romance

Felix Orbus Series
Possessed by the Leonid King[17]
Taken by the Tigerite[18]
Loved by the Leopardine
Saved by the Servali

Forgotten Gods Series
Forgotten Gods: Volume One[19]
Forgotten Gods: Volume Two[20]

Romantic Suspense
Madeline[21]

---

13. https://books2read.com/pumpkinspiceandspeeddating

14. https://books2read.com/allIneverwishedfor

15. https://books2read.com/orcschristmasromance

16. https://books2read.com/hauntedheartsmb

17. https://books2read.com/leonidking

18. https://books2read.com/takenbythetigerite

19. https://books2read.com/forgottengodsvolumeone

20. https://www.amazon.com/kindle-vella/story/B0BSDMBHMC

21. http://books2read.com/u/mg18BR

Passion[22]
Deep Cover[23]
Contemporary Romance
Turning theTables[24]
Repairs[25]
Chocolate Kisses[26]
Chocolate Krinkles and Two Kris Kringles[27]
Books and Suits: A Friends-to-Lovers Romance[28]
Belgravia Security [29]
The Man with the Umbrella[30]
Off-Court[31]
Risky Business in Rovigo
Historical Romance
Alliance[32]

Read the next page for an excerpt from
the cozy-but-spicy paranormal romance

The Minotaur's Valentine

---

22. http://books2read.com/u/3n5DX6

23. https://books2read.com/deepcover

24. http://books2read.com/u/mv1R18

25. http://books2read.com/u/br1oVZ

26. http://books2read.com/u/mg1oYz

27. http://books2read.com/u/mVRwkJ

28. http://books2read.com/u/49LMB0

29. https://www.amazon.com/kindle-vella/story/B09DDHWF3C

30. https://books2read.com/themanwiththeumbrella

31. https://books2read.com/offcourt

32. https://www.amazon.com/kindle-vella/story/B0B4F2RB94

The Minotaur's Valentine

S.C. Principale

Milo has finally met the girl of his dreams. She's funny, into 80's metal, loves animals, and wants to be a vet.

And that might come in handy since he's half-bull—a minotaur, to be exact.

But Libby is 100% human and not even aware of the monsters and magic that exist in her new town of Pine Ridge, New York. Everyone tells Milo to be patient and stay in the shadows. Libby's smart and she'll eventually figure out that something's different about this innocent-looking suburb...

Libby Ingersol loves Pine Ridge, but it's lonely being the new girl in town. As another Valentine's Day looms, single Libby is desperate to get out and mingle. When she tries the Pine Ridge club scene, things go wildly wrong.

Can a shy minotaur who wears his heart on his hoof make things go right and salvage Libby's Valentine's night?

The Minotaur's Valentine is a feel-good monster romance with a cinnamon roll hero. Just a warning... cinnamon isn't the only spice you'll find in this happily-ever-after tale of monster love!

Chapter One: Milo

THE NIGHT MARKET IS exactly what it says it is. It's a market that's only open at night. It looks like one of those flea markets or farmers' markets that are set up in the civic center parking lot or a school gym during winter break. In the case of the Pine Ridge Night Market, there are about two dozen small stalls set up in the empty lot behind the Pine Loft Coffee Shop. We sell everything from homemade candy and potpourri to weapons for the discerning demon hunter and pre-made potions for nervous spellcasters.

Obviously, you have to know where to look. (And when to look. We're not open every night.)

And humans... humans aren't excluded, especially not humans who've lived in Pine Ridge for a long time, but most won't see the Night Market the way I do.

I don't have specially enhanced vision or anything. No superpowers. I'm just your average, twenty-something minotaur. I put on my jeans one hoof at a time, just like everyone else.

"Milo. Can you fix my watch fob?"

"What's the trouble, Mr. Minegold? Ooh, hey, J.J." I take the watch from the tall, thin, distinguished man wrapped in a black frock coat and bright tartan muffler. His adopted grandson, J.J., is strapped to his hip in one of those stretchy baby-sling contraptions. I look around for something to give the kid, something that won't kill him. I reach under the stall into my big red tackle box and take out several inches of silver chain. "Here you go, little man. Oh!" I draw back at the last second. "It's silver. Can he touch it?"

"Silver doesn't harm Jesse Jakob." Mr. Minegold savors the name, letting his accent become more pronounced as he caresses the curly little head. "Jesse Jakob, you naughty mite! You have tossed off your wooly hat. Your mama and papa won't like that. I must retrace my steps, Milo. I confess I was lingering too long at the fudge stand!"

"I can understand that, Mr. Minegold! I'll look at the watch fob, and you find J.J.'s hat." I wave them off. J.J. waggles his chubby fist, which is now curled around the silver chain.

Dang. Kids are cute. Even human kids. I know J.J. isn't fully human, but he looks human. His dad, Jesse, is a vamp (so is Mr. Minegold), and his mom is... something demon-y? I don't know the details, but she is gorgeous.

My brother, Bill, would tease me if he were still living in town. He'd call me out on my interest in interspecies couples. As soon as Bill turned twenty, he moved back to the family homestead in Greece. He has a beautiful wife and two kids now. He'd also tell me that I'm running out of time to find a girl. I'm almost thirty. Minotaur women like their bulls young, that's what he'd say.

But I don't want to marry a person based on their outer shell, that's what I'd tell him.

And that's how the fight would start. That's how the same dumb argument always starts. And every time, my parents snort and exchange glances and go take their coffee into the kitchen.

I force my focus back to Minegold's watch. I press the fob on the thick, brassy case, careful to keep it pointing at the floor.

Plink.

A thin wooden stake clatters to the cement. It was only a quarter of an inch wide, tipped in silver, and reinforced with an iron core. It *should* have shot out with the force of a small, lightweight missile. "Ahh. The spring action is gone," I mutter, retrieving the stake from where it had landed between my hooves. It was supposed to spring out with a pretty hefty punch so that its razor-sharp tip and inner core (fully encased in wood) would penetrate deep enough to take out a vampire or a werewolf at close range.

Of course, I'm not advocating the killing of *all* vampires and werewolves. The established supernatural community of Pine Ridge is mostly peaceful and dedicated to keeping evil-doers out of our fair little city.

Mr. Minegold, who has been here since the end of World War II, organized a neighborhood patrol long, long ago to drive out or exterminate undesirables. My grandfather came over around the same time as Minegold. But since minotaurs in rural New York have a little trouble blending in, my family has always hung out in the shadows, worked nights, and made friends with other night-dwelling creatures, like Mr. Minegold. He can get around okay in the daytime as long as it's cloudy, but he prefers the night and stays inside during the day whenever he can.

Minotaurs protect. We guarded King Minos' wife and children against his insane rage by taking them into the labyrinth and pledging we would die before they were harmed. Greek history can say what it wants, but minotaurs have always been friends to the weakest among us. In the modern age, that usually means we make the firepower to hunt the *real* monsters.

I slip my headphones (the wireless kind so they don't get tangled around my horns) over my head and cue up Metallica on my phone. "Hey! Mr. Minegold?" I shout down the row of market stalls.

"Yes, Milo?" He turns at once. Vampires have amazing hearing.

"You need a new spring! Twenty bucks and twenty minutes?"

Mr. Minegold beams and waves back, earning smiles and curious looks from the people pushing past him. "You are a godsend! See you in twenty minutes!" He jiggles J.J. on his hip, unearthing a blue knitted cap with a fluffy white pom pom and ear flaps. "Ah! J.J.! There's your hat! Did you have it stuffed in my pocket this whole time? You clever little dumpling!"

My God. Kids are adorable...

I turn up the volume.

Chapter Two: Libby

Have you ever had coffee so good you want to take it back to bed with you? Maybe whisper in its ear and coo a few sweet nothings?

Why, yes. I am single, thank you.

But, that perfectly describes the cinnamon streusel coffee from The Pine Loft Coffee Shop. It was delicious and decadent, sweet and full of warm spices. And cheap. Criminally cheap.

Everything in my new town is ultra affordable. My godmother says that I should consider it a red flag.

"There's nothing cheap about New York, Libby!" Aunt Karen had lectured a few months ago, her thin arms crossed over her bony chest, staring at me with her wild, not-all-there eyes before turning back to her blaring television.

My godmother is a lot like a feral cat, whereas me, I'm a stray. She didn't want to take me in, and I didn't want to stay with her. When she and my mother were best friends back in high school, "Aunt Karen" became my godmother. Then my mom went to work at a daycare where I could come for free, and Aunt Karen moved in with a way-older guy, discovered daytime television, and developed a taste for flavored vodkas. By the time my mom passed away when I was eighteen, Aunt Karen was all alone. Rich, lecherous "Uncle Amir" had been done in by a spectacular cardiac arrest in a strip joint while choking on a cigar and trying to get change from a five out of a neon bikini.

I didn't want to live with Aunt Karen, even sans the not-so-dearly-departed Uncle Amir, so I was a stray. On my own, surviving on scraps of part-time jobs, and a few months of my mother's Social Security benefits before they cut me off.

I went to a cheap college and lived on campus. Antonia College isn't the jewel of the state education system, so they offer perks for coming back each semester, and bonuses when you take summer classes. I had no complaints. I think Antonia is kind of feral, too. It's in the

Endless Mountains of Pennsylvania. It likes to hide from prying eyes, but if you show it a little love, it's decent.

When I graduated with an animal science degree, I found a job as a vet tech. I found a cheap apartment in a cheap town.

Aunt Karen had lectured more when I made my dutiful pilgrimage to see her after graduation. She blew cigarette smoke at her enormous flat screen, obscuring the evil face of a pseudo-psychologist who embarrassed people on television for money. "It's a scam. You'll see."

"It's not a scam. I know people from Pine Ridge. We were buddies in college."

That was a stretch, but Aunt Karen didn't need to know that. When I was a freshman, there was a gorgeous, adorable melanin-challenged couple, Sophie-Something and Jesse-Something Else. They were seniors, and already engaged. Because of the dismal size of Antonia's enrollment, seniors and freshmen were often in the same electives. We ended up in Literature of Ancient Civilization together, sitting in the back row during evening classes. (I worked afternoons at a little taco joint in town.) When we were forced to introduce ourselves during one of the weekly "Pair-and-Share" events the professor had coordinated to discuss Aeschylus and Enheduanna, I told them I was from Allentown, Pennsylvania. It turned out Sophie was from Philadelphia, making us practically neighbors. Jesse was from Pine Ridge, New York, right over the state line.

Sophie and Jesse made his town sound like a dream come true—friendly, little, full of beautiful people and places. They never mentioned how affordable it was, but when you're bored in class and you start looking up random crap on your phone... Well, I couldn't believe my screen.

Sophie and Jesse were planning to get their own place after graduation. They showed me some of the houses they were looking at one night when the antiquated overhead projector overheated and the professor insisted we all sit and wait patiently for it to cool off enough to come back to life.

That's right. I said two college seniors were buying a *house*. At first I figured one of them must've had money, but then a little more talking and a little more squinting at the phone revealed that Pine Ridge real estate seemed to be quite a bargain.

And if they could afford a mortgage, maybe I could afford to rent a room. Or even a whole apartment with a kitchen?

My other option was moving in with Aunt Karen, who had started telling me that I should try to find a "sugar daddy." Uncle Amir 2.0, or a town that sounded too good to be true? I was going to gamble on something that at least sounded like it wouldn't induce vomiting.

Aunt Karen was right there with me on the "too good to be true" part. While I packed the few items I had stashed in her spare room, she trailed after me, wailing in a voice that set off the neighbor's chihuahua. "That little hick town in the mountains sounds too good to be true. You've only been there for a weekend! This is a crazy risk, Lib-Lib. You should move in with me. You don't know *why* it's so cheap! I bet all the babies have birth defects! I bet it's near a nuclear testing site. A sewage station! A slaughterhouse!"

"I stuck around for the summer, Aunt Karen, but I have to go. My lease is signed. My job starts the second week of September. Look, if it's anything like you said, I'll move back. I promise." I may or may not have had my fingers crossed behind my back at the time.

Chapter Three: Libby

WHERE WAS I?

Oh, right. Aunt Karen, She-Who-Is-Hysterical. Despite ear-splitting pleas and the arrival of Renaldo or Rudolpho (some swarthy guy with chest hair that resembled roadkill) in his red Boxster, I tore myself away from Allentown and started my new life.

I moved to Pine Ridge in September. It's now January and I haven't seen any babies with two heads, haven't been exposed to sewage or radiation, and the only unreasonable expense is my coffee addiction. The Pine Loft takes a tenth of my paycheck, but I blame that on my own weakness and the fact that I pass the place on my way home from the clinic. I don't get out much, but I think Pine Ridge is perfect.

The only thing that would make it better would be a social life.

Oh, I go out with friends—sort of. It really is a small little town. I asked Dr. Peterson, my boss, if he knew of a couple named Sophie and Jesse, and he did. I looked them up and we've had dinner a few times.

Everyone is friendly, really.

But people seem... guarded or oblivious. Is that mean to say? I don't care, it's true.

There seem to be two kinds of people in this town. Group One includes people who will smile and chat, always super interested in you, but revealing only little, vague basics about themselves. Group Two includes people who smile and chat, talking a ton about themselves, but asking very little about me, the new girl.

I've decided, whether I'm right or not, that this bi-oddity (new word, go me) is because I'm new here. This is a tight-knit town, according to Jesse. (His last name turned out to be Smith.) I figure that people don't want to invest in me too much in case I leave and break their little hearts.

Well, I've got nowhere else to go, so I'm staying.

Sophie, who has only been here a few years longer than me, already seems relaxed. I've seen her in the store showing off their little boy, surrounded by a gaggle of old granny-types, looking like a queen with the heir to the throne.

Jealousy is a bitch.

I'm not jealous of Sophie! I just... I want a family. I want to *fit in*. I've been a loner for a long time, ever since I started realizing that the poor kids on food stamps with single moms don't *quite* fit in, no matter what the teachers said.

So, using the new pastel blue planner my boss had given me for Christmas (stuffed with gift cards to the bookstore, the sushi place, and The Pine Loft), I decided to change that. I had a planner. I was going to plan.

One foggy night last week, with Metallica's *Whiskey in a Jar* blaring as I savored my on-the-way-home cup of coffee, I opened the planner and actually looked at it.

It was pretty straightforward. There were spaces for monthly, weekly, and daily notations. I flipped past the first two weeks of January and discovered a Goals and To-Do Lists section. Dr. Peterson had even left me another present. "Oh, my gosh. I love my boss." Two vinyl sticker collections, both full of metal band logos from the eighties! I would have to ask him where he got such a perfect gift.

But back to the to-do list. I grabbed the matching baby blue gel pen that was stuck through a loop on the side of the planner and wrote:

Have a social life.

Stop living on coffee, cheese puffs, bananas, and sushi.

Find a club.

Get a date.

Chapter Four: Milo

THERE AREN'T ANY OTHER minotaur families in Pine Ridge. The only female minotaur in town is my mother. When we traveled to Greece for my brother's wedding, there were gorgeous girls everywhere. Girl minotaurs, I mean.

I wasn't into them.

After the reception, my dad sat me down on the back of the private yacht my new sister-in-law's family had chartered. My father was a little tipsy. (It takes a LOT of ouzo and champagne to make a minotaur tipsy, in case you're wondering.) He asked me if I was into bulls instead of cows, and I told him no. Then he asked if there was someone back in Pine Ridge that had my heart. I told him no. He asked if I was one of those aromantic types, only he was slurring so it sounded like he asked if I was *aromatic*. After I sniffed at my suit for a few minutes, I told him I didn't smell like I'd bathed in anise, which is what drinking too much ouzo makes you smell like.

By that time, my mom came back on deck, looking for us. My father got this completely unhinged, lustful look in his eyes and started chasing her around the boat.

I was severely tempted to jump overboard and swim ashore.

The truth is, I'm probably one of the most romantic people I know—but no one else knows it.

Minotaurs have a thing for protecting and serving. Acts of service are our love language. I dream about having a wife I can protect and help. She'll look up at me adoringly. She'll be so small next to me that every time I'm around her I'll feel like I'm her living shield, a proud warrior—not just the guy who makes poison rings and recalibrate weaponized watches.

Yes, I said she'd be small next to me. Small and possibly on the helpless side. I admit it. I have a damsel in distress thing, but I'm not some neanderthal brute.

I blame history.

Pull up a chair.

My people were not always called minotaurs. We existed before that whole King Minos crap. We have been around as long as anyone else, human or "monster." Humans feared us, the same way they feared other half-man, half-animals. The peaceable taurosapiens pulled back into the shadows, forming secret rural communities. Every community had an underground lair equipped with escape tunnels and traps to prevent violent humans from attacking the clan.

And then King Minos found out that his wife had become friendly with a local blacksmith (taurosapiens like metal). The way my mother tells it, Pasiphae was nothing more than a friend to the smith, who she had commissioned to make armor for her oldest son, the Prince.

Minos, who was already two hammers short of a forge, decided she was having an affair and went on a murderous rampage, killing one of his own children. My ancestors of course then urged the queen and surviving royal children to take refuge with us.

Well, you know how it is when you're thrown together with someone day after day...

Yeah. Eventually, Pasiphae and Aspro (the smith) were secretly married and had a bunch of little half-human, half-taurosapien babies. And we started being called minotaurs. (I think we should have been called *Pasi*taurs. Why give that murdering idiot any credit? But you can't change two thousand years of history overnight.)

Ever since I saw the picture in mom's old history book, I've been a hopeless romantic. The picture is an old ink illustration that shows Aspro blocking the labyrinth entrance. His eyes are glowing red, his horns are glinting, and his nostrils are flaring. One hand holds a huge broadsword. The other arm is pushing Queen Pasiphae behind him. She's looking up at him with such utter love and adoration.

I want that. I want a woman I would die for and a woman who would be by my side, adoring me as much as I adore her.

That isn't going to happen in Pine Ridge.

There are two kinds of people here. One, there are people who know about the magical energies and entities who live here. They play it cool. They know that everyone isn't what they seem. They're all (99% of them) nice, normal-ish folks. What about the second group?

They are incredibly, stubbornly blind. They walk around with witches, wolves, succubi, and whatever else we have on tap, thinking that everything is normal. According to those people (all human), some of their neighbors are just a bit "eccentric."

The people in the second group would all be dead by dinner time if Pine Ridge weren't such a safe place to live.

Either way, I'm not going to find a woman who needs me here. If she's a vampire, a werewolf, or a witch, she'll be able to take care of herself and probably won't want me being my overprotective self. If she's a normal, oblivious human, she won't ever meet me. If she did, she'd run in terror, and that's no way to start a relationship.

Chapter Five: Milo

THE NIGHT MARKET OPENS at dusk, but the stall owners who can tolerate sunlight tend to come a little before so they can set up and not waste a single second of selling time.

Stalls are set up in a grid between the light poles in the lot. There are three rows. The ones closest to the street are run by residents who are human or who can pass for human. They also tend to sell stuff human "tourists" would buy, like crystals, fudge, hand-embroidered clothing, and more run-of-the-mill stuff. It's not any kind of "human-looking equals better" mentality, believe me. It was decided a long time ago, back in the fifties when the Night Market was first getting set up, that this arrangement would help the more "unique" vendors stay safe. After all, no matter how oblivious a human is, he or she will notice if you're about seven-feet tall and have horns coming out of your head. My stall is in the back row, the corner spot. It's a prime location.

Christmas, Hanukkah, Yule, Kwanzaa, and Solstice weren't too long ago, so there are still a dozen strands of multi-colored lights strung up between the poles. I think we should leave them up all year. It gives the market a bustling, festive air, and that's important in cold, foggy, mountain towns in January. Festive, fun places attract customers who want to browse. Otherwise, people go straight to the stall they need, buy their potion or bat wings, and get the heck back home to their nice cozy houses.

"Milo! Hey, man!"

"Leo! Good to see you! Back from touring, Mr. Big Shot?"

Leo is a werewolf who is also in a local band. (It's a pretty big deal in the NYC club scene, but he never brags. Actually, he rarely talks at all.) His wife is a witch. They're some of my best customers because they're part of the "Neighborhood Watch." It's not a full moon, so I don't hurry to put my silver-tipped goodies away.

The stocky, auburn-haired man grins at me. "Out again next weekend. We'll be gone for a solid week."

"Ah. Looking for something to fend off those city demons?" I start moving weaponry around, sliding choice pieces forward for Leo to see. Everyone knows violent demons love big cities. Their kills blend in and get blamed on drug dealers and gangs.

"Actually, no. I'm packing Robbie. What else do I need? Plus, Tessa and Charlotte will be with us."

I nod. The two-man band usually travels as a foursome, two sets of best friends, two couples. My heart stabs me in a way I wasn't expecting.

"What can I get you, then?" I ask in a gruff, clipped voice that shocks the hell out of me.

Leo doesn't seem to mind. "Can you make me something pretty?"

I take out one of my tackle boxes. Tackle boxes are great for holding tiny tools and metallic parts like springs and screws. My boxes are covered with all kinds of band stickers. Skin Deep, the band that Leo is in with Robbie, another local (and vampire), has a fair amount of signage on my boxes. Leo sees the stickers and smiles.

"I gotta tip you better," he mutters, hands in his pockets.

"Well, I'd never say no to that." I have a black velvet drape on my table every night. Just because I'm showcasing deadly weapons doesn't mean I can slack on presentation. Right now, I clear a space and put down a selection of poison rings and some of my "daintier" weapons.

Leo looks at a black leather band that has a shiny silver box in the center. From the filigreed box came a knitting-needle thin dagger of shining silver. From the other side was a wooden rod of the same length and thickness with a silver tip.

"Don't trip." My voice is just a rumble in the dark, protective instincts nudging up in my chest. "The silver makes for easy penetration. The wood will slip right through the heart. It'll kill a vamp or a werewolf."

"Hell, that'll kill a human," Leo points out, never losing the half-grin on his face. "Anything in the heart, dude, beating or still. How does it work?" He lightly taps the center of the metal box with its ornate design.

"Telescoping barbs controlled by a catch on the band. It has a safety. The barbs resist pressure, however. An effective weapon that I can demonstrate." I bend down to my insulated lunch box at my feet and pull out a cantaloupe. I'm a vegetarian, and I usually eat one melon per night during my "lunch" break. If I get to use it as a demo first, that's fine. "Let's say this represents a human head."

"Let's say it doesn't. I believe you without puncturing an innocent fruit. How much?"

"Fifty."

"A steal. I'll take it. But can you make me something else, too? Something that isn't a weapon. A necklace?"

I flex my thick fingers, fingers that have a light coating of hair, the same as any bull. These mitts are big, but not clumsy. Still, I wouldn't consider myself adept at jewelry making. I've never really tried it unless it was to conceal a weapon. "There are two other stalls here that sell jewelry, Leo."

"Yeah, and they're both good places, but not what I want. I like your work. Your style. You put something of longing into the metal. Like a little piece of your soul, man."

I blink down at my wares. Really? My soul was in there? Maybe an occasional piece of hair, but... I shrug. Leo is a good customer and he doesn't talk much. That speech contained the most words I've ever heard him say at one time. If it means that much to him, I'll do it. "Sure, Leo. When do you want it and what did you have in mind?"

He hands me a drawing on a creased piece of staff paper. Two interlocking metal hearts, one covered with leaves and flowers, one covered with thorns and spikes. Leo and Tess.

Dang it. My eyes were instantly welling up. The wolf and his witch. My voice cracks, "Two weeks?"

"You're the best, Milo. You know, some woman's going to be so lucky when she finds you."

Leo walks off. I fold the paper carefully and hide it in my tackle box. I feel a tiny sliver of hope in my heart. When Leo speaks, it's important and he means it.

Lucky to find me.

I'll be lucky to find her, too...

Continue reading for an excerpt from
CrossRealms: Healing Hope
by S.C. Principale.

Sometimes two broken people make one whole...

Hope Maguire has always been a loner, both by choice and necessity. She'd learned from a young age not to expect anything from anyone, and that suited her fine. In her line of work, friends would be nothing but liabilities anyway. Most Hunters don't live long, so why get attached? When she's assigned to Malcolm, a stuffy, inexperienced Guardian of the Guild, and then sent to work with the team (ugh!) at the Creek Valley CrossRealms, she's sure it's going to be disastrous.

Self-fulfilling prophecy much?

Approached by a third party and asked to inform on her fellow agents, Hope thinks she's doing the right thing—until it's revealed that she has been a pawn in a deadly double-cross. Now, assassins are after her, and it's run or die. Too bad a near-fatal attack has left her as weak as the prey she used to stalk. Hope knows she is as good as dead. No one will save a Hunter who turned on the good guys. Right?

Malcolm Mansfield-Smythe has always regarded Hunters as tools for killing demons and little else. When his rebellious Hunter betrays them all and then ends up on the chopping block herself, it's tempting to forget about her and keep being the empty, by-the-book man he's always been. Except... he doesn't want to be that hollow automaton anymore, and he doesn't think Hope wants to be a cold-blooded weapon, either. A daring (but poorly planned) rescue leads to a life on the run. Forced to rely only on each other, can two enemies find a way to become friends— or even more?

Healing Hope
Territory

APRIL 2006

"Winters Interventions." Harold Winters picked up the phone at the front desk. Typically, he remained closeted in the back of the agency, but he was currently short-staffed. This investigative agency, which handled paranormal issues as well as the mundane spousal affairs and stolen property, was simply a cover. Oh, his true work dealt with the supernatural as well, but much more intimately.

Harold Winters was a Guardian of the Guild, the secretive and elite group of men and women who possessed the knowledge to train those who could see through the Mists. The Mists cloud most human eyes to the supernatural elements among them.

His receptionist was one such person, and as such, she was out helping on an assignment, tracking down whatever had been terrorizing a rather rundown area of Creek Valley, home of the California CrossRealms, a place where the Heavenly, Earthly, and Hell Realms were separated by only a thin margin.

"It's me," Beryl, the receptionist in question, chirped cheerfully. "Maddox and I killed a big scaly demon by Scarlet's. He was going to ravish mc in the back alley, but then he said that might not be a good idea."

"Who, the demon or Maddox?" Winters felt like he had to double-check. His ravishing receptionist was a reverted succubus, after all. Sex was her second nature, a perk for her lucky human fiancee, the stalwart Maddox.

Beryl made a noise of disgust. "Maddox! I'm not into scales. Plus, Celeste and Auggie are here. Also, it's Friday. We haven't had a nice, demon-free evening in weeks. Well, present company excluded."

"I'll pass on the invitation. We *are* rather slammed at the agency, you know." He loved his agents dearly, despite the clear rules that stated Guardians of the Guild should remain firmly detached from them, especially given their startlingly high mortality rate. "I shall stay here and consult with our recently seconded Guardian."

"You two just want to get rid of all the Americans and then drink all the tea and say words like snog and knickers," Beryl huffed. "I don't like Mansfield-Smythe. He's a pompous ass. Not a *lovable* pompous ass like you are. He says Celeste and Auggie shouldn't work together, and Maddox and I can't have sex on my desk. It's *my* desk!"

"Technically it's my desk as I own the premises and all the furnishings, and I happen to agree with him on that point."

"But Maddox says you'd have a stroke if we used *your* desk."

"I am *not* having this conversation."

"I don't like him. He treats us like robots."

Winters pinched the bridge of his nose to stave off the headache he felt surging forth. For a full decade, he'd worked in Guild Headquarters in London. He oversaw a much larger area with many Guardians reporting to him. He regarded all of them with cool, precise detachment. Only a few years in the Creek Valley CrossRealms with a bunch of young upstarts had turned him soft. Oh, he could assist and train his entire team of young Hunters, Warriors, wiccas, and field agents, even associate with the occasional willing Darkling. But five minutes on the phone with Beryl....

She was still talking about Mansfield-Smythe's many faults. "... never goes on field assignments, wants our reports typed and handed in like we're pupils at some freakshow school, never trains in hand-to-hand with us, never even takes his tie off! I think he irons his underwear. And maybe his hair. If you ask me, it's a waste of a cute face and a nice posh accent."

"I did *not* ask you and he's simply doing what other Guardians do, what *most* other Guardians do. *I* am the aberration, not him. Also, he's quite right to recommend that couples do not work in the field together. It can cause distraction and hinder successful missions and investigations."

"You also have way more at stake and you can't let the baddies win. Look, you're old. You have way more experience than he does. This is his first field assignment, right? You teach him! Don't let him corrupt you."

Winters grimaced against the receiver, "My dear, I'm already considered corrupted and irredeemable by most of the Guild. If Felicia hadn't led this team to victory against the dark forces so many times, they'd have stripped me of my rights and titles, my pension and my salary... even my lapel pin."

"Not the sacred lapel pin." Beryl laughed and turned. A strong hand was kneading her shoulder pointedly. "Saving innocent people makes me horny. Maddox, too."

"Dear Lord."

"Just tell everyone who wants to meet at Scarlet's that we'll be waiting for them. In a dark corner behind some potted plants."

Harold Winters hung up, muttering, "Since when does a crowded hole-in-the-wall club like Scarlet's have potted plants? And I'm not old!" He was only forty-two. Mansfield-Smythe was in his late twenties. He supposed that did seem young to Beryl. "Comparatively speaking."

"Winters?" Felicia Montgomery, Winters' surprisingly petite top agent, poked her head in, a strained smile on her face. "There's some girl here. She says she's a new agent."

"What?" Winters practically fell off of his chair. "New— I haven't asked—"

A leggy brunette sidled in behind Felicia, her siren-red tank top and hip-hugging jeans painted onto her curvy body. "You didn't have to ask, Boss Man. I'm just a gift." She smiled seductively at the open-mouthed Guardian. "It's your lucky day, Mal," she purred, sitting on the edge of his cluttered desk.

Harold practically fainted with relief. "Malcolm! There's a... lady here to see you."

May 2006

"You wanna come with us to Scarlet's?" Felicia tried to make their recent addition, a field agent from the New York area, feel welcome. The entire male population of Creek Valley had certainly done their part.

Hope Maguire gave the smaller, sun-kissed blonde a sex-siren smile, her cherry-black lips parting sensually as she tossed her mane of dark hair. "Nah. Got a hot date."

"I'm surprised Mansfield-Smythe lets you off the lead," Nox was slouched in the back, polishing a lethal-looking blade. He never even looked up, or he would have caught the sudden bitterness on Hope's face. It wasn't a dig at the brunette Hunter, but her stick-in-the-bum Guardian.

Both his barb and his refusal to acknowledge her sex-on-legs posturing rankled more than she'd care to admit. No one owned her. And no way in hell she'd want a pasty, pale vampire, even if he was utterly fuckable, those sharp cheekbones, that accent, those eyes.... Nah. Screw it. Her Warrior senses went haywire whenever she was around him.

"Shut up, Nox. Winters paid you. To use the British slang you love to ruin my ears with, 'shove off.'" Felicia sent a withering glare at the Darkling turned informant-turned-occasional-backup.

No one needed to notice that the glare lingered, meeting his piercing blue eyes for a little too long.

Hope felt a whip crack in the middle of her spine. It was true. What the Rogues said was true.

Nox lifted his head, nostrils flared. Fear? Sex? Adrenaline? He kept his eyes on Felicia. "I'm not invited to Scarlet's, Huntress?"

"You're only here so I don't kill you and because we can't handle Guild business and Winters Interventions business at the same time. Someone must be brewing something." Felicia tore her eyes from his with an effort.

"Yes, so much so that you have to bring in the hired muscle and the slut bomb," Nox chuckled darkly. "And Guardian-the-Younger."

Hope, AKA the slut bomb, drew a stake from her waistband as casually as most would check their phones. "Well, since the slut and the Guardian are here, it seems like they don't need you anymore. I'll just save Winters some money." *And put a stop to what's brewing... Little Miss Innocent can't see the Big Bad Wolf wants to take a bite out of her.*

"Don't!" Felicia pulled Hope's elbow sharply.

"What's wrong, Valley Girl? I'll get you another vamp. One who knows his place." Hope shrugged the smaller woman's arm off, never losing her smile.

"I don't want another vampire! I don't want this one." Felicia felt truth wriggling in the back of her brain. She and Nox weren't friends or anything, but they had a mutual truce. They helped each other. Sometimes... sometimes she thought it might be worth giving her heart to someone again, or at least letting it out of its cage.

"You already had one vamp. That's what everyone says."

"Liam's a decent vampire. He has his human soul. He works for the Guild."

"Ooh, freaky girl." Hope cocked her head appraisingly. "I've heard some Warriors get off on it. The risk. The rush. Maybe I *should* try it myself." Her eyes lingered over Nox's taut body, rising slowly, blade resting on the bench at his back.

"Leave her alone," Nox said in a flat voice, resisting the urge to let his fangs slide free.

Hope's eyes traveled between Felicia and the vampire. Nox didn't have a soul, but he didn't kill. He had some "truce" with Winters and his privileged little pets. All of them were so cuddly close to one another, all "Besties" and "Bros." All bonded. Practically inbred.

Throw in the vampire.

Corruption. Contamination.

"Awww, look at that," Hope breathed. "Got yourself a pet, Montgomery? Is he a good little lapdog? Or more of a pussy?"

A lot of things happened at once. Nox lunged and growled, Hope's stake was raised again, and Felicia jumped in the middle.

"Stop! Nox helps us, he doesn't hurt anyone!" Felicia's fingers locked on Hope's elbows, forcing her raised arms to her sides.

"Mind your mouth," Nox snarled at the struggling brunette.

"I'm surprised she doesn't mind yours. You like the bites, Blondie?" Hope knew she was burning bridges. She didn't care. The Rogues would be in charge soon enough.

There was a crack and a snap. Felicia broke the stake in her bare hand, her Warrior strength on full display. "What the hell is wrong with you?"

"I was just going to ask you the same question. I'm outta here. I'll pass on the drinks. I'm not really into the red stuff," she panted, humiliated. That short little blonde couldn't necessarily beat her, but she could force her to a draw. Hope stormed out.

She was done with those losers.

'YOU WERE RIGHT. YOU guys were so right. They've crossed the line, all of them." Hope paced the gray box-like room.

"The first vampire was a warning. That the Guild ever accepted Montgomery's lover, even with his human soul restored... They wouldn't have if she and Winters weren't so influential. You see how that ended."

"Hot vampires. It's like the gateway drug, man." Hope chuckled grimly.

The shadowy figure continued. "Then the succubi. The witches. There's another vampire among them now, not a soul in sight. He killed several Heaven Fallen in the past, you know."

Hope didn't know, but she nodded as if she did. She never let anyone see a weakness, even a tiny one like ignorance of a simple fact. She'd had a Guardian once. Nice lady. Prim and annoying, rattling on about Mists and magics. She ignored most of it, except for the parts about monsters. She vaguely remembered hearing about Heaven Fallens, too, Warriors and Hunters that had died in battle and been returned to earth with extra powers, way beyond what normal Hunters and Warriors had. So Nox had killed some of them? More to the vamp than she'd thought.

"Nox is more than just an informant from what I've heard. He's bedding Winters' team leader?"

"Miss Perfect? Yeah," Hope lied again, comfortable with lies, far more than the truth. In the weeks that she'd come to be around the little group of agents, she'd come to hate them all. They all... pretended they weren't hurting. They were okay and happy, one big Partridge Family with a side of the undead. Felicia was the worst, a Warrior like her. Blondie clearly wanted to bond... but there was nothing they could bond over. Felicia was living a lie. Warriors and agents don't have friends. They don't have families. They don't have careers and dreams. Felicia still went home to Sunday dinner with her mother, for fuck's sake! She went to college. College.

Like a real girl. Normal girl.

"Maguire, if you don't want this chance, I have a dozen agents more experienced and willing. Let's not forget that you failed to keep you last Guardian alive." The man in the shadows spoke, leaning forward to reveal gray stubble and pulled tight over long jaws.

Hope swallowed hard. That was a low blow, but she deserved it. Her Guardian had been the first one to believe she wasn't some psycho chick, some drug-whore, seeing monsters. She helped Hope to get out of the last mental health facility the state had put her in. They worked together for a little over three months before a demon ripped the middle-aged Guardian in half, right before Hope's horrified eyes.

She was only nineteen when it happened.

She was twenty now, a lifetime in months, barely a year, turning harder than she already was.

I'm an effing diamond.

"I want this chance. Tell me what to do. I'll put that vamp in the ground, you know I can. I've killed—"

"I know you've killed many demons in your short time as a Warrior." The man rose. "I'm sure the Guild has been appropriately grateful?"

Hope hesitated. She ran after her Guardian's body hit the ground, unable to look at the two halves, still twitching. Abandoning her post and turning to her more familiar lifestyle of running, taking, and stealing for survival, the Guild had paid her nothing for the better part of a year. She would have a few weeks' pay soon, now that she'd reluctantly reported to the cardboard cutout, Mansfield-Smythe.

"They're grateful enough," Hope shrugged.

"But we are more so. We are exceedingly grateful to have you as our ally. We can pay you handsomely, take care of you as you deserve to be cared for, an asset, not merely an accessory."

Honeyed words, spoken in a factual voice, a tiny current of the trans-Atlantic running through it. Winters and Mansfield-Smythe had enough toys in their sandbox. She was a lone wolf, meant to stand out. Meant to be feared.

"I'll do it. Anything you say."

"Welcome to the Rogues." The man extended his hand, the rest of his body still bathed in shadow, a key in his palm. "I believe you'll enjoy your new accommodations, a luxury flat. Far better than the slum you've been bunking in."

Hope's cheeks flushed. They knew where she was staying? "Sounds good. What do I call you?"

"Sir."

He rattled her. She never showed that. "Oooh. I could dig it. Strong, silent... shadowy. Strong hands. Strong other things?" Maybe a little spanking, a little choking, a lot of hair-pulling.... She was tired of men who couldn't keep up. She'd guess from his voice that he was in his late fifties, early sixties, way too old for her tastes, but her tastes hadn't always mattered when she needed to trade favors. Powerful, though. Obviously powerful. She liked taking the powerful men to their knees, even if they made her get on hers first. "Why don't you come over here, Baby, and show me?" Sex was a good way to keep them off-balance, too. They thought they were the predators, but oh no. These days, men were always her prey.

"Stop. That sort of talk is detrimental to the cause. There will be no fraternization." The man's voice rang with contempt.

"Sorry. Sir." She hated that word. Both words, actually. Sorry was a word for losers. Well, losers who would admit they were losers. "What's my assignment, Sir? I've infiltrated. Informed."

"You've burnt your bridges there, Maguire. They'll never welcome you back into the fold now."

Hope felt a shiver run through her sinuous body, not the erotic kind she liked. As much as she hated them, Montgomery and her little crew had tried. Mansfield-Smythe was a prick, but he never hurt her. Aside from the demons, they were good people. Even the demons were pretty harmless.

She could never admit mistakes. Back to that weakness thing. Hope waited in silence for the man to answer her question.

"Winters is being controlled and corrupted. Whether he is aware or not, we can see what's happening, not with that foolish demon-worshipping witchcraft, but with pure science. The energy disturbances are worsening considerably. Soon there will be a Realm Rift, if not a full tear, a total breach. Winters and his team are no longer fit to safeguard this CrossRealms. The Guild itself is not fit. They've been hoodwinked into believing that association with Darklings can be tolerated. It cannot. If they're not stopped, we may lose Creek Valley to the Hell Realm."

Hope swallowed. "That would suck."

He ignored her attempt at understatement. "It's time for new blood to control our efforts in the Mortal Realm. The Guardians are stagnated and weak, misaligned." The English accent grew more pronounced. So did the glint of madness in the gray-blue eyes. "The Rogues must control the California CrossRealms, or we may lose this town, then the state. Demons will flood the realm and spread. We must not be stopped by half-efforts."

"Yes, sir." This sounded like action. Hardcore, the war is on, guns-a-blazing action. The shiver returned, this time moving lower, resting between her hips.

"Winters' agents are too loyal to him to turn him over to the Guild or to stand down for the Rogues."

"Yeah, I've seen that. It's sick. He's Daddy Dearest to all of them. And that snotty twerp, Mansfield-Smythe, is bad news in a whole different way."

"Precisely. He'll be recalled soon."

"He will?" Hope frowned briefly. How did this guy know the Guild's plans for their prim and proper Poster Boy?

"It's customary to recall the Guardians of a post for debriefing after a tragedy. Once we're in charge, he'll have no need to return"

"What? What tragedy?" Hope shook her head. Had she lost the thread? They were going to prevent the tragedy before it could happen. She hated being called a hero or anything sappy like that, but that was kind of her deal— even if she was pretty bad at it.

"The death of Mr. Harold Winters. I expect him to be removed within the week. I'd appreciate it if you could take out the blonde bitch, too. The wiccas, as well. The succubus and the vampire are a matter of course. The rest are of little consequence."

"But... Winters is a human." Hope cocked her head, stomach churning.

"And?"

"And... I...."

"I don't have time for him to die a natural death. And of course, since you know my desires, I'm afraid I can't really wait for you to die a natural death, either."

Hope jumped at the unmistakable click of a safety going off. "I'll do it."

"Excellent." The man let her see a cold smile for a split second. "Then, when I appoint a new Guardian, I shall place you as his chief agent."

"Guardian?" She cocked her head.

He waved away the slip of a tongue impatiently. "For want of a better term. A Rogue Commander. Now, go. Don't try to contact me. I will contact you. After all," he handed her a piece of paper with an address typed on it, "I know where you live."

Made in the USA
Middletown, DE
02 October 2023